T. W. H. Brydie,

Midcalder.

FAIR GAME

ABOUT THIS BOOK

The connection between your diminishing meat-ration, the Great Grey Man of MacDhui, and the descent of lawlessness on the empty glens of the Highlands, may seem to be obscure. But to Alan Kinnear they became as clear as crystal, or at least, as the amber waters of Loch Coraig, beside which he sought to create a masterpiece but only found his fate—and a very different fate from that which he seemed to invite by his impulsive efforts in the cause of law and order.

Nigel Tranter has given us many novels set in his beloved heather, but none surely more gripping than this tale of present-day large-scale deer-poaching amid the great forests, the green corries, and the wind-swept summits of the high Cairngorms.

Novels by

NIGEL TRANTER

★

MAMMON'S DAUGHTER	HARSH HERITAGE
TRESPASS	EAGLE'S FEATHERS
WATERSHED	THE GILDED FLEECE
DELAYED ACTION	TINKER'S PRIDE
MAN'S ESTATE	FLIGHT OF DUTCHMEN
ISLAND TWILIGHT	ROOT AND BRANCH
COLOURS FLYING	THE CHOSEN COURSE

FAIR GAME

NIGEL TRANTER

Fair Game

WARD, LOCK & CO. LIMITED
LONDON AND MELBOURNE

First published . . . 1950

MADE IN ENGLAND

Printed at the St Ann's Press, Timperley, Altrincham

WITH a deepened purr, the large Sunbeam-Talbot lifted easily to the last rise of that rising narrow road, shuddered, but only disdainfully, to a succession of pot-holes, and slewed round into the level stretch before the Lodge. The big man driving, while still he muttered automatic profanity at the pot-holes, uttered something approaching to a sigh of relief. He had been afraid, as he had driven up that lengthy and winding track—for it would be absurd to call it a drive —noting the state of its surface, and the condition of the fences and walls and so on, that he might well be confronted with some tumbledown ruin at the end of it. But the place looked reasonably respectable, at least from this range. The frown on the man's heavily handsome features relaxed just a little.

The house lay before him, on its natural terrace, long and low and many-gabled, after the fashion of Highland lodges, but with something like an incipient tower at one end. The motorist approved of that tower, with its ironwork at the top—it gave the place some style, character. It was a pity about the clutter of wooden buildings reaching out at the other end, though. These people were astonishing. Behind, to the north, the outline of a small tree-clad hill framed the grey-stone house—and its timber excrescences— in the sombre hues of a pine-plantation. And behind that again, the hillside proper lifted in great sweeps, through scattered natural forest, turning bracken and burgeoning heather, to the bald stony crest of a long ridge. The golden sunshine of a late-August after-noon was doing some rather wonderful things to a belt of quartz-shot rock up there, not to mention the spray from a number of cascading streams, but naturally the man in the big car was not interested in observing anything of the sort. He was an emi-nently practical man.

With a nice precision the Sunbeam-Talbot swung round over the expanse of water-bleached pebbles from the river-bed, that did service for a gravel sweep before the house, and drew up at the pilastered doorway below the tower—more style and character, here. The man leaned out.

"This is Glencoraig Lodge, I take it?" he demanded.

The young woman perched up on the window-ledge, two casements along from the door, nodded over her shoulder. "It is," she agreed, and, for some reason, probably because she *was* perched up there, and the man had a very authoritative sort of voice, she added, "As ever was."

"Ummm," the motorist said, and took a closer look at the front of the house, noting such things as the jaded state of the paintwork, the greening stain on the masonry below a leaking rone, and a cracked pane in one of the upstairs dormers—all the sort of things a practical man would note. "M'mmm," he said, and opening the car-door, got out.

The young woman, from looking at the man, followed his gaze along the frontage of the house, and then came back to her own person, her chamois-leather, her window. By twisting just a little, so that her body came between the brightness of the sunlight and the newly-polished glass, she could see herself as in a mirror. And what she saw gave her no satisfaction, evidently, for she frowned. Also she bit her lip. As the man was getting out of his car, she glanced down at the ground, four feet below her, and at the kitchen-chair that acted as a step half-way between. And at that she frowned too, with an almost imperceptible shake of her head. She had on her oldest stockings, and . . . well, it just wasn't suitable. She stayed where she was.

The newcomer stretched himself, as a driver does after a long journey, and yawned frankly. He was a heavily-built man, but tall enough to carry his weight well, dressed in a plus-four suiting of a sporting and vivid green-and-white check, and wearing one of those fore-and-aft tweed hats known as deer-stalkers. Yawning again, he turned and strode up the two or three shallow steps to the open door. As an afterthought, he glanced along towards the window-cleaner.

" Somebody about, I suppose ? "

" Well . . . yes," she admitted.

" Right. Tell them I'm here then, will you." That was a command. " Tell them Major Crosbie's here."

" Crosbie . . ! " She enunciated the name with difficulty, with almost a croak, indeed. " Good gracious ! "

But he did not notice. He did not notice even her clambering down from her perch, inadequate hosiery and all. He had stepped through into the tiled vesti-bule, as any man would who did not make a habit of hanging about on doorsteps.

Thither, presently—but only presently—she followed him. And, considering the relative brevity of the delay, she had made a surprising transformation in her general appearance. She had whipped off the scarf that had bound her hair, and shaken loose quite a noteworthy head of dark-brown curls, undis-ciplined but effective. She had discarded likewise the print wrapper that had enfolded her, and now stood revealed in a thoroughly efficacious outfit of high-necked, ribbed, and short-sleeved jumper of navy-blue, and a kilted skirt, of authentic if somewhat faded hues. Also, by some means, she had managed to wipe off a wide smear of honest dirt from her brow —though, the extemporised mirror having failed her in this, she had overlooked the fact that it continued round her temple and down below her ear. Sundry tidemarks about her bare arms, too, might have been noticed if any keen scrutiny had been made.

Major Crosbie, however, was not making any such —at least, not of the girl. He was not that sort of a man. He did withdraw his critical gaze presently, though, from a rather moth-eaten stag's head bearing a pair of magnificent twelve-point antlers, that decorated the vestibule wall, in recognition of the fact that the young woman was still hanging around, and gawking, and not carrying out his perfectly explicit instructions. He frowned, and tapped on the tiles with the toe of his shoe.

The other frowned a little, too—possibly because she was also flushing slightly. "You *did* say Crosbie?" she wondered, "Major Crosbie . . . from London?"

"Naturally," her visitor returned. "Who is about the place? Mrs. Macpherson?"

"Not Mrs. Macpherson, no. Only Miss . . ."

"Well, tell Miss Macpherson I'm here, then."

The girl cleared her throat, and turned to look past him, back through the doorway, to all the towering summits of the Cairngorm Mountains. "I'm sorry . . . I'm afraid *I'm* Miss Macpherson, Major Crosbie."

"Good Lord! You . . . !" The man stared at her. "Oh. Ummm. Well . . . I'm sorry. I had no idea. of course." He fumbled to remove his tweed hat. "Damn it, I couldn't be expected to know . . ."

"Quite," the girl said, stiffly, and her chin rose fully a couple of inches. "You couldn't be expected

to know I'd be cleaning the windows! But I was.
You see, we hadn't expected you for fully a week
yet.''

"Oh, actually it will be after that before I move in.
I can't make it, for a fortnight at least. But no harm
in that—the stags won't suffer for being left a week
or two . . . or will they?'' He paused, as though
significantly. "No—I've been up at the grouse in
Ross-shire, and thought I'd look in here, on the way
South, to see what the accommodation is like, and
what staff I have to bring, and so forth.''

"I see,'' Miss Macpherson said, frigidly. "If
you'd given me a ring, or dropped us a line, I might
have been able to receive you more suitably. But
don't you think you'd better come inside? I imagine
we can find a corner somewhere, where we can
discuss, er, business.''

"Quite,'' the man acceded. Quite is a very useful
and expressive word.

She opened the glass door into an inner hall, and
ushered him in. Here, there was a woman down on
her knees scrubbing the parquet floor. The Major's
glance went down to her, warily.

The girl spoke up, at his back, clearly. "No,
Major Crosbie—this is not another member of the
family! This is just a friend of our's, giving us a
hand. Mrs. Cameron, the keeper's wife.''

"M'mmm,'' the man grunted.

"Och, a fine day it is, too, sir—but hot for the
scrubbing,'' the lady on the floor mentioned. "Yes,
then—it is so.''

"This way, please,'' the younger woman directed,
indicating a door on the right. "And do watch the
paint—it's wet. It would be a pity to smudge it. I'm
rather proud of it, actually—another of my accomp-
lishments, you see. I paint, as well as window-clean.''

"Indeed.''

"Yes. This is the dining-room. And here's a plan of the house. That chair's been dusted, I think—do sit down. Now, what information can I give you, Major Crosbie?"

"Well, shall we start with the staff? What staff is available, here?"

"That's easy," the girl said. "None. None, at all. Hence the window-cleaning. Though perhaps, Mrs. Cameron out there might be persuaded to give you a hand a couple of afternoons a week, if you asked her nicely. You've come to the depopulated Highlands, you know, Major Crosbie. I told you that, in my letter, you'll recollect."

"Ummm," said the Major. "The accommodation, then . . . ?"

"Dining-room, drawing-room, breakfast-room, gunroom, ten principle bedrooms, six servant's rooms, and some extra accommodation outside, if needed. But I told you that, too, didn't I?"

"Well, yes. I suppose so." The man smoothed his crisp military moustache. "Actually, what I really wanted to hear about, were some further details about the sport, here." He glanced at his hostess, and then away, away out of the window, across that vast panorama of pine-forest and soaring hillside and dizzy peak, slashed with steep valleys and beetling precipices. "I've been up in Ross-shire, as I was saying . . . and there was a man there who knows Colonel Mallinson . . ."

"Ah!" said Miss Macpherson. "I see."

The Major spoke carefully. "This man, this friend of Mallinson's seemed to think . . . he got the idea, that . . . well, Mallinson didn't seem to have very good sport here, last year? That's what this man had heard, you see . . ."

Quite as carefully, the girl answered him. "On

the contrary, Colonel Mallinson, I am assured, had
excellent sport . . . though he didn't grass a great
many stags.''

"Three, I heard," Crosbie mentioned, heavily.
"Exactly three."

"Three, yes," the young woman acceded. "But
the Colonel's methods of stalking were striking, and
quite original. I understand that his previous experience of this sort of thing had been gained entirely
in India. On shikari, I believe, is the expression.
The effect was tremendous—only, our deer were not
quite up to it, I'm afraid."

The other coughed. "Still, you know—three stags,
out of what you claim to be a thirty-stag forest . . . !"

"Major Crosbie—I am only a woman, and I
wouldn't be indiscreet enough to suggest that anyone
so militarily prominent as a full colonel could be
anything but a first-class shot. But the fact remains
that his, shall we say, approach, was not always
entirely successful. Having a rifle-bearer, an ammu-
nition-bearer, and a flask-bearer, as well as the
keeper, and a couple of pony-gillies, made a magnificent show, and impressed the whole neighbourhood
—but unfortunately was apt to impress the deer, too.
The stags were there—and they're still there, Major
Crosbie."

"I see. So you think there'll be plenty of sport
for me?"

The other touched up her hair, and then, noticing
the state of her wrists and forearms, promptly put her
hands below table-level again. "The conditions have
not altered since I wrote to you," she answered,
striving to keep her voice steady. "Glencoraig is a
forty-thousand acre unfenced forest, with other still
larger forests east and south of it, with ample cover—
almost too much woodland—and good, reasonably
accessible high ground. The deer are plentiful, and

the stags in pretty good shape. I said it was a thirty-stag forest, in my letter, and I stick to that, naturally. All things considered, I think the rent asked is reasonable. It is only half what we were taking, pre-war."

"Quite. Quite. But conditions are very different from pre-war, unfortunately. And this area has become rather popular, of late, I hear, with trippers and walkers and so on. If you're liable to have hikers and pests of that sort straying all over the place, then the stalking is bound to be affected?"

Miss Macpherson drew a long breath. "To some extent, perhaps. But we don't get what is generally known as trippers, here—we are rather remote for that. And the hikers and climbers, very sensibly, mainly confine themselves to getting to the Cairngorm peaks as quickly and by as short a route as possible, and so stick to one or two well-defined paths. I don't think you need worry about them straying all over the place—especially during September, when the hiking season is getting past."

"I'm glad to hear that," Major Crosbie said, though he did not altogether sound it. He was drumming his fingers on the table. "Miss Macpherson —as I tried to find my way here, I'm afraid I got rather lost, I drove up the wrong track, over there somewhere," and he gestured out over the wide basin of the forest with his hand. "I got quite a long way up, before I realised I was wrong—the road was becoming quite, er, impossible, even for these parts! But it was car-tyre tracks that led me up there. And away far up, just before I turned back, I passed two plain vans tucked into the bushes, off the track. They were fairly well hidden, but I have, h'm, well, shall we say, a trained eye? Just what d'you think those vans were doing up there, Miss Macpherson?"

The young woman bit her lip, and, though the man

did not see it, her hands clasped themselves very tightly in her lap. " I couldn't say, off-hand," she said, and though she tried to *sound* off-hand, it was not a very successful effort. "Possibly they'd brought up a party of climbers, heading for the Bealach Pass. They might even have been tinkers—they're quite mechanised, nowadays—collecting reeds and wands for their basket-making . . ."

" Or they might have been poachers ! " the big man put in, deliberately.

" They might, of course." The little laugh that followed that, was not reflected in her eyes.

" Miss Macpherson—do you have much poaching hereabout? You are fairly near the main road."

" No more than other forests, similarly situated, I should imagine." She swallowed. " We are five miles from the main road, you know."

" But you do get *some* poaching ? " he insisted.

" Naturally." And suddenly she flared. " Did you ever know a Highland property where there was *no* poaching, Major Crosbie? Highlanders are only human, you know. But perhaps you haven't *had* much experience of renting forests, to date ! " That came out like a rifle-shot, itself.

The Major frowned, but went on with his tapping. " You have not very many keepers, I understand? In fact, it would be accurate to say that the place is under-keepered? Is that not so ? "

" Major Crosbie ! " The girl jumped to her feet. " I gave you all this information when I sent you the particulars of let. Which particulars you accepted, presumably, when you agreed to rent Glencoraig for this season. We have only the one permanent keeper and stalker, though there are one or two other men, small farmers and so on, who can be drafted in during the actual stalking season, when they're finished with their harvest, to give a hand. I told you all this. If you are not satisfied, if you wish to withdraw from your bargain, we would not wish to hold you to it, even if it is somewhat . . . unusual. I would suggest, since you are obviously in some doubts, that you go and see our keeper, John Cameron. But, unfortunately, he is out on the hill today.'' She half-turned away. '' Now, if you will excuse me, I have a great deal of work to do—many more windows to clean ! So . . .''

Major Crosbie got up. '' Very well,'' he said, stiffly. '' I understand. But *you* understand, that if the place is seriously under-keepered, and consequently badly poached, then my sport is bound to be seriously affected.''

'' I understand that, yes.''

'' Good. Then I won't trespass further on your, er, valuable time, Miss Macpherson.'' In silence he followed her out, and to the front door.

There, she faltered, her Highland conscience pricking her. '' I'm sorry not to be able to offer you any hospitality, Major Crosbie, even a cup of tea—but we have nothing up here, as yet. The cupboard is bare. If you care to call down at Coraigmore, where we live, of course . . .''

'' Not at all, thank you. I'll be staying tonight at the Duke of Gordon, at Kingussie—I'll be there in less than an hour.'' He eased himself into his car, and shut the silver door. '' I'll see—I may come up and have a word with your keeper tomorrow, though I may not have time.'' Formally, he saluted the tip of his deer-stalker. '' Good afternoon, Miss Macpherson.''

'' Goodbye,'' the other said. After a brief pause, and a quickly-drawn breath, she opened her mouth to say something further, but her words were lost in the whirr of the self-starter and the strong revving of the engine.

With a brief and military nod, Major Crosbie flicked in his gears, and the big car moved forward, crunching loudly over the bleached pebbles.

And as it slid away down that long and pot-holed drive, that was really only a track, the girl stared, not at it, but away and away to that awe-inspiring vista of forest and towering peak and plunging cliff. And if her eyes were dry, her lips trembled.

CHAPTER II

THE youngish man leaning on the counter twirled one of the dud half-crowns nailed thereto reflectively. " So, apart from this Mrs. Macdonald, you can't suggest anybody who is likely to have a room available—that is, not till you get to Aviemore ? " he said.

" That is so, yes," the policeman answered. "Och, it's difficult, I know—but there's not that many houses in it, at all, sir, you see. There's just only the one bit hotel, and I was hearing Alec Macphail saying they'd have to be having Jessie—that's the maid-lassie—out into a caravan, so's to be giving her room to somebody . . ."

" Yes—but I don't want a hotel, anyway," the younger man interrupted. " A hotel's no use to me, at all."

" Och, yes—they're expensive, the hotels, right enough," the policeman nodded sympathetically. " It's the season, see you . . ."

He got no further, with the door thrown open, and a big man in green-and-white checked tweeds striding in with masterful tread. Instead, he eyed the checks and the deerstalker with knowledgeable respect.

The newcomer ignored the lounger at the side of the counter, and came straight to the point. "Constable," he said crisply, " I want some information from you. I hope you can give me it."

" Och, I hope so, too, then, sir," the policeman agreed, cautiously.

The lounging youngish man cleared his throat rather loudly, but said nothing.

"Quite," the new arrival observed. " My name is Crosbie—Major Crosbie—and I'm interested in the shootings and stalking at Glencoraig. I want to know just what the position is about poaching, in this district."

" Poaching, now is it ! " The constable sounded as though that was an interesting but academic, almost an original, subject. " You mean . . . poaching, just ? "

" That's what I said, isn't it ? "

" That is so, yes." The other accepted that. "Poaching. I'ph'mmm. Well, now—there's poaching and poaching, whatever. What sort of poaching would it be you're interested in, sir ? "

The big man's brows came down. " Constable," he said, " I'm not interested in a treatise on poaching, if that's what you mean. I want to know how much poaching goes on in the neighbourhood—on Glencoraig, especially."

The other rubbed his chin. " Och, well now, I've heard that now and again there could be a bit fish lifted out of one of the Coraig pools . . ."

" It's deer-poaching I'm mostly concerned with."

" The deer, is it ? Well, I daresay there's maybe a deer or two taken off the hill—but myself, I have never seen it done, mind you." The constable was a fair-minded man, obviously.

" I see," the Major said, grimly. " There *is* poaching going on, then ? I thought so. On what scale ? "

" Scale, now ? " The law scratched a bald spot with the chewed end of a pen-holder. " That is a different question, whatever, as you might say." He glanced at the lounging man for support.

But the Major was not a major for nothing.

B

" I want an answer, Constable," he snapped.

" Surely, sir," the policeman agreed, though he sighed as he said it. " It is an answer that I'm just thinking up for you." He was entirely solemn. " The folks in this place, Coraigbeg, are very law-abiding, see you. Och, they're not what you'd call poachers, at all."

" Then who does the poaching? Outsiders? "

" It must be, indeed, sir. Outsiders, yes. That is it. Outsiders, in their damned cars."

" Exactly what I thought ! " Crosbie snorted. " Why couldn't you have said so at first, man ? How much of it is there ? I've heard rumours about these scoundrels. Are you going to tell me—or must I go to your Inspector at Kingussie, or wherever he is ? "

" Well now, sir—I wouldn't just be troubling Inspector Grant. No. No. The Inspector's a right busy man, with all the forms he does be having to fill up. Forbye that, he's not that likely to know much about conditions on Glencoraig, I'm thinking. Likely he'd just be sending you back to my own self, indeed."

The big man leaned over the counter, his jaw quite visibly out-thrust. "Look, officer," he said distinctly, " I happen to be acquainted with your Chief Constable. In fact, I've just been shooting grouse with him, in Ross-shire."

" Is that a fact, sir ? Then you have the advantage of myself, for I scarcely know the gentleman, at all —though I've heard that he's a very nice sort of gentleman, whatever. Och, it is a big county, Inverness . . ."

The third figure, at the other end of the counter, seemed to find trouble with his respiration at this juncture, and the remainder of the policeman's information was lost in a gust of alarming coughing.

Major Crosbie was very patient—his patience has

been remarked on, before. " Answer me these simple
questions, please, Constable. One. Have you heard
of poachers in cars raiding Glencoraig? "

" Och, well—I've heard it suggested, yes. Myself,
as I say, I have never seen any . . . "

" Two. Has Miss Macpherson, or anyone else
belonging to the estate—the keeper, for instance—
spoken to you about such poaching? "

The policeman considered the ledger in front of
him, fixedly. He seemed to be thinking deeply—at
least, he took an appreciable time to answer. " Yes,
then," he said, at length. " It has been mentioned,
as you might say."

" By Miss Macpherson? "

" Yes."

" I see. And did you take any steps—do anything
about it? "

" I did, yes."

" What? "

" Och, I went out, and watched, as you might say.
But I never saw a poacher, at all. Wasn't I after
telling you that! "

" How many times have you been out watching?
Once? Twice? "

" Och, more that that, sir. Many times I have been
out. But never a poacher in it."

" Disappointing."

" That is so."

" But the poaching still goes on! "

" That is so. At least, well . . . they do be saying
so." The law looked a little confused.

" Who says so? " The Major's voice rose.

" Well . . . just folks, sometimes. Talk, it is, you
know . . ."

" Does Miss Macpherson say so? Answer me,
man? "

" Maybe she does, then. But . . ."

" I knew it ! " Crosbie cried, in triumph, and his fist crashed down on that counter. " Just what I thought. The place is poached to death ! And she as good as denied it. That comes pretty near to false pretences, I imagine." He looked at the policeman, and actually smiled—his first smile that afternoon, indeed. " Thank you, Constable," he said, " You've told me all I need to know—even if you were a trifle slow in coming to the point. It looks as though your Miss Macpherson will have to be looking about for a new tenant ! "

He was at the door, when the lounging individual spoke, his first contribution to the conversation—since a cough, however eloquent, scarcely deserves such a description. " You did indicate that you were an Army man, didn't you ? " he mentioned, interestedly. " Judge Advocate General's Department, I imagine ? "

" Eh . . ." In some surprise, the big man turned to stare, apparently taking cognisance of this intruder for the first time.

" I was at a Court-martial, once," the other went on, pleasantly informative. " Most instructive. I was in the Army for only a few years, myself—a temporary gentleman, you know." To which, as an afterthought, he added a pious " Thank the Lord ! "

His further reminiscences were cut short by the violent slam of the police-station door.

For a little after the noise of the car had died away, the policeman and the last speaker eyed each other thoughtfully.

" Aye," the former said, at length. " I'ph'mmm. A right military gentleman, that. From London, likely, or some such place."

" Undoubtedly," the younger man agreed. " He

seemed, rather, to have something on his mind. A poaching complex?"

"That is so, yes." The constable sighed. "Och, it is a right bad business for Miss Fiona, this. I did the best I could, but . . ." He shrugged, and sighed again .

"Miss Fiona . . . ? That'll be the Miss Macpherson he was talking about?"

"Just that. Miss Fiona, the old laird's daughter. And a hard row she's had to hoe, that one, ever since the Admiral died. Och, it's right sorry I am for her. And this looks like just another dinger for her—it does so."

"You mean, the prosecuting-counsel, who's just been cross-examining you? He's going to cause trouble?" The enquirer after accommodation settled himself more comfortably, both elbows on the counter, his chin propped on his hands, prepared to listen, obviously he had lots of time.

"He's after backing out of taking Glencoraig, man —you heard him surely?" the other said. "And that'll be a sair blow to Miss Fiona—she's not that likely to be getting it let to anybody else, this late in the season. Bad, it is—bad. I don't know what they'll be doing now, at all."

"Hard-up, are they?"

"Och, yes, these sort of people are all that, nowadays. But the Macphersons of Coraig are worse than hard-up, see you. They have nothing at all, but just the estate, now. Poor enough they were when the Admiral was in it—and don't I know it, and my own father under-keeper, and having the devil's job itself to be getting his wages at the end of a month. But since the Admiral died five years back, and the taxes and the death-duties and all, they're just about done for, whatever. Och, it is hard on the likes of them, yes."

" It is," his companion agreed. " But inevitable, I suppose. The end of an epoch. The old order changeth, and all that. Better that they should just accept the fact, probably, and get out. Not try to hang on, against the tide. The day of the prosperous landowner has gone for good, I'm afraid."

" Maybe you're right, sir—and for some of them, it's maybe good riddance, too. But the Macphersons of Coraig are a wee thing different, see you. They have been there that long—since ever there were Macphersons in Badenoch. As long as Cluny himself, they say. I never heard tell of any others before them. Just part of the place, they are, as you might say."

" And she—this Miss Macpherson—is the last of her line, is she ? "

" No, no—there's the young laird, her brother, in it. But he's no more than a bit laddie—still just a cadet at that Dartmouth-place. So it all does be falling on Miss Fiona, since her father died—for her mother's not that much use to her, the feckless, sickly, girning body. She's had the bad luck, has Miss Fiona. And now, this ! "

" It's a big thing for her, then—this letting of the deer forest ? "

" Och, it means just everything. It's all they've got, like I was saying. Barring the timber, that is—and she says she won't cut any more of that, she'd rather they packed their bags, she was saying, than cut the forest down. They couldn't let the place during the war, and they couldn't get it back into shape, at all, till last year. Even then, they couldn't let the Lodge itself, for the soldiers had been in it, and left it in a right mess. The tenant they had last season—a colonel, he was—had to stay in the hotel here. This was the first year they'd be having the Lodge taken, since thirty-nine. Och, a shame it is—and all the fault of those damned poachers ! "

The other looked up. " So the Major was right, after all? Your folk here are not quite so law-abiding as you suggested? "

" Tcha—it's not the folks here, man, at all. It's these gangs of ruffians out of the towns, with their cars and trucks and their automatic rifles. Sheer bloody murder, it is. They raid the forests, kill everything they can put a burst of shells into—and wound twice what they kill, blast them! They sell the meat—stags, hinds, calves, anything—on the black-market at wicked prices, so it's profitable the game is. I've heard they'll be getting as much as £10 for a big beast. And half the trouble is, they scare the deer right off the place for days afterwards, weeks maybe—and that's ruination to the stalking. Just ruination."

" I get it. That's what's worrying our friend the Major. But can't you do anything about it? You police, I mean? "

" Och, it's not so easy, at all." His informant shook his head. " It's a big place, mind—forty or fifty thousand acres. What's one man, or two or three either, to that, whatever? And these borachs are the rough boys, too—there was a keeper killed by them over Dalinblair way, just a month back."

" Yes, I see it's not a one-man show. But why not bring in more police? Make a real job of it? Get the local man-power mobilised. Surely it's a big enough thing to warrant that? Your Chief Constable, or whoever is responsible, would surely agree to that? "

The other rubbed his chin. " Likely enough, yes —I shouldn't wonder. But that has not just been asked for, see you, by the estate. It would have to be asked for, to be sure. And myself, I doubt if Miss Fiona would be wanting the likes of that, at all."

" But, Good Heavens, why not? It's the obvious

answer to this organised law-breaking, I'd have thought?''

"Obvious, yes—och, yes, it is obvious enough, sir. But it is just a wee thing too obvious, maybe. You see, if there's to be lots of police in it, and the local boys too, then it's not going to be kept all that quiet, at all. There's going to be a proper stramash—and that means talk, publicity, see you. The papers are going to write about it. And bang goes Miss Fiona's chances of letting the place ! It's not a good thing, whatever, for a deer-forest to be known to be having these damned poaching gangs at it—it's the last thing she wants, the lassie. She's been having the hard enough time letting it, as it is. Och, no—she's not wanting any field-day, that one.''

"I see." Nodding slowly, the younger man admitted it. "I catch on, now. Looks as though your Miss Fiona's in a bit of a spot. Either way, she gets it in the neck, eh?''

"It's right you are there, man—and doesn't she know it ! Och, I tell you, it's hard . . .''

The high ringing of a telephone-bell interrupted him, and getting off his stool the policeman moved over to the fireplace, and lifted the instrument off the mantelpiece. "Police-station, Coraigbeg," he intoned, frowning with official concentration.

But quickly his brows lifted, and his voice became almost avuncular. "Och, is that yourself, Miss Fiona. B'damn, wasn't it myself just talking about you ! Och, no—nothing of the sort, at all. Uh-huh. Yes, then. Su—u—urely. What's that? Vans, is it? Two plain vans—and up the Edart road. So—o—o ! Right away up, is it . . . and at the side of the road, hidden, sort of? Uh-huh. M'mmm. Aye. Right—I'll away up and have a look. Och, yes—I've had my tea. I'll be up there in an hour, on my bike. This gentleman that was telling you—it'll be the same that I've had

in here, asking about the poaching! Yes, he was,
indeed—it's sorry I am. A great pity, whatever. Aye,
he was the one for the questions, him. I'ph'mm. Yes,
then. I'll call in at Coraigmore on the way back, and
let you know. That's right. Goodbye, Miss Fiona.''

Business-like, and buttoning up his tunic, the
constable returned. '' Well, that's me for the road,
then. A couple of vans in it, up Glenedart way—and
yon Major-man after finding them.''

'' Poachers, you think ? ''

'' Och, maybe not, at all.''

'' Wanting a hand ? '' the other enquired. '' I'm
able-bodied, unattached, and I've been through an
unarmed-combat course in the Army ! ''

'' No, no—nothing of the sort, man. It's just
investigating I am—not looking for a tulzie, b'damn.
I'll be fine, never fear. Now—you'll be for trying
Mrs. Macdonald, her I was telling you about? Yes.
It's just down beyond the loch, there. You turn right
at the first bit road after the loch, and you go through
the black wood a bit. You'll find a burn coming in,
with a plank bridge over it, and after that the path
forks. Take you the right fork—the other leads down
to the loch-shore, and Coraigmore House, where
the Macphersons live. Your track leads on another
half-mile through the birches, to Mrs. Macdonald's
—it's above the loch, too, but further along. Her man
used to be a forester about the place. You'll find it,
easy. You'll like it there fine, if it's not a lot of
company you're wanting. A mile and a bittie, it is—
no more.''

'' Thank you. You've been very kind. You think
she'll take me in, then?''

''Surely she will—if you tell her I was sending you.
Sandy Cattanach, say. I'll be seeing you, then, for
sure—och, I'm often about there. What would they
be calling your*self*, now . . . ? ''

"Kinnear. Alan Kinnear." He paused for just a moment, as if expectantly. And then added. "From Edinburgh."

"Edinburgh is it? Och, but man, there's good folks from all parts!" the other admitted handsomely. "Good day to you, Mr. Kinnear."

CHAPTER III

ALAN KINNEAR shouldered his pack, got his pipe going strongly, and strolled down the road towards the loch. As has been said, he was a youngish man. but he was a lot more ' ish ' than that—tallish, slenderish, fairish, plainish; in fact, he was not a particularly outstanding-seeming person at all, an impression which he emphasised by the habitual air of casualness that he wore like a garment—but which was exposed for the sham and pose it was, by the pair of intensely alive blue eyes, which he could by no means hide nor veil. Those eyes, indeed, if they were his only claim to distinction, were noteworthy, and were apt to leave the final impression of the man on all but the most superficial. He was dressed, now, in a suit of well-worn greenish-brownish Harris, from which the shagginess had long since departed, patched at elbows and cuffs with leather, and in stout brown boots of distinctly ex-Army appearance. Hatless, with his wavy fairish hair, not over-short, requiring frequently to be tossed back from brow and temple, he had a moderately-sized rucksack on his back, and a stalwart ash-plant walking-stick in his hand, and he swiped randomly, impartially, at sundry unoffending wayside thistles and ferns as he strolled down the road, with the sun at his back.

But his eyes, those questing urgent eyes, were not on the ferns and thistles, nor on the road either—which no doubt accounted for his deplorable aim. Though the prospect had by no means burst newly

upon him—hadn't he been looking upon it, from
some angle or other, most of that day?—it nevertheless still held his gaze. Which was not remarkable;
there was a challenge, a magnetism, about the
scenery that he was walking into, from which few
even habitual non-observers could escape. And this
man, Alan Kinnear, was far from insensible in such
matters. Indeed, it was that tremendous vista,
growing and working upon him all day as he had
walked northwards towards it, that had decided him
that here he would, he *must*, rest his caravan, pitch
his tent awhile; that had assured him that here he
could work, with all the dare of that outflung
challenge for urge and inspiration; that had sent him
looking for accommodation; that had taken him to
the police-station and Sandy Cattanach; that now
took him down that hill towards the loch, and Mrs.
Macdonald. He had reason for his preoccupation,
then, with so potent a view.

It was the scope and sweep of it all that had
impressed him first, almost overwhelmed him, as it
was bound to do by its very proportions, but rather
it was the colour, and the mutability of shadow-
etched perspective, that entranced him, now. The
levelling sun, it was, that was the craftsman there,
of course—but what material it had to work on. The
long level loch below him, sheerest blue slashed with
glittering gold and stained with violet shadow, the
yellow strand beyond, and then the great sombre
waves of the pine-forest, olive to black, mile upon
mile of it, splashed with the brighter green of
clearings and the delicate lemon of the already-
turning birches, lifting up and up to the purple
leagues of the heather above the tree-level, out of
whose massive flanks again thrust the proud
shoulders of the Cairngorm giants, bathed in the
flooding refulgence, their prodigious peaks, soaring

buttresses, and cliff-bound plateau a brilliant back-cloth of vivid hues—the flush of pink granite and the angry weals of raw red earth, the emerald seams of burn-channels and the tawny scattering of the deer-hair grass, the black of the frowning crevices and glooming corries, and the stark white of patches of eternal snow. And over all, despite the golden radiance of the westering sun, that blue grape-bloom that is synonymous with Cairngorm. Scope there was for preoccupation, there.

Down at the reedy head of the loch, the man leaned over the stone hump-backed bridge that spanned the outflow of the Coraig River on its way to the Spey, and stared across the wimpling waters. Over there, above the farther shore of the loch, he could see three houses amongst the open birch-woods, a small cottage, timber-built, with a red roof, probably of painted iron, a tall grey stone house, creeper-clad and with the look of age—no doubt the Coraigmore house of the unfortunate Macphersons—and much farther along, he just could glimpse the gleam of what must be the whitewashed walls of Mrs. Macdonald's establishment. A mile and a bittie, the policeman had said. The bittie was fair enough, but the mile, now . . . !

Kinnear turned off the road at the first opening beyond the loch, as he had been instructed, and found himself on a sandy track that led straight into the gloom of a pine-plantation. It was silent in there, as well as dark, and the soft murmur of the wood-pigeons made the only sound to the place, the man's footfalls being muffled on the carpet of the pine-needles that already overlaid the sand and gravel of his track, and the hurrying legions of the ants making no noise about their urgent business. That quiet was a good thing, too, and he walked in its resin-scented hush appreciatively, till the gurgle and chuckle of

a stream prevailed over the cushats' gossip, and he
was at the brink of a sizeable burn whose clear amber
waters plunged and eddied over smooth basalt slabs
and polished granite pebbles. From its wooden bridge
Alan watched the glancing shadows of darting trout,
and nodded sagely to himself—and to the burn's
laughing mockery and the pigeons' soft reproof.

Beyond, the pines gave place to open woodland,
green glades of graceful birches and rust-tipped
junipers, where rabbits scampered, and glimpses of
blue loch and purple hills were framed between the
white boles of slender trees. There had been a sawmill here, not so very long before, but already the
rabbits were burrowing in the saffron hill of sawdust,
and the wide-scattered bark peelings were all but
hidden beneath the yellowing bracken.

After the sawmill, the track forked, as Cattanach
had said; at least, another track, broader, but in
much the same condition, joined it from the east, and
swung away south-westward—no doubt, the main
avenue to the House. Kinnear considered it and its
implications for a little before drifting unhurriedly on
through the verdant aisles of the birch-wood. All
things in good time, he told himself; meanwhile,
there was nothing to hurry about in all the world, for
him—hadn't he come all this way just to be quit of
hurrying and rushing and bustling, to unwind his
mind, to relax and uncoil the tension of his wits,
screwed up by the tempo of the life he lived, to make
a reality out of that pose of nonchalance and casualness that he wore so assiduously, so that he could
work as he had it in him to work? Well, then!

In that spirit, and therefore determinedly casual,
he presented himself some ten minutes later within
the rustic porch of the whitewashed house upon the
green knoll above the spreading loch, and knocked
on the door. And though he leaned shoulder against

the pine-trunk doorpost, and whistled under his breath as he waited, that was all part of his so necessary pose, too. He was not casual, at all, about this pleasant two-storeyed house cradled in the green forest, that looked out on the one hand, into all the sun-filled south and west, across the shining waters and lifting wine-red moors to the long ridges and aloof summits of the Monadh Liaths, and on the other, over the tree-tops, to the towering spectacle of the lofty Cairngorms. He was going to be a very disappointed man if Mrs. Macdonald did not come up to scratch.

When the lady of the house appeared, it was not at the door but from round the gable-end, heralded by a scattering of domestic fowl and a couple of vertical-tailed cats—the man might have known better than to look on the front door as other than an emergency exit. She was a small trim elderly person, with tightly-coiled white hair, a complexion like a red-cheeked if slightly wizened apple, and a pair of washen-blue but piercingly keen eyes. And if her lilting Highland voice was as mildly gentle as soft music, those eyes—quite as noteworthy as his own—could well counteract any wrong impression given.

"Well, now," she said. "A very fine evening it is, and it August. And I've seen the midges worse, whatever."

"Er . . . undoubtedly." Alan Kinnear agreed. "This will be Balnahard, I take it, and you'll be Mrs. Macdonald?"

"Och, yes—none other," she nodded. "Just that. And if it's that scoundrel Sandy Cattanach that was after sending you, then it's my sympathy you have, young man, and you with the long walk for nothing. It's just a disgrace to the Force, he is, that one—and often I've told him so!"

Crestfallen, the man gazed at her, almost incredul-

ously—for her voice sounded sweeter than run honey.
" Oh, I say . . ." he faltered, " This is . . . discon-
certing." He shook his head. " I mean . . . how did
you know ? "

" Och, what else would be in it, then, and you with
the name of myself and the place on the tip of your
tongue ? A room it'll be that you're wanting ? And
what makes Sandy Cattanach think that I've got the
time to be looking after folks that do be wanting a
holiday ? Myself, I have never had a holiday in my
life, whatever."

Her caller tried to insert a plea, here, but the
melodious demulcent voice went on, unheeding.

" I am not against the holidays, see you, for them
that do be needing a holiday, but why should an old
woman the like of myself have to be looking after
strong young men that do be rushing up hills and
falling off rocks all day, instead of doing something
useful ? The last one yon Sandy was after sending
me—the last one that I was foolish enough to be
taking in, that is—he fell off the Sgoran, there, and
had to be fetched back on a garron, and hadn't I the
nursing of him for six weeks, and him with a broken
leg to him. Och, he was a nice enough lad, and
harmless—sort of English, just, you know—but I
told Sandy Cattanach, I said, no more climbers, at
all . . ."

" But I'm not a rock-climber, Mrs. Macdonald !
And I'm not English—I'm not even on a holiday,
really," the man insisted, " I'm only . . ."

" You're one of these hikers, aren't you—with
your stick and your pack on your back ? Och, it's
the great trouble the hikers are, too, stravaiging about
the place, and setting the trees on fire, and putting the
deer off the hill . . ."

" I'm not a hiker, either, and I promise not to
start a single forest-fire, or break a leg, or make any

other sort of trouble, Mrs. Macdonald." Kinnear had
quite forgotten his nonchalance, now. "But I do
like your house in the woods, and I'm sure I could
work here. I wouldn't take much looking after,
really . . ."

"Work, is it? And what sort of work would you
be doing at Balnahard, at all?"

"Well, I am a writer, you see, Mrs. Macdonald."
He coughed a little. "Alan Kinnear, the name is.
And I feel that the atmosphere here is just what I'm
looking for. I . . ."

"A writer! Well, now!" The old lady opened her
eyes wide. "You mean, a real writer—you write
books, is it? Or just for those trashy newspapers?
You'll not find anything for the newspapers at Balnahard—you will not!"

"No—it's books, all right," the other assured.
"But not very important or valuable sort of books,
I'm afraid," he hastened to disclaim. "Just detective
stories—thrillers, you know. But I do feel that here,
I might write something better—get it started, at
anyrate."

"Detective stories! My goodness, d'you tell me
that, now! Murders and gangsters and such-like, is
it?"

Kinnear swallowed. "I'm afraid so," he faltered.

"My, Oh my—but this is a treat, indeed! There's
nothing I like better than a good murder or a kid-
napping, or a gang-fight. Man, man—come away in.
Dearie me—you'll be fair starving. Have you had
your tea, at all? Goodness gracious—and the long
walk in it! Come along—och, never heed the front
door—this way, now . . . Och, well, now—a detective-
writer . . . !"

Alan Kinnear beamed at his hostess, as well he
might. Fed royally, on boiled eggs, cheese, oatcakes,

C

scones, heather-honey, and fruit-cake, rested, and installed in a delightful coom-ceiled bedroom upstairs, facing out to all the challenge of the high-tops—he had selected that in preference to one at the other side, facing westwards across the loch, for the sake of the early-morning sun, and what that bracing vista was expected to do for him—and given the run of the undoubtedly little-used parlour for the mechanics of his trade, he now had received directions for the short exploratory stroll he was going to take himself before dark, as well as the chaperonage of a small but ardent black spaniel that quite evidently foresaw possibilities in the newcomer.

" Mrs. Macdonald," he said, " I know I'm going to enjoy myself here—but what's better, I know I'm going to be able to write here, write something worthwhile. If a masterpiece comes out of Scotland next year, the chances are that it is going to be Mrs. Seana Macdonald of Balnahard that is responsible ! "

" A masterpiece, is it to be—out of Balnahard ! And is it to be a poisoning, or a shooting, or a knifing —or just the blunt instrument, whatever ? Have you got that far yet, at all ? "

The man puckered his brow. " Well . . . I'm afraid that wasn't exactly the sort of thing I'd intended, this time. You see, my idea in coming up here, away from all my accustomed haunts and habits and friends, was to try and write something entirely different, something altogether more meaningful and significant, more profound, if you like—a novel that has depth and purpose instead of merely speed and action." He paused, and grinned, ruefully. " But that must sound fearfully priggish and egotistical— self-important, and all that. It's just that I feel that I've got into a rut, a pleasant and reasonably profitable rut, but a rut nevertheless—and I've come here to see if I can get out of it."

His hostess shook her white head. "You go your
bit stroll, Mr. Kinnear, and think about all the decent
folk just waiting to read your next detective-story,
and the two-three clever ones that'll wade through
your fine deep significant masterpiece and pick it to
pieces, and consider you which is the most important,
at all. Off with you, now . . . and would it not be the
good idea to have a thriller in a Badenoch glen, for a
change, and only the likes of Sandy Cattanach to
interfere with the detecting of it ! Go on . . . and don't
be letting that Specht be losing you."

So Alan Kinnear went strolling again, down towards
the loch, this time, behind the bounding joyful
rabbit-chasing Specht, and along over the sand and
pebbles and bleached wrackage of the shore. It was
quite a different world, now, grey and shadowy and
wan, stark almost, with the sunset no more than a
memory, and a cold breeze across the water setting
little splashing wavelets lap-lapping along the shingle,
and sighing amongst the birches. But if there was less
of colour and detail and feature to be seen, there was
more of life and movement, the quiet unhurried
fundamental life of the wilderness. Along the loch-
strand the busy columns of midges were like truncated
pillars of smoke for the man to dodge, and out on the
water itself the frequent plops, so much deeper than
the splashing, told of fish not disinterested in the
teeming insects. On all the greensward the rabbits
were legion, and over the swaying tree-tops the
whistle and beat of wings marked the swift passage
of more mallard to swell the raft of duck that quacked
sleepily out in mid-loch. From a reedy dell nearby
a wild pheasant croaked discordantly, and down
amongst the shallows a pair of oyster-catchers were
at their flitting and restless crying. Other things there
might have been, too, that saw and heeded and went
their silent ways into the shadows, but Specht's

assiduous ranging precluded observation. The man was well enough content with what the evening showed him.

Presently, a light in front of him gave Alan pause, till he perceived that it must come from a window of the tall house of Coraigmore, set amongst shadowy slopes above the steel-grey speculum of the loch. Not wishing to blunder into gardens or desmesne-lands, he turned away from the water, and climbed up between green tree-clad knolls and rioting bracken, towards the higher ground. He reckoned that if he moved at a tangent north-eastwards, he would strike that avenue that he had crossed soon after the sawmill site, and so would be able to turn back to Balnahard along the same track by which he had first approached it.

It was much darker amongst the shaws and glades of the trees, and not very good going, with many fallen and decaying trunks to trip the unwary walker, as is the way of birch-woods. There were frequent belts of sodden ground which had to be crossed or circumnavigated, and often he was over the ankles in surface-water and red mud, and squelching in the lighter shoes into which foolishly he had changed to rest his feet. Also, there were cattle in the wood, strangely enough, great vague shapes, all horns and hair, that materialised out of the juniper clumps, and plunged away heavily, puffing and snorting and crackling the bushes, and sending a benighted and un-initiated traveller's heart into his mouth with ridiculous regularity. And once a huge bird, a capercailzie perhaps, or a monster, or even a jabberwock, burst from under his very feet, and went hurtling away into the deeper fastnesses with a prodigious crashing that was one more affront to the watching brooding spirit of the night. Alan Kinnear was not sorry when, unexpectedly, he found his feet on the firm grit and gravel surface of the road, and saw the pale gleam of it stretching away left and right into the gloom. He turned right-handed, and strode out more manfully.

He had quite forgotten the existence of the dog, when an excited yelping broke out from no great distance ahead, intermingled with, first, an alarmed whimpering, and then a woman's high-pitched and imperious calling. These sounds continuing unabated —though both the yelping and the whimpering seemed to be getting rather more distant as the moments passed—the man hurried forward.

Round a bend in the track, he came on a young woman standing, apparently stamping her feet. " Damn that Specht ! " she was crying, " Confound, curse, and damn it ! " And raising her voice still higher, she called, " Sal—ly . . . Sal—ly . . . Sa—a— lee—ee ! "

From deep in the mirk of the woods Specht's ecstatic barking, in high pursuit obviously, came back to them, though the unidentified Sally's unhappy whimpering was lost in distance.

Fairly evidently a marathon was in progress.

" H'r'mmm," the man said, not so very confidently. " Good evening."

The girl glared at him—at least, he suspected that she was glaring, though the light was not so very good for observing the finer nuances of expression. " Why can't you keep that wretched brute under control ? " she demanded. " *Always* this is happening." And turning away, she resumed her ululations towards the farthest forest.

" I'm sorry," Kinnear said, " Exceedingly sorry. But I wasn't to know . . . I'd no idea, you see . . . Specht and myself are only newly acquainted, as it were."

" Specht," the young woman said deliberately,

" is an over-sexed, under-bred little hooligan. And
Sally's just, just the opposite. He just persecutes
Sally, that's what he does. Specht shouldn't be
allowed out, except with somebody capable of con-
trolling him ! " Biting, she was.

Involuntarily, the man frowned. " Indeed," he
said, " I will keep that in mind."

" Do," he was adjured. " I don't know who you
are, but I expect you're one of Seana Macdonald's
hikers ! " That was practically an accusation.

" My name is Alan Kinnear," he told her stiffly,
" And though I am staying with Mrs. Macdonald, I
am not a hiker."

" That is something, at anyrate . . ."

" And I'm sorry about your dog, Madam. If you'll
inform me where to deliver it, I will see if I can, er,
retrieve it for you." He was diginity itself.

" Don't be ridiculous ! " the other fumed. " Listen
to it—just listen ! " Certainly, Specht sounded a
long way off, and still going strong. " What chance
would you have, or anybody else, of following up
that ? No—Sally will turn up, wheenging at the door
in the middle of the night, wet and bedraggled and,
and demoralised, and Mother will be angry and all
upset again." She produced an incipient toss of the
head. " And it's not *my* dog ! I wouldn't own a
brute with as little spirit as that ! Good *night* ! "

" I can well believe that last, at anyrate ! " the man
gave back, with some little vigour of his own. But it
is improbable that she heard him, for already she
had swung on her heel and gone striding off down the
avenue.

Alan stared after her, from under knitted brows,
till the dusk swallowed up her light but energetic
figure. Of all the hussies, the harridans, the scolds
and unmannerly shrews ! Spitting at him like a wild-
cat, for what was obviously no fault of his ! Was

this a sample of the famed Highland good manners?
The Macpherson wench, for a certainty, the policeman's Miss Fiona—with all the authentic haughty
arrogance of her kind ! No great loss, by jove, if she
and her type were on the way out ! Slashing violently
at a convenient juniper-bush with his stick, the man
resumed his walking. But now he did not stroll, he
marched up that whitely glimmering track, his cloak
of casualness a casualty beyond recovery.

He was into pine-forest, heather-bedded, and
stumbling out on to a slightly wider road, a county
highway probably, with a couple of telephone wires
to it, before he realised that, in his indignation, he
must have missed the path on the right that he had
intended to take, missed it possibly by quite a margin
—for he would not like to say for just how long he
had been stalking up that avenue. He was peering
left and right and then backwards, trying to decide
which way to go now, when, heralded by a faint
metalic rattling, a figure loomed out of the dark, a
tall bulky figure, on a bicycle, rather noticeably without a light.

"Well," he said, recognising that flat-topped hat,
even in the gloom. "Caught your poachers?"

The policeman dismounted. "Och, is that yourself,
sir. Did you find your way to Balnahard, then, and
Mrs. Macdonald?"

"I did, yes—and she's put me up. Though I don't
know whether that is any thanks to your advocacy,
or not ! But what about the poachers?"

"Man, devil the poacher, or the van either, did I
see, whatever. There was tyre-tracks in it, in the
mud, yes—but they could have been the Major-man's
own car. Och, but there's two-three side roads they
could have left by, see you. If the light hadn't failed
on me, maybe I could have found the tracks of them

—but what would be the good of that, at all? Hech-aye." He sighed, but not very dolefully. " I'm just away down to be telling Miss Fiona."

The younger man snorted. " Then you'd better be prepared for fireworks—especially as you've no good news for her. I've just seen her down the road, there, and she's in a foul temper. A thoroughly ill-natured young woman, she seemed to me—just a termagant."

" Och, she's not so bad as that, at all—though I'll not just deny but what she's got some go to her," the constable objected, loyally. " And she'll have had a right trying day, mind—and yon mother of her's would be upsetting a saint. A wee dog, she's got . . ."

" I know all about the wee dog! " he was interrupted, " And if you happen to come within kicking distance of the brute, down there, give it the toe of your boot from me—and double the same to that devil-spawned Specht of your Mrs. Macdonald! "

" Och, is that the way of it, then ! " The policeman chuckled.

" It is," Kinnear said sourly. And stiffly, he went on. " Now, will you be good enough to direct me the shortest route back to Balnahard?"

" Yes, yes—that's easy, now. Just you carry on along this road a bittie, and the first on the right takes you down to it. You'll be seeing Seana Macdonald's bit letter-box on the corner. You'll not miss it. Cheerio, then—and will I be telling Miss Fiona you think she's a ptarmigan ? "

"Do," Alan Kinnear instructed, definitely. "Good-night."

The sound of the constable's laughter as he mounted his bicycle, came back to the incensed pedestrian. It struck him that the fellow didn't sound terribly depressed about losing his poachers.

CHAPTER IV

THE larks shouted, the breeze whispered amongst
the heather-stems, the white clouds sailed across the
washen blue vault of the heaven where the black
speck that was a buzzard wheeled and soared, and
Alan Kinnear lay on his back, one hand behind his
head and the other plucking idly at the blaeberry leaves,
and knew with utter certainty that life was good. He
had climbed Sgoran Dubh—the easy way, admittedly,
but then wasn't it his first day amongst the real
giants?—he had sidled down the long ridge to Càrn
Buidhe, and, deserting the high ground, he had
plowtered across a great basin of dessicated peat-
hags, standing water, and nodding bog-cotton, and
then, muddy, sweating, but undaunted, he had
clambered up the steep pointed hill of Meall na
Corrie, slabbed granite and layered basalt like a
slated roof, just for the hell of it. Now, with the glow
of achievement upon him, as well as that of the afternoon sun, he lay relaxed and at ease, well below the
piercing winds of the tops, and with all the land
spread out below him, while the sweat dried on him
and his prowess grew on him, and he knew content.
For, after all, this was only his third day actually on
the hill. He could think of tackling Braeriach, tomorrow . . . no harm in thinking !

He had had perhaps ten minutes of his ease and
content, when his relaxation was suddenly and
effectively banished. The unexpected crack of a rifle
is apt to have such an effect. He sat up, even as the

41

vicious report echoed and re-echoed from all the score of hillsides around him.

That shot had come from not so very far off— below, and to the right somewhere, he imagined. Though it was hard to tell, exactly, with the upheaved nature of the land, and all the echoes to complicate impressions. He scanned all the ground about him, above and below, but could see nothing significant. He was about to get up, to make for the summit of a nearby rocky knoll which would give him a wider prospect into a deep corrie below and right, when abruptly, involuntarily, he threw himself down again into the thin heather. The figure of a man had appeared, tiny, but evident enough, climbing up out of the gut of the corrie, on its farther flank. Alan reached for his binoculars.

They were a good pair of old German glasses, Goertz of Berlin, reaching to twelve magnifications, and through them, though the climber was all of a mile away, the watcher could make out the details clearly enough.

As well that he had crouched down, he decided, for the marksman was no sporting gentleman or tenant, that was certain, judging by his clothing and carriage. He was a dark young fellow, dressed in a shapeless jacket of stained and faded aspect, and what appeared to be blue dungaree trousers, with a cloth cap worn well to one side of his head. And he carried what looked like a service rifle—at least, its bulky lines had none of the grace of your sporting weapon. He climbed swiftly and well, but with an unmistakeable air of furtiveness. That was either a temporary keeper, which seemed highly improbable, or one of the odious poachers.

His glasses sliding on ahead, Kinnear sought to find the target—for by the man's urgent gait, he had not wasted his shot. But he could pick out nothing against that background of heather, peat-hag, out-crop and faded deer-hair grass, all in connatural affinity with the red deer's protective colouring. He was switching back to the man, when out of the corner of his naked eye, he glimpsed movement high up where the corrie tailed away into the bald brow of the hill. Following up quickly, he was just in time to focus on a herd of fully a dozen deer, in swift and graceful flight, all long legs, russet flanks, and bobbing white sterns, before they were gone, over a fold of the braeside. As far as he could make out in the moment or two he had, they were all hinds, females.

Back at the man, Alan watched him avoid a green apron of surface water and bog, and then, half-hidden behind a little ridge of heather, stop and bend down. That would be why he had not discovered the kill—it was lying behind that ridge. He watched the fellow take off his jacket, and, rolling up his sleeves, turn to stare long and carefully over the entire spread of that far-flung vista. Crouching his lowest, as the other's gaze travelled methodically up towards his own position, Kinnear lowered his binoculars, that they might not reflect the sun, and then, reminded of the reality of the distance between them, recog-nised that the chances of his being seen, lying flat as he was and with outcropping stone all around him, were infinitesimal.

Satisfied, apparently, that that world of the high places was empty indeed, the other knelt down in business-like fashion. Though Alan could see only his head and shoulders, and sometimes not that, it was obvious by his forward-bent position and the motions of his body, that he was working hard. Gralloching and bleeding his kill, undoubtedly. It did not take very long—perhaps three minutes in all. The man was an expert, evidently.

The watcher considered his own situation. What was the best thing to do? If this was a poacher, as seemed fairly certain, what ought to be his, Alan Kinnear's programme? No good barging down there just now, in any gallant effort to catch the culprit red-handed. The man had a rifle, and these individuals were said to be pretty desperate characters. There might well be others involved, too—probably were, for they usually worked in gangs, by all accounts. And there was no sense in dashing away and trying to get help, at this stage—the nearest available help would be five extremely rough miles away, at least, and the police-station eight. Best just wait and see what eventuated—this chap couldn't move a full-grown stag away on his own anyway.

Which seemed to be just where the witness was wrong. Straightening up, the man below him had another look around, then reaching down, he dragged what was soon seen to be the steaming entrails over to a nearby peat hag, and pushed them in, kicking down the black soil and roots to cover them. Back at the kill, he wiped his gory hands and arms with grass, put on his jacket, slung his rifle across his back by a cord, and stooping again, commenced to move backwards, bent almost double.

Surprised, Alan watched, as he saw the stag being hauled from behind its cover. He had it by the hind legs, which were tied together. It looked a big beast, and the weight obviously was a severe strain on the dragger. From his own small stalking experience, he knew that a full-grown stag could weigh anything from twelve to sixteen stone. Lifting his eyes from his glasses, Kinnear glanced downwards. The fellow was a good mile above the tree-level, with a levelish shelf before him, water-logged and peat-pocked, then a steep scree-lined slope, and then a typical stretch of heather-coated, outcropped hillside, to cover. Surely he was not going to attempt anything such?

But his poacher was no tyro, most evidently. He was not trying to drag his burden downhill, at all, but sideways, and after a comparatively short period of back-breaking haulage, he got the carcase into a burn-channel. There he paused, and tied one of the antlers to a foreleg, presumably to prevent the head from jerking about and catching in roots and projections, and on the bed of the stream he proceeded to splash and plunge his way down, the stag slipping over the polished stone and rounded pebbles much more readily than amongst the clinging heather. When he reached the steep slope, he heaved the beast out of the burn, and attaching a length of rope to the hind legs, he started to pull and run sidelong, slantwise down the hill, the corpse rolling and slithering and pitching, not behind him, but almost alongside, the pull of gravity and the drag on the rope being skillfully counterbalanced. Only once or twice did the thing get nearly out of control. It was quite an able piece of work.

Where the gradient levelled off again, the man halted, necessarily, and glanced along, calculatingly. Alan followed the line of his gaze, and perceived what he was making for—an ill-defined path through the heather, only a deer-track undoubtedly, but still a track. Dragging his trophy along by main force, once more, and painfully slowly over the uneven and sodden ground, he got it into a hollow near to the track, and there, putting down his rifle, he set about pulling armfuls of heather, under which he soon had the stag completely hidden. Thereafter, setting up a tiny cairn of three small stones, set one upon another, nearby, and with only another very brief glance around, he strode off downhill. After five minutes or so, he was swallowed up amongst the stunted pines that were the high outriders of the vast forest that clothed all the low ground, right to the very banks of Spey, in its sombre green.

Alan Kinnear pondered. Had he gone to collect colleagues operating elsewhere amongst the hills? Or had he just buried himself in the cover of the trees to lie low till darkness enabled him to come back to deal with his quarry in anonymity and safety? The former, probably, for one individual could not man-handle that meat down to any road and waiting transport. In which case, the fellow was not just lying there within the cover of the forest, watching the hill, and he himself could risk rising up and making his get-away, without too probable observation. But what was to be his route, his immediate objective? Time seemed to be the decisive factor. It was now turned five o'clock, and it would be dark by eight or eight-thirty—or dark enough for these customers to come back to finish their work. The nearest house on the Glencoraig forest was probably the keeper's house, not far from the Lodge—but that was all of five miles. In this sort of country, he would not cover that in under two hours—and it would take just about as long to get back. By the time that the keeper, an elderly man he was told, had been able to gather some little assistance, it would be too late. He could telephone the police-station from there, but even that would only produce Sandy Cattanach on his bike. Cattanach might have means of raising reinforce-ment quickly, of course—but the time lag was too great . . .

There was one other possibility. Earlier on, from the top of Càrn Buidhe, he had looked down into Glen Àrdoch, and had scanned that long narrow glen with his glasses. And he had descried two or three houses in it, one quite close at hand, nearly directly below, and all but hidden by its sheltering belt of black pines, a whitewashed place of some size, with what looked like a fairly decent road leading to it. A place like that, remote as it was, would quite likely boast a telephone. And, if he calculated aright, by skirting above this corrie here, and over the ridge beyond, he would only have to cross one small shoulder of hill and he would be right above it—no more than two-and-a-half miles, at most. That was halving the distance that he would have to cover, and therefore the time. If he could do that in an hour—most of it would be downhill—then there might be some chance of getting help up in time. Also, the route to it being in entirely the opposite direction, if he *was* seen by the poachers, on his way, they would be less likely to consider him as dangerous.

His decision made, Alan took his bearings carefully on that hollow wherein lay the bloody evidence, and on such local landmarks as were relevant, got to his feet, and retraced his steps up along the empty face of Meall na Corrie.

He was well over the ridge, and striding hugely across a wind-swept plateau of faded tussocky deer-hair, before it occurred to Alan Kinnear to ask himself just why he was doing all this, and with such urgency. After all, it was none of his business, really. He had no particular fish to fry for the deerstalking sports-men—especially if that oaf Crosbie of a few days before, was typical. He had stalked a stag or two himself in his day, but never on a conventional deer-forest. And he had no reason to put himself out too strenuously in the cause of these haughty Macpher-sons—the only member of the family he had come across had hardly gone out of her way to be charming! In a way, weren't his sympathies rather with the poacher, who was taking a risk, pitting his wits against entrenched authority, a tough country, and

the wily and difficult deer on its own ground, than
with the landowner who claimed a whole vast
countryside and all on it as his private possession?
That would be true for the individual, the casual, the
old-style poacher. But this new organised and large-
scale gang poaching was a different matter entirely,
and one at which his every sporting instinct rebelled.
And this Macpherson girl was having a tough time,
and putting up a game fight, apparently—however
much of a shrew she might be! At least, the local folk
were all loud in sympathy with her, and strongly
partisan. Mrs. Macdonald had given her lodger quite
a homily on the subject of poor Miss Fiona. In any
conflict between a young woman struggling against
odds, and the forces of gangsterdom and spivvery,
there could be no question as to where his sympathies
lay—however impersonally—and on to which side
he must throw his weight. No man worthy of the
name could stand idly by in such a situation, surely?
Well, then!

It was a little farther than he had calculated to that
ridge above Glen Ardoch—or perhaps he was not
quite so fresh as he had thought—and it was nearly
six-thirty before, hurrying and sliding and stumbling
down the steep glen-side, he approached the dark
plantation that enfolded the lonely whitewashed
house, farthest outpost of man in that high wilderness.
He rejoiced to note a line of poles carrying telephone
wires, marching up from far down the glen.

It was evidently a small shooting lodge—no doubt,
Glenardoch Lodge, if he had taken the time to look
it up on his map—and the sort of place where his
present mission should gain a sympathetic reception,
at anyrate. But from the single plume of blue smoke
that rose on the evening air from the chimney
crowning the small domestic wing to the rear, it
looked as though the place might well be occupied

only by a caretaker or something of the sort. These
were bad days for letting sporting properties. Alan
made for the back door, and knocked.

A great barking of dogs greeted his summons,
which sounded a hopeful note, and presently the door
was opened by a middle-aged woman backed by
three wide-eyed children and a couple of doubtful
retrievers. She smiled pleasantly and remarked
inevitably on the excellence of the weather.

To her Alan, still a little breathless, spilled his story
and his request. Poachers on Glencoraig, working on
the hill Meall na Corrie. This the nearest house.
Could he telephone to the police at Coraigbeg?

"Surely, surely," the woman agreed, "Och, the
poachers—they're aye at it, the devils. It is bad for
Glencoraig, yes, with the three roads out of it. Ourselves, we are not so bad, with just the one road up
the glen, and it can be watched and blocked. But it's
the pity that himself is not at home to be giving a
hand, and him away down at K'ussie, for the day. It
is so. But come away in, and telephone, to be
sure."

Through in the unlived-in front portion of the
Lodge, amidst the glassy stares of the ranked stags'
heads, Kinnear asked Exchange for the policeman's
house at Coraigbeg. But it was only Mrs. Cattanach
who answered. No, Sandy wasn't at home, at all—
wasn't it his day off, Wednesday, and him away at
the fishing up the glen somewhere. But could she take
a message . . . ?

Perplexed, the man frowned. Could she tell him,
then, the Glencoraig keeper's name, and whether he
was on the telephone?

But apparently that, too, was no use. John
Cameron's house was not on the telephone, really—
not on the public line, anyway. He had an extension
from the Lodge, but as there was nobody living in

D

the Lodge itself just now, there was no through communication. A pity, but there it was.

Thanking her, if only briefly, Alan rang off. There seemed to be only one course left to him, now—to get in touch with the police at Kingussie. Wasn't there an Inspector there? It was much farther away, of course—fifteen miles, anyway—but they might be able to rise to a car. He turned to the instrument again.

Yes, this was the police-office, K'ussie—none other. And yes, Inspector Grant was in it. And who would be wanting him, and for why, at all? Who? Och, well then—just wait a wee whilie, and the Inspector at his supper . . .

The bearer of urgent tidings waited his wee whilie, tapping out his impatience on the hall-stand. At length, certain background noises resolved themselves into a man's authoritative voice.

" Inspector Grant speaking."

" The name is Alan Kinnear—but you won't know me," he was informed, " I am staying in the Coraigmore neighbourhood just now. I'm phoning from Glenardoch Lodge. You know . . . ? Yes. Well, I saw a stag poached on Meall na Corrie, this afternoon. Meall na Corrie . . . oh, well, one of the hills on the Glencoraig forest, about three miles from here. Yes —shot by a tough-looking customer, obviously no shooting-tenant, with a service-rifle. He has hidden it amongst the heather, and I've no doubt means to come back for it after dark. No, I don't think he saw me. You'll know a lot more than I do about the large-scale poaching going on around here . . . ? Yes, it looks like a chance to catch up on it. I know Miss Macpherson of Coraig, and Constable Cattanach, too are very worried about it. I tried to phone Cattanach first, but it's his afternoon off, apparently. Yes. I'd have tried the Glencoraig keeper, but he's not on the phone. No. Yes, this is the nearest house—at least, as far as I know. No—I shouldn't think so. That's right—I saw only the one man, but he might have had accomplices about, down in the trees, maybe— you know what all that forest is like. You will . . .? Oh, good. In a car? Yes, I suppose one of the Glencoraig roads would bring you up nearer to the actual spot, but it would complicate contacting me. Definitely. And it would be much more likely to alarm the poachers, wouldn't it? Oh, yes, I think so, from here . . . even in the dark. I took careful note, all the way. How long? It's ten-to-seven, now . . . Yes, I dare say it will. I'll just wait till you come, then. Very good, Inspector. Au revoir."

Alan made his way back to the kitchen. " The Inspector's coming up, himself, in a car," he told the woman. " He says he ought to be here in about three-quarters of an hour. I've to wait for him. I'm sorry to be such a nuisance."

" Och, it's nothing of the sort you are, sir. Sit you down, and have a bit of supper with us. Cold rabbit-pie, just—but you'll be hungry after the hill. It's glad I am to be seeing a fresh face, and that's a fact —it's few indeed we see up here, whatever. Dearie me—it's himself will be the angry one to be missing this! Head-stalker he is, on Glenardoch, and a hot one on the poachers. Draw in your chair, now. I'll have the tea mashed in just a minute . . ."

CHAPTER V

ALAN KINNEAR had heard all about the difficulties
of letting, and therefore of keepering and maintain-
ing, the deer-forests in these degenerate times, before
Inspector Grant and two other policemen arrived
in an old Austin, at about twenty-to-eight—even if,
for the last quarter-of-an-hour at least, he had been
hard put to it to keep his mind on the conversation,
and not following his eyes away down the glen-
road, or up to the fading light of the heavens.

They set off without delay, up the long ascent out
of the glen, in the shadowless clarity that precedes
the gloaming, with all the hills settling down around
them into the aloof brooding that serves them for
sleep. And after the first confirmatory exchange of
question and answer, they had little to say to each
other; it was not the time and the place for talking,
moreover they needed all their breath for their
climbing. Also, perhaps, the Inspector, if not his
minions, had had other plans for that evening. The
swish of the constabulary's leather leggings through
the heather, the chink of steel-shod boots on stone,
the labour of heavy breathing, and an occasional
grunt, were all the sounds that they produced to
challenge the weary curlews at their calling, and the
abiding quiet of the night.

It was twilight before they reached the top of that
long hill, with Alan becoming ever more anxious
about the light. For most of the way up, he was a
good dozen yards ahead of his companions, and even

then having deliberately to restrain himself. But he did not seem to be able to transmit much of his urgency to the Force; they took that climb at their own pace, concerned it seemed, with their own inscrutable thoughts, and impetuous and excitable Sassenachs, poachers, or the night itself, could wait for them. The Inspector, of course, was by no means a young man.

Crossing the high plateau, Alan realised that it might not be so simple to return straight to the desired spot, as he had assumed. Picking out any sort of landmarks in this half-light was no easy matter. On his outward journey, he had repeatedly looked back, to fix in his mind the route to return, but now, in the strange levelling nebulosity of the dusk, nothing stood out with any definitude, save the stark ultimate outlines and ridges of the high tops, withdrawn and infinitely remote. For all that, he did not allow any faltering in his leading. His war-years as an infantry-officer had taught him that such was fatal, the unforgiveable failure—much more so than leading confidently in the wrong direction.

Eventually, however, they came out on the second ridge not so very far to the left of the great corrie—and since there was only the one on that hill, to give it its name, it must be the right corrie. It gloomed deep in purple shadow below them as they skirted along its rim, and, far beneath the vast spread of the pine forest, lay like a black pall upon the outstretched land.

Keeping as closely as he could to what he hoped was the line of his previous approach, Alan led the way down. He felt that they must be terribly conspicuous, that he wanted to crouch, to creep, to hide somehow, not to march stolidly downhill like this; but quite obviously the police were not going to do

anything so undignified and ridiculous. And no
doubt they were right enough; he supposed it was
sufficiently dark, anyway, and they would probably
never be seen against the gloom of the hillside. It
was just the *attitude* that seemed wrong, somehow.

Approximately where he thought that he had lain,
in the afternoon, and watched the poacher, he
stopped, to take his bearings. But it was difficult.
Distances were all untrustworthy, and there was no
certainty about anything, even of hummocks and
hollows and outcrops five or six yards ahead. Any
one stretch of that braeside looked identical with any
other. However, the presence of the corrie was a
great help—after all, the stag had been shot on the
side of it, and near the foot. That burn-channel that
the poacher had utilised as a sort of shute—that
would be the stream that flowed out of the corrie,
of course. And the fellow had stuck to the burn till
the first levelish stretch reached a markedly steeper
slope, before slanting off at a tangent on his tactical
glissade down towards the tree-level. To make for
the burn, then, seemed the obvious course.

They found it easily enough, its quiet murmur a
friendly thing in that grey solitude. Following it
down, it was not difficult to perceive where the
gradient increased—the stream itself told them that
by its own enhanced eagerness. The judging of the
correct angle of the man's and the stag's descent
was not quite so simple, but they had to take a chance
on that. There might possibly be scrapes and foot-
marks to show on the scree and bare ground, for the
slope was too steep here for the heather to grow
strongly; but the light was insufficient to make any
such apparent, and they could not risk the electric
torches that the constables carried strapped to their
belts.

Where the descent shelved off again, they paused,

to listen. No sound broke the stillness save the muted aggregate whisper of their own and a hundred other tiny burns, and the sibilant sigh of air drifting over the high places. Looking for the deer-path, they spread out, and moved on.

They found two or three tracks, running approximately parallel, and were getting much too far advanced, Alan felt, when a quiet call from one of the constables brought them all to his side. He had stumbled, quite literally, into the essential hollow itself, and uncovered part of the carcase, the underside of which gleamed palely against the darker heather. They were not too late.

The Inspector stooped down, and cleared away some of the heather from the head, running his hand over the tall antlers, still tied to the foreleg. " A switch ! " he said, " Fancy that, now."

His coadjutors felt the horn, likewise, and seemed impressed. Kinnear, enquiringly, followed suit, and found the antlers to be entirely devoid of points, or tines, save the projecting brow-trays, and, of course, the white-tipped apexes. There was none of the branching galaxy that is the sportsman's pride. But the beast seemed to be a big one, fully-grown and well-developed.

" Uh-huh," the Inspector commented, " Just so." And, peering around, " Better be finding another bit hollow for ourselves, then."

" There's one just over there—about ten yards, only," Alan mentioned. " I fell into it, as I came."

" Fine," Grant said, " We'll just be having a bit seat to ourselves."

So they sat and waited amongst the tall heather, while the night grew darker about them, and the stars began to glimmer in the deep blue above. It was very quiet. Only a cock-grouse that they had

disturbed in their advance, kabek-kabeked crossly,
sleepily, every now and again, from somewhere
nearby, to underline the stillness.

The custodians of the law still were uncommuni-
cative, sunk in deepest thought, presumably, and it
was more for conversation's sake than for information that Alan returned to the subject of the carcase.

"You seemed a little bit impressed, Inspector, by
that stag—by the fact that its antlers had no points,"
he mentioned, low-voiced. "Is that very unusual?
A switch, didn't you call it?"

"A switch, yes," Grant agreed. "Och, you see
them now and then, but not that often. A damned
nuisance they are, indeed, on a forest—a right
menace, as you might say."

"Indeed? How's that?"

"Och, well, when the stags are fighting, there, at
the back-end they aren't doing each other that much
harm, at all—the points on their horns do be keeping
them from digging deep, see you. But a switch,
now, is a different story. Those horns are just like
bloody swords, whatever—they'll run right through
another beast. Och, they're right killers, the switches,
and them putting down much bigger and better beasts
than themselves. Many a forest's had a switch as
king of it, a miserable shilpit brute, like enough, but
taking the most of the hinds, for all that. So you get
breeding from the wrong stock, see you—and that's
bad for the forest. Aye, the switches are better away,
every time."

"I see." Kinnear nodded slowly. "Though I
don't suppose these poachers were taking the welfare
of the forest into much account when they shot the
brute!"

"Likely not," the other admitted.

"I expect it was the best proposition in the herd,
for him to grass. I only got a glimpse of the others,

but as far as I could see, they were all hinds. And
they're not in season yet, are they?''

"That is so," Grant agreed. "Not that these
borachs do be caring much about a thing like that.
Och, they'll be shooting anything, just anything."

"Aye," one of his associates substantiated heavily.

"Uh-huh."

The silence returned.

Twice in that long waiting, Alan imagined that he
heard the faint and distant sound of a car-engine—
but on neither occasion did his companions admit to
hearing anything. Anyway, they calculated that the
nearest track up which even the most determined
driver could coax a vehicle, would be fully two miles
distant. They'd heard of these people using jeeps,
admittedly, but no jeep would get very far in that
forest down there. And there was the well-doing
Coraig River in between.

The Inspector lay back in the heather, and seemed
to sleep, an example that one of his juniors was
prompt to follow. The other chewed rhythmically
and continuously at nothing in particular, in a
strangely bovine fashion, eminently suitable for the
static passing of time—perhaps a speciality developed
in the Force. Alan Kinnear alone was restless and on
edge.

For all that, it was the cud-chewing constable who
heard the sound first. Stopping only momentarily in
his mastication, he said, "Garron," and relapsed
into his rumination.

His colleagues sat up, listening.

"Uh-huh," said Mr. Grant, at length. "Just the
one."

"Aye."

Still Alan could hear nothing, beyond the quiet
continuous susurration of wind and water. "Afraid I
don't get it," he admitted.

It was almost a couple of minutes before he made it out, the muffled clop-clop of broad hooves on the heather; and by that time the sound was from very close at hand, for he could also identify the creak of harness and the metallic clink of a chain. That it came from along their deer-track was apparent. And he had thought that he had good ears! But even when the policeman had first spoken, it could not have been far off. It was astonishing that, in all that hush, such a sound should not have reached them earlier. Perhaps the fact that it proceeded from below them accounted for it, or that the drift of air was in the wrong direction, or that the faint but unending sough that emanated from the great pine forest was a more potent sound that was palpable . . . .

They were all peering along the line of that deer-path, but it was ten o'clock now, and fully dark, and as yet nothing was visible. Their hide-out was actually nearer to the line of approach than was the cached stag, though set-back well from the track.

Quite suddenly, the horse materialised out of the gloom, without any transition, at about forty yards or so. And strain their eyes as they would, they could make out only the one man at the beast's head.

In silence they watched as the little cavalcade came up, drew level, and then, only slightly past them, halted. It was quite obvious now that the man was alone, and though the watchers were keeping an eye on the track behind him, there was neither sign nor sound of followers.

Leaving the horse standing, the fellow stepped into the heather, directly towards them, most evidently casting about to locate his cache. Alan held his breath as the poacher came close, to within a few yards of them, But then, apparently recognising some land-

mark, he trended off to the left, fairly quickly found
what he sought, and returned to lead his garron up
to the stag.

Kinnear glanced at the Inspector enquiringly, but
that man shook his head. " Let him be, a wee," he
ordered, beneath his breath.

They heard the man's expelled breath, as he bent
to clear away the covering heather, and his brief
word to the horse, as he manœuvred it into
position. Then there was the rattle of a chain.
Evidently the kill was going to be dragged along;
Alan had wondered how one man was going to hoist
a couple of hundred-weights of meat on to even a
short-legged pony's back.

There was a certain amount of manipulation of the
chain, and then another command to the garron.
"Wait," the Inspector whispered, " Let him come
to us. If he was bolting, we'd never be getting him
in this dark."

There was some sense in that.

The garron was being urged forward now, and they
could hear it straining at the weight it had to drag
out of that hollow, and the scrape of its hooves on
the stones. Then it was on to the path again, and
coming towards them, its load scuffling and bumping
behind it, the chain clanking. There was noise
enough to cover the Inspector's orders.

" Donal'—you round the back, to the other side,
in case he makes a bolt for it. You too, Angus—but
bide you at the back. You, sir—grab the garron.
Right? Come on then ! "

It was all rather an anti-climax, the four of them
rushing out on the lone unfortunate like that. The
victim didn't help, either; he didn't bolt, or put up a
fight, or even loose a flood of invective. The only
remark he made, was " Whoa, Nell—whoa, lass ! "
and so stood, waiting for them.

"Aye, then," Grant said, mildly enough. "Would that be a stag you've got there, man?"

"It might, then," he was answered, resignedly. And then, as the other leaned forward to stare into the gloom. "Losh, the polis is it, and all!"

"That's right," the Inspector nodded, "Just that. You wouldn't be after poaching this stag, now, would you?"

The stranger shrugged, and said nothing.

"I'ph'mmm." The older man came closer for a look at his captive. "Who would you be, at all, now? Your name, man?"

Still the man held his tongue. One of the constables switched his torch full on him, and the Inspector's voice came quickly.

"Put off that light, Donal'. There's maybe others in it." To the prisoner, he spoke more sharply. "Is it alone you are—or is there a gang of you?"

The poacher frowned, shaking his head. "What for would there be a gang? There's just myself in it."

"Aye. Maybe." Grant sounded unconvinced. "What did you say your name was?"

"I didn't say it was anything," the other pointed out. "But it's Fraser—Archie Fraser."

"Uh-huh. Well, Archibald Fraser," Inspector Grant chanted, suitably solemn, "I hereby charge you with illegal possession of game, the property of Ewan Macpherson Esquire of Coraig, trespassing in pursuit of game, and poaching—all indictable offences. And I have to warn you that anything you say may be taken down, and may be used in evidence against you." He took a deep breath, and resumed his normal voice. "Have you anything to say, at all, then?"

"Devil the thing," the culprit said, grimly.

"Right, then—you're coming along with us, see

you. You're coming to the station." He looked from
the delinquent to the horse, and then over to his
colleagues, and tipping back his peaked cap,
scratched his head. "Now, what the hell are we to
be doing with this shelt, and the damned stag,
then?"

They considered that poser awhile, in silence. "A
bad road to be taking the garron, up over the hill,"
one of the constables volunteered.

"It is that."

"Och, we'd never be getting it over there, whatever, all night," Grant declared, "Especially with
this stag in it." He cocked an eye at the last speaker.
"Angus, man—you'll have to go down with it, I
doubt. Nothing else for it, at all. Take it down to
John Cameron's house, at Glencoraig Lodge—he's
the keeper. Leave the brute with him, and the stag
too. It'll be the nearest house, I'm thinking, that
direction—and he should be getting the stag, anyway. It'll be rough-going till you get across the
Coraig, but after it'll not be that bad."

"Aye," the constable acceded, but unenthusias-
tically, "That is so."

"You know John Cameron's house?"

"Och, yes—I know it fine. It'll be the getting
there, with this lot, that's the trouble."

"There's a bridge down just below the waterfall,
there," the captive mentioned, helpfully. "And a
track all the way down the glen, after that. Even a
polisman couldn't miss it!"

"Enough of that from you," Grant said, but
without heat. "I'll be sending the car for you, when
I get back, to John Cameron's. What about yourself, Mr. Kinnear?"

"I'll just go down the glen with the constable, I
think. It's on my road, more or less." Alan told
him, "If you want me any time, you can get me

care of Mrs. Macdonald, Balnahard, Coraigbeg."

"Och, I'll mind that, yes. You'll likely be needed as a witness. Well, then—it'll be goodnight to you . . ."

"See you," the malefactor interrupted, "before you're for off, you'd be better to be after hoisting that stag on the garron's back. She'll go more easy that way." He seemed determined to be helpful— even if he did add, "I wouldn't trust a polisman with a horse of mine, this way—you'd have the legs broken on her!"

The Inspector ignored the addendum, but acknowledged the wisdom of the first suggestion. "It's right enough, she'll travel better on top," he agreed, "Come on—we'll get it up."

So, unhooking the chain from the stag's hind legs, the five of them got busy. Undoubtedly, the prisoner did most of the work, or, at least, had most to show for his efforts. Somehow they got the heavy carcase draped across the garron's broad back, and tied down with a rope that was part of the poacher's equipment.

This done, the company split up, without further delay. The last communication that passed between the two parties, came from the felon.

"Keep you along this track, to the second bit burn," he shouted back, "and follow it down. It'll bring you right to the river, and you'll be hearing the waterfall. And look you after that garron, mind, or I'll be having the law on you, by heaven!"

And that was Archie Fraser.

It was a long and weary trudge that followed, and Alan for one was practically asleep on his feet before they reached the cottage of Cameron the keeper. The man Fraser's directions had stood them in good stead, and they had found his two burns, and a track of sorts following the second one down across rough hillside and then through dark heather-floored forest right to the rushing headlong Coraig River, a track that the sure-footed garron negotiated without difficulty or much in the way of guidance from the men. At the river they could hear the roar of the waterfall nearish at hand, and down below it, perhaps half-a-mile, they found the rough bridge of pine-logs. That half-mile along the river-bank was the most trying stretch of the journey. After seeking vainly to find a possible route for the horse along its rocky, slippery, tree-strewn course, they gave it up and left the brute to find its own way—which it did so ably that they followed behind, quite content to play second fiddle. Once across the bridge, however, it was plain if tedious sailing; only the interminable plodding down an endless sandy road between the black walls of the pine forest, and only the scuffle and clop of the garron's hooves and the occasional cry of a night bird, to break the silence—for Alan soon gave up any attempt at conversation with his companion, who seemed to be well content to chew his way right to the end of the road. This Angus was the first really inarticulate Highlandman that it had been his lot to come across. No more than half-awake, then, he arrived at the door of Cameron's cottage, sometime in the region of twelve o'clock that night, footsore and bone-weary, and stood swaying by the garron's head while the constable knocked up the unfortunate keeper.

John Cameron's reception of his untimely visitors was conducted from an upper window, with the aid of an electric torch. The exchange was mercifully brief, confined to essentials, and for once, carried on mainly by the policeman. He conveyed the compliments of Inspector Grant of Kingussie, announced the red-handed capture of a poacher on Glencoraig, now in custody, indicated the stag which was herewith returned to its rightful ownership, and requested that the accused's garron be taken care of till such time as proper arrangements could be made for its disposal. All in considerably fewer words than it takes to tell.

Cameron, as befitted a man ravished from his good lady's side, was prepared to accept that, accept anything meantime, content to make his enquiries at a more suitable hour. He directed that the stag be dumped in the cart-shed and the door shut on it, that the garron be turned into the bit field beside the cow, and left there, and wished his visitors godspeed. One parting remark, he made, before he closed the window, jabbing with his torch.

"That beast looks to me sort of like Archie Fraser's grey shelt," he said.

"Archie Fraser's grey shelt it is," the law confirmed.

The keeper banged down the window-sash.

And on that note, Alan Kinnear fumblingly helped to loose the stag so that it fell on the cart-shed floor, stood while the garron was conducted through a gate into a little field, and lurched off again down-hill, towards Coraigmore and Balnahard, leaving the unaffected Angus to ruminate to his heart's content on a tree-trunk at the road-end, till his car came for him.

On Alan's eventual greeting by an anxious, irate, and eloquent Mrs. Macdonald, armed ready with bandages, lint, and restoratives, and the halting explanations that were all he was capable of producing, we will draw a compassionate veil.

CHAPTER VI

By noon next day the district of Coraig, the parish of Inverardoch, the province of Badenoch, perhaps the entire county of Inverness, knew that Archie Fraser, Dalnamuick was locked up in Kingussie on a charge of poaching, of actual *poaching* mind you, and Glencoraig deer into the bargain—and all on account of an interfering Sassenach, a non-account summervisitor, a meddlesome tourist, just one of Seana Macdonald's hikers. Was ever the like of that heard before, at all, my goodness !

The news arrived at Balnahard by the Post, who brought it, along with the mail, at approximately eleven o'clock. Whereupon, Mrs. Macdonald waited no longer with her sluggardly boarder's breakfast, but marched upstairs with his porridge and eggs, knocked loudly on the door, and walked in, to complete the remainder of the waking-up process partly by hand and partly by word-of-mouth.

"What's this I'm hearing about your last night's ploy, Mr. Kinnear, then?" she demanded of the blinking and tousled-headed lodger. "Don't be saying that it's the truth that Simon the Post's been after telling me?"

"Eh . . . ? Last night . . . ? You mean, about the poaching?" Alan yawned. "Is that it—this police-business? Not knowing your postman's version, Mrs. Macdonald, I can't tell you whether it's true or not." He was mildly quizzical, with the gentle forbearance of a patient man wakened out of

E
65

well-earned slumber to answer foolish if well-intentioned questions.

"He is saying you had Archie Fraser, Dalnamuick arrested for the poaching!"

"Well," the man said, modestly, "it's perhaps a little strong to state that I *had* him arrested. After all, I was only the link, as it were, between the police and the guilty party. But in essence, the story is true enough. Archie Fraser was the fellow's name, at anyrate."

"Goodness gracious me—d'you tell me that! But this is bad, bad. You shouldn't have done a thing like that, at all, Mr. Kinnear. Och, I'm right disappointed in you. Dearie me—this is terrible, whatever."

"Why? What's wrong with it?"

"Wrong? Och, everything's wrong with it, then." Mrs. Macdonald pursed her lips, and shook her white head. "Archie Fraser would never be doing a thing like that."

"But he did, just the same. I saw him do it, with my own eyes." Alan still was smiling.

"Och, no—not the poaching, see you. Not Archie?" That was definite.

"But I saw him shoot the brute, I tell you," the young man declared, strongly. "I was there. I saw him gralloch the beast and drag it down-hill, and come back for it in the dark. I saw the whole thing."

"Och, maybe he'd lift a bit stag off the hill, now and again, Archie—but, my goodness, he's no poacher, whatever. You've just made a terrible mistake, Mr. Kinnear—you have so."

"But, hang it all—this is ridiculous! He didn't deny it, when he was charged . . ."

But old Seana Macdonald dismissed such reasoning as irrelevant. "Just you take your breakfast, and away with you along by the twelve bus to

K'ussie, and get him out again," she directed.
"That's the best thing, see you. Och, he's a nice
lad, Archie, and likely he'll not be holding it against
you, if you're explaining that you didn't understand
it, just."

"But, look here . . ."

"Eat, you," his landlady ordered, crisply, making
for the door. "You haven't that long, at all, and
the bus coming through Coraigbeg at twelve-ten.
You'll be needing all your time. Hurry now." And
the door closed, very unmistakeably.

"Well I'm damned!" said Alan Kinnear.

He was completing his toilet, when Specht's barking heralded the sound of a man's voice downstairs,
and presently Mrs. Macdonald was calling up,

"Here's the police for you, now, Mr. Kinnear."

"All right—I'll be down in a minute," she was
told, not very genially. It was a frowning face that
the man continued to consider in his mirror.

But when he got downstairs, it was Sandy
Cattanach whom he found waiting for him. "Man,
Mr. Kinnear—this is a bonny basket of trouts you've
landed for us, whatever!" he charged, without
preamble, without any reference to the fine day it
was, even, head ashake.

"Good Lord—you too!" Alan complained,
"What's all this in aid of, I'd like to know?"

"Och, it's Archie Fraser, Dalnamuick. Damn it,
you've got Archie in the jail, man. What came over
you to be doing a thing like that?"

"What came over Archie confounded Fraser to be
poaching stags, is more like it!" the younger man
returned with spirit, and with reason. "Who is this
Archie Fraser, anyway?"

"Archie? Och, Archie's the tenant in Dalnamuick,
the bit farm along the road, here—the second place

you come to. Always there's been Frasers in Dalnamuick—damn't, they've been in it just about as long as the Macphersons themselves. He's all right, is Archie—sergeant in the Lovat Scouts, he was, and got the M.M. at yon Alamein place. Och, I used to play at the bowls with his dad, whatever."

"Yes—that's all very well. But he *was* poaching, wasn't he . . . ?"

"No, no—not poaching. Not what you call *poaching*, see you . . ."

"You mean, he had permission to shoot that stag?"

"Well, now—I wouldn't just say he had permission, exactly," the policeman declared, more cautiously. "Not just what you'd call permission, maybe. But, man, there's no harm in it, at all . . ."

"That is so, yes," Seana Macdonald confirmed, from the kitchen door, where she stood, an interested observer. "Many's the bit haunch and chop I've had from Archie, indeed."

"H'rr'mmm," said P.C. Cattanach, hurriedly. "Och, aye. No, no—you'd never be calling Archie Fraser a poacher, whatever."

"Look—let's get this straight." Alan besought him. "This deer-forest of Glencoraig is either still let to that Major Crosbie, or is being attempted to be let to someone else? Right? Today is the second of September—so the stalking season's started. The place is being poached to death—so much so that the owners are having the greatest difficulty in letting it, and they, and the police, indeed the whole neighbourhood, are greatly concerned over the whole business. And yet, when I lay a poacher by the heels, caught red-handed and not denying his guilt, everybody rounds on me as having done something terrible, put my foot in it, and generally upset the entire district! I can understand it, in a way, if his neighbours are distressed, he being some sort of local worthy—but it's hardly a sound attitude for the police, surely ? ''

'' That's right enough, in a manner of speaking, Mr. Kinnear, but . . .''

'' Tell me this, then. Had this Fraser any legal right to take that stag, yesterday ? ''

'' Well, maybe not just exactly a legal right, no—but nobody would have thought anything about it, see you, if you . . .''

'' Not even Miss Macpherson ? ''

Sandy Cattanach coughed. '' Well, I'm not just committing myself as to what Miss Fiona would be saying,'' he hedged, carefully. '' Not but what she's a sensible lassie, and knows fine when to shut her eyes, like. But man, there was no need for Miss Fiona to be brought into the likes of this, at all . . .''

'' Well, I'm blest ! You beat me, I must say ! Here I was, thinking I was doing her and her blessed estate a good turn—and you too, Cattanach—and now you turn round and tell me . . .''

'' Och, if you'd just got in touch with myself, before you went bringing in the Inspector, there would have been none of all this, at all . . .''

'' But I tried to, man—I phoned your house. But you were away fishing, somewhere.'' Alan snorted. '' Poaching, too, as like as not ! ''

'' Now, Mr. Kinnear ! '' Cattanach protested, with dignity. '' Uncalled for, that is, yes.''

Alan ignored him. '' I tried to get hold of the keeper, too—but he's not on the phone, direct, or so your wife said. What else could I do but ring Kingussie ? I thought I'd got hold of the gang that's ruining the place. Inspector Grant didn't seem to find anything wrong with my actions, anyway.''

'' Och, it just happens that the Inspector isn't knowing Archie, at all. You can't be blaming the

Inspector, with you handing him Archie in a bag, just. What could he do, the man, but run him in—and what can he do now, but hold on to him, too? Och, it is bad, bad.''

'' Mrs. Macdonald has some hare-brained idea of me dashing along to Kingussie right away, and getting him out, somehow. I suppose she means for me to withdraw the charges, or something of the sort. But it wasn't me that charged him . . . it was Grant himself.''

'' Yes, indeed,'' the old lady nodded. '' And you'll be missing your bus, unless you're off this minute. Unless maybe you take Sandy's bicycle . . . ? ''

'' Och, that's no use at all, Seana,'' the constable declared. '' Archie's charged, before witnesses, and in custody. It isn't for Mr. Kinnear, or the Inspector either, to be withdrawing the charges. Nor yet Miss Fiona, either, and him caught red-handed, as you might say. It is in the hands of yon Procurator-Fiscal, now—and that means the Sheriff, whatever. And you know what like the Sheriff is about the poaching. There's been that much of it. Hech-aye. I doubt even if he'll be getting bail.''

'' Och, poor Archie, the lad.''

'' As you say, yes.''

There was silence in that pleasant sitting-room for a little, and then Kinnear spoke abruptly. '' I'm sorry,'' he said, '' Very sorry, about it all. But I don't see that I acted wrongly in the circumstances, as they developed—not knowing your peculiar local idiosyncrasies. It's most unfortunate, but . . . well, I'm sorry.''

And turning about, he strode upstairs again, heavy-footed, and left them there.

Alan Kinnear *was* sorry, too, about the whole wretched business, for Archie Fraser—and for himself, likewise. For, while it all was no fault of his, and his conscience, even his self-esteem, was undisturbed, that was more than could be said for his susceptibilities, and his peace of mind. What man of his pen could work effectively with the entire neighbourhood looking down its nose at him, treating him with the hostile and frigid politeness reserved for lepers, excisemen, and the like—what writer of even frivolous detective fiction could produce any sort of work, let alone a masterpiece under these conditions? Indeed, had it not been for the fact that almost certainly he would be required to give evidence locally at Fraser's trial, he probably would have packed up and left the district, however topographically and atmospherically suitable it was. Though, again, he might not. There was an obstinate streak in that man—there has to be, in any writer, who, at say Chapter Two of even the veriest pot-boiler, can face up to the prospect of compiling another eighteen such, another three hundred pages, another ninety-thousand reluctant words; obstinacy, mule-like and pig-headed, is a prerequisite—and that streak was aroused more or less automatically by the opposition encountered, and increased proportionately as the evidence of the latter grew. A trying and deplorable attribute. What probably set the seal on his decision to dig in his heels, to ride out the storm, was Mrs. Macdonald's minatory account to him of a talk that she had had with Miss Macpherson of Coraig. It seemed that the peculiar and vixenish young woman was no more reasonable and consistent than were the rest of her less responsible neighbours, in that she as fully deplored the arrest of the wretched Fraser, being apparently quite ungrateful for the service performed on behalf of her brother's property and estate. Even, according to Seana Macdonald, she had used the term " busybody." Nothing could be calculated more effectively to ensure that Alan Kinnear set his teeth, and stayed put.

But if stubborn and headstrong, he was not entirely an unsympathetic individual, and his indignation was not directed against the other unfortunate victim of circumstances. As has been said, indeed, he was sorry for this Archie Fraser. For undoubtedly, the fellow appeared to be likely to catch it in the neck. Everyone was at one on that. For the new Sheriff was known to be very hot against the poachers, and had warned recently that maximum penalties were to be the rule, in an effort to stamp out this pernicious business that was disturbing the peace of Highland Scotland. Thirty days seemed to be the accepted computation of what was coming to him, thirty days of September—and his harvest not in! Thirty days at any time was a bad thing—but thirty days in September was a disaster.

Kinnear's sympathy was not entirely theoretical. That was why, two mornings later, he took the sandy road through the pines to Dalnamuick.

CHAPTER VII

THE Fraser establishment at Dalnamuick, too large
to be termed a croft, but not, by Southern standards,
to be accounted a farm, lay perhaps a mile-and-a-
half through the forest from Balnahard, and con-
sisted of about twenty acres of arable and something like a thousand of euphemistically-called rough
pasture.

This latter, of course, was nothing more than
natural scrub, woodland, heather, and hillside, on
which could be supported hardy blackfaced sheep
at the rate of say one per four acres, and a few shaggy
black cattle.

Unfortunately, during the months of winter
and early spring, such rudimentary grazings
had to be supplemented largely—hence the vital
importance of every inch and scrap of those stony
and oddly-shaped acres of tilth, on whose thin oats,
potatoes, and turnips, the survival of beast, and
therefore man, depended. And September was
harvest time.

The house and steading crowned its own low green
hill at the edge of the forest, and around it its little
patches of field, yellow corn, blue-green roots, and
the grass of the infield, made pleasant splashes of
colour after the sombre hues of the pinewoods.
Behind, the outliers of the great hills rose almost at
once, through turning birch and bracken. As Alan
approached up a steepish stony track, he noticed an
old bent man, scything away at the far corner of

the cornfield, a picture of patient husbandry as old as time.

Kinnear knocked at the door of the house—the back door, it was, for he had learned so much, at least. A young woman answered it, a child in her arms. She was an open-faced, mild-eyed creature, pleasant if slightly harassed-seeming—and if she was not very tidy about her hair and apparel, hadn't she her excuse? The man's compunction smote him like a blow.

"Good morning," he said, and with little confidence and certainly no casualness behind his voice. "You will be Mrs. Fraser, I expect?"

"I am, yes. It is a fine day, again. Hush you, Kirsteen, now."

Alan coughed. "My name is Kinnear," he said, and waited.

"Och, yes—you'll be the gentleman that does be staying with Seana Macdonald, Balnahard. I thought that, sir. Can I be helping you, at all?"

"No—or at least, yes, you can." That came out in something of a rush. "You can accept my sincere regrets that I should have been the cause of so much distress to you."

The young woman wiped the baby's mouth with the tail of her apron. "These things do be happening, sir," she said, with a quiet acceptance that was less critical even than resignation would have been.

"Yes, but I do want you to realise, that if I'd known all the circumstances, if I'd fully understood what was involved for your husband, I'd, I'd . . ." the man's word's tailed away. After all, what *had* he done that was wrong, or even inadvisable or indiscreet? Hadn't he done just what any more or less responsible individual would have done in the circumstances? In essence, he certainly had done nothing to apologise for—and yet, *in effect*, look what

his action had brought about! This pathetic
creature . . .

But Jean Fraser was not being pathetic, only
practical, reasonable, helpful. " You would be doing
what you thought was right, sir—and that's the thing
that we all must be doing, at the end of it, whatever."

Actually, in the state of mind in which Alan
Kinnear found himself, he would have preferred that
she had produced reproach, revilement, raillery,
instead of this calm fatal acquiescence. It would have
been easier to counter, easier to bear, easier on his
self-esteem. " Look, Mrs. Fraser," he said urgently,
" I thought I'd caught one of these poaching gangs
from the cities—these thugs that are ruining the deer-
forests. I thought I was helping the estate, helping
the neighbourhood, which depends on the estate to
such a large extent. You must believe me, that if I'd
realised it was a local man just, er . . . well, just
having a bit of sport, I'd have looked the other way,
forgotten the whole thing."

" Quiet you, Kirsteen, now—hush, will you," the
woman crooned. " That is kindly said, sir. It is a
great pity, indeed, the way things have turned out.
But Archie knew the risks that was in it—always I
was after telling him. Och, myself, I was against it
from the start, whatever. But Archie is that keen on
the rifle, and could be seeing no harm in it, at all.
The deer do be eating our corn, and he says he is
taking nothing more than the laird owes him for the
damage they are doing. You cannot be blaming
Archie too much, and him young, and liking his
sport. In the winter he does be shooting the hinds
for the Macphersons, and he is the best stalker in the
place, indeed." She shook her head, wistfully. " He
is not a bad man, at all, Archie."

" Of course, he's not—I realise that, perfectly,"
Alan cried, unhappily. " It was all a misunderstand-

ing, as far as I'm concerned. He was no more
criminally-intentioned than I was maliciously-
intentioned. It's just a miserably unfortunate hash
of circumstances. They say the road to hell is paved
with good intentions, don't they!" He shrugged.
"But what's done is done, unfortunately, and no
amount of saying I'm sorry will help much, will it?
But what I *can* do to help, what I want and intend
to do, is to give a hand with your harvest here, Mrs.
Fraser."

"Och, dear me, no—not at all, sir. There is no
need for such a thing—never be thinking it."

"But I mean it—I want to help."

"You are kind, sir—but we will manage fine, I
am sure. Och, yes—fine."

"Will you?" Alan raised sceptical eyebrows.
"How many have you got, to do it?"

"Well," she looked away, "there is Old Callum,
there . . . and my own self . . ."

"Yes?"

"And, and there will be neighbours to be giving
us a bit hand, to be sure . . ."

"Are the neighbours not at their own harvest?
Not that you've *got* many neighbours, have you?
Not within miles, anyway?"

"That is so, yes—but they will not forget us,
likely. Och, Kirsteen, now—ssshhh then, ssshhh."

"And how much corn to be cut?" the man went
on, unrelenting.

"Just about the fourteen acres—no more."

"And only a scythe to cut it with?"

"No, no—there is a reaper, once the lanes are cut.
It is not a binder, at all—but it cuts quicker than the
scythe, whatever."

Alan nodded grimly. "Mrs. Fraser," he said,
"obviously, you need every scrap of assistance you
can get—you owe it to your husband, don't you?

We all know what the weather's like hereabouts in September, and how full advantage of every possible moment of decent weather must be taken if you're going to get your corn in. I'm no expert, I assure you—I've never tried even to work a reaper. But I'm able-bodied, and I can tie up sheaves. What's more, I'm going to—and right away. I can't write— which is my job—because I'm not in the right frame of mind. And I've nothing else to do. This sort of thing, harvesting, is just what I need. So you'll be doing me a favour by letting me help. No—I mean it. You're not getting rid of me."

Jean Fraser tried to frown, but she was not the sort of young woman that had any aptitude for frowning. " Och, goodness me," she sighed, " What would Archie say to this, at all ? "

" Archie, if he had any sense, would say, ' Make him work ! Keep him at it. Work him overtime. If anybody's asked for it, he has ! ' And he'd be right ! Now—where do I start ? "

The woman smiled then, and to Kinnear, that smile, faint as it might be, was something to be proud of. "Come you, then, and I will take you to Callum," she said, " He is hard of hearing, Callum, but I will tell him. This way, it is."

And so, Alan Kinnear went to work in the small slantwise fields of Dalnamuick, alongside a rheumy-eyed deaf old greybeard, who crooned to himself tunelessly as he swung his scythe, and every now and then leant on its curved handle to stare fixedly at the nearest hill-top, or at the Bealach Pass, or it might be, into infinity itself, for periods as long as ten minutes at a time—as indeed he might, for that view was well worth the staring at, even after a life-time of it. It did not take the novice long to appreciate the suitability and wisdom of such a procedure, either, as he straightened an aching back above the levelled oats—even if he did not go in for quite such lengthy trances in the process.

His job was to gather up the cut stalks, pathetically short and thin as they were, into armfuls, form a rope twisted out of themselves, and tie this round the bundle to form a sheaf, and to set up every ten such sheaves alean against each other, into a stook. These stooks had to be carefully and compactly built, so as not to blow down, like a ridge-pole tent open at both ends, and heedfully placed at the right angle so that the prevailing wind might blow through them and dry the sheaves. Also, at this stage, they had to be set where they would not be in the road of the reaping machine when it was brought in. All this Alan learned gradually out of much patient instruction from the ancient—mainly by demonstration, for as well as being deaf, Old Callum—a Fraser, also, apparently, but no relation—seemed to be largely speechless, though he laughed and chuckled cheerfully the while, and his wordless tuneless singing went on practically without ceasing.

By lunch-time, a margin for the reaper to work in had been cut right round the first field, and the sheaf-making and stooking was catching up. Alan borrowed Archie Fraser's old ram-shackle bicycle, and rattled back to Balnahard in excellent time thereon. He did not divulge to Mrs. Macdonald just what he was up to; he and his landlady at the moment were on slightly distant terms.

In the afternoon, they got on famously. Old Callum was started on to cutting the lanes for the second and smaller field, and presently Jean Fraser herself came down to join them, wheeling the baby in an ancient go-car. Between them, they got the sheaves and stooks finished in the first field in little more than an hour—for the young woman laboured

strongly as well as deftly—and were able to follow
the old man, and soon, to be working practically on
his heels. On learning that there was a second scythe
hanging on the wall of the stable, Alan went to fetch
it, to try his prentice hand. But for all Callum's
mirthful efforts at instruction, the girl's gentle if
pink-faced encouragement, and his own determination, he could make nothing of it, digging the point
into the ground, flattening but not severing the oat-
stalks, and cutting only thin air—to the decided
danger of his legs. Reluctantly he laid it by, while
there was any scythe left, and resumed his gathering. Old Callum was greatly tickled—so much so
that he was prevented from continuing with his own
scything for a time that Alan at least considered was
out of all proportion to the entertainment provided.

However, in mid-afternoon, another harvester
appeared, a stocky elderly man, grizzled but high-
complexioned, and dressed in a plus-four suit of
rather less ancient tweeds than were usual amongst
the farming folk, and who eyed Kinnear just a little
askance. He was introduced by Jean Fraser as John
Cameron, the gamekeeper, and shook hands with
formal civility, if withal a wary eye. Thereafter he
took the second scythe, and removing himself to a
safe distance on the other side of Callum Fraser,
began to cut, apparently an expert. Since, very soon
thereafter the young woman went back to the house
to make the tea, the scything quite noticeably drew
ahead of the sheafing again. Undoubtedly old
Callum was much relieved; he could contemplate
the view in peace, once more, without all this
unseemly haste.

They took their tea sitting on sheaves where they
worked—though John Cameron made only a token
gesture of it, drinking a brief cup and hurrying back
to his scythe on the plea that he had had his tea before

he came; Alan surmised that it might well be the
embarrassing company that was at the back of his
urgency. For himself, it was pleasant to sit relaxed
on the sheaves in the warm regard of the afternoon
sun, and let his aching muscles ease themselves,
drinking bitter strong tea and chewing innumerable
buttered scones, what time his eyes feasted in their
turn on all the array of peak and buttress, glen and
corrie and pass, that was spread out for their delecta-
tion. Also, he exchanged a word or two with his
hostess, smiled in sympathy with some of the more
pronounced chuckles of the permanently diverted
Callum, and fed surreptitious morsels of scone to a
lean black-and-white collie that had taken up its
stance beside him.

Afterwards, all four of them resumed their labours,
till it was time for the woman to take the baby up
to the house. By seven o'clock, with the sun already
sinking in level glory behind the long ridges of the
Monadh Liath, the margins of the second field were
cut, the sheaves made and either stooked or set up
against the fence, and all was ready for the reaper,
on the morrow.

Disclaiming the young woman's grave thanks, and
assuring her that he had enjoyed his day and that he
would be back first thing tomorrow—she told him
not to come too early, as the dew would not have
dried off sufficiently till ten or so—Alan Kinnear
walked back to Balnahard through the gathering
shadows, tired, stiff, with a griping pain in his back,
and his hands burning and full of thorns and the
jags of thistles. And he yawned as he went, not once
but many times, and felt less dissatisfied with life
and himself than he had done since he lay on the
broad shoulder of Meall na Corrie three days ago,
before the confounded shot was fired.

He even wrote a little, that night, after supper—

till he fell asleep over his notebook by the sizzling birch-log fire.

But next day, he did not go up to Dalnamuick, at the back of ten. It rained with a dour and heavy persistence that offered no hope of lessening. There would be no harvesting that day, And the next, it was just as bad, with this time a blustering wind behind it to lash a cowering world. This was typical Highland harvest weather. Alan Kinnear, in between brisk walks in the groaning dripping woods, cudgelled his brains, chewed his pencil, and made surprisingly little impression on his new notebook.

And on the third day, when a pale gleam of tired sunlight illumined the still grey morning, and he repaired to Dalnamuick, hopefully, it was only to be told that there could be no cutting that day, either; the corn was not only sodden wet, but partly beaten down by the wind. Nothing could be done with it, as it was. If it was a bright and breezy day, it might lift and dry off well enough to cut tomorrow. Och, they would be hoping so, whatever . . .

Alan, at a loose end, restless, and with his lunch in his pocket, turned his face to the high hills, and commenced to walk, long-strided.

F

CHAPTER VIII

PANTING, Alan Kinnear reached the crest of the rise,
and halted on the very lip of the declivity, eager
eyed. It was not only his climbing thus far that set
him panting, either; it was a form of excitement, the
sheer challenge of what he saw. He was perhaps
two-thirds of the way up Beinn Dearg, a great lump
of a brown heather hill with an almost flat summit
nearly touching four thousand feet. But however
flat the top, it was far from dull—from this side, at
least. He was facing into a great amphitheatre that
his map called Coire Ruadh; but it was more than
any corrie—it was a vast basin gouged out of the
side of the mountain, level about its floor, and
cradling therein a little blue loch, while behind, its
walls rose almost sheer for practically a thousand
feet to the summit plateau, a majestic frowning
precipice of seamed and fissured and riven red rock,
proud, defiant. There are many such amongst the
Cairngorm giants, but this was considerably further
south and west than most of them, by itself amongst
lesser hills. Alan had espied just a glimpse of it—
the cliff, that is—when he had climbed the Sgoran
that other day. Beinn Dearg, the hill itself, was
plainly visible from Coraig and the Spey valley, all
its brown western flank and level summit; but it
gave no hint of this tremendous corrie from that
angle—or indeed, from any angle offering a distant
view. This secret was hidden in its own red heart.

There was no question, of course, but that the

man must climb up there—anything else was unthinkable. He had spoken truly when he had told Mrs. Macdonald that first day that he was not a rock-climber—he was not, in that he did not make a special practice of climbing rocks, though he had done some climbing in his day. But that did not mean that he was precluded from tackling an ascent, where one just pushed itself forward—as here—any more than, because he was not a hiker, he must not go for a walk. And he was just in the pent-up, urgent, vaguely-frustrated mood for it.

He had not brought his binoculars—since it was a day's harvesting that he had set out to do—but the air, as so often after rain, was of a crystal clarity that threw every feature of the rock-face into sharp relief. He sat down, and sought to pick his route and plan his assault.

There were innumerable cracks and fissures on that startling façade, and the man knew enough of the business to realise that however sheer it might appear from out in front, it was not indeed anything like perpendicular as a whole. A number of white cascading burns were his guide; by their progress, streaming, scoring, splaying, or sheerly plunging, he could plot the approximate angles of descent. There were one or two areas of overhang to be avoided, as there were certain greenish aprons of smooth rock-slide, that could spell disaster. But likewise, there were not a few good buttresses, with suitable traverses, and at least two tall crevices that might almost be termed chimneys. Altogether, he could visualise a reasonable and not too daring ascent, which at the same time would be exhilarating, by no means child's-play, and infinitely worth doing, especially in his present frame of mind. He finished the last of his sandwiches as he decided how it was to be done.

Cheerfully, he made his way down into the floor of the corrie, and almost immediately raised a flock of perhaps a dozen grey and white speckled ptarmigan, which swept off round the half-moon of the amphitheatre in whirring alarm. It was while watching them that the man perceived what he had not realised before—that the corrie was full of deer. If he had had his binoculars, no doubt he would have picked them out previously, but now they were obvious enough because they were all on the move. There were dozens of them, scores, possibly even hundreds, in herds large and small, little groups, and individuals, russet-brown, white-rumped, grace-ful-bounding creatures, mainly hinds and calves, though there were a fair number of antlered stags too, drifting with as effortless an ease and deceptive a speed as the racing cloud-shadows themselves, out of that vast rock-bound punch-bowl. For perhaps thirty seconds the man watched them, in admiration and a little wonder—for he had never seen so many deer at one time, before—till the last pair of puck-like ears and the last pair of antlers, each silhouetted only for a moment, had disappeared over the various skylines, and the place was empty under the sun.

Then, wondering that Fiona Macpherson or that man Crosbie, or anybody else, should be in any way perturbed about the possible shortage of deer, he moved on around the stony shore of the lonely brood-ing lochan, to the scree-choked base of his towering precipice.

From the tumbled rock at the foot, his climb looked easy, so easy that he was debating whether it was worth all his exhilaration back there. Crossing sideways up the scree was not difficult. The ground slipped away from under his feet admittedly, but by moving lightly and quickly, and never lingering on any step, he was able to keep well ahead of all the little avalanches that he started. Two hundred feet or so up, where this rubble ended and the more or less upright face of living rock began, he paused for breath before he started the climb proper.

A great step or plinth, roughly forty feet high, and running along the entire base of the cliff, was the next obstacle. Admittedly it was highest and most difficult at this southern end, where Alan had elected to climb, but any advantage in using the other end would have been lost promptly by reason of the highly daunting remainder of the ascent on that side. The stone was pink granite, and worn smooth by weather and water, but there were sundry seams and cracks in it, to provide hand and toe holds, all running slantwise with the structural formation of the rock. And the plinth was by no means perpendicular; sixty-five degrees, probably would be its pitch. Also, the stone being granite, it was firm and not liable to crumble beneath him. Without hesitation, the man went up it, making for a fairish ledge from which a burn tipped over whitely.

It was an excellent satisfying piece of climbing, with nothing in it to assail his confidence, with the rock warm in front of him, and the grips sure to his touch, and enough of them to provide all the step-ladder that he needed. He climbed well, relying on his feet to push him up, not his hands to pull him, and he was up that forty feet to his ledge in no more time than it takes to tell.

He had intended to work up the next section, which was a steep slope of slabbed and broken stone, by means of the higher channel of the burn afore-mentioned, which had carved a gutter for itself in the rifts of the rock. But once on his shelf, he thought better of it; there was a more satisfactory course a little to the left, a burn-channel also, but old and dried-up this time, whereas the other was fuller of water than he had bargained for—the rain of the last two days would account for that. This alternative route was a better proposition altogether, and though it went up in a slightly different direction, it led to another buttress that seemed to offer quite as effective a further means of ascent as the one for which he had been heading. Alan took that dry burn-channel forthwith.

There was a good deal of this slabbed and sloping rock, volcanic basalt this, overlying the core of granite, and spilling down the hillside in successive layers, like icing on the side of a cake. It had been eroded further up and down, to the basic granite, but this portion had remained, presumably because of the temporarily eased gradient. Slippery brittle stuff, it would have made difficult and dangerous climbing, had it not been for the one-time burn's patient activities in scoring a deep wedge down it, in places right to the subjacent granite. On all fours the man made good going up its something over one hundred yards, raising himself perhaps two-hundred feet in the process.

He was slightly over half-way up his ascent—but with the real climbing still to come. Everywhere along the cliff-face, at this stage, great buttresses thrust out and up, vast towers of granite soaring through hundreds of feet to naked pinnacles, and to all intents perpendicular. Up, in the re-entrant angle between one of these and the sheer rock wall of the hill, his route now lay—or, rather stood. It was as good a time as any to have a breather.

Sitting on the sun-warmed stone of that dizzy eyrie, Alan Kinnear considered the perspective of half Highland Scotland, and found that it was very good. Southwards, above the Tromie hills, he looked towards all the uplands of Atholl, and thence over the rugged peaks of upper Badenoch to the long long rift of Laggan, leading the eye down past Alder to the great hump of Ben Nevis itself and the blue mountains of the sea-girt West. Directly opposite, beyond the wide green strath of Spey, the long ramparts of the Monadh Liath barred all prospect other than their own serried ridges, and further round still, Coraig and its woods and loch were hidden by the hog's-back of Creag Follais; but northwards, over the far-flung forests of Rothiemurchus and Abernethy and the brown hills of Findhorn and of Cromdale, there was no limit, no sufficient barrier, across the moors and verdant coastal plain and gleaming firths to Ben Wyvis itself, and all the hazy sentinels of Ross. It was a vista breath-taking in its immensity, holding and magnetising the eye—which, perhaps, is why it was not till the man was dragging his bemused gaze back to the task on hand, that he noted the tiny figures, far below him admittedly, but near-at-hand indeed compared with the distances his eye had been covering. Three of them, there seemed to be, down there, on a spur of green hill-side, perhaps a mile below and to the right of the entrance to his Coire Ruadh. They appeared to be standing still. A pity that he had not brought his glasses with him, for he could make out no details. Not that it signified. If they were more climbers, then good luck to them. And if they were more poachers, by Heaven, then let them get on with it ! They were safe from interference by Alan Kinnear, at anyrate !

He turned back to his climb. His ladder, between the converging faces of cliff and buttress, looked alarming at first glance, but was not so in reality, provided that the climber kept his head and developed no fits of cramp or any imperative urge to use both hands about his person—which could be said with equal force about entering a bus. There seemed to be ample in the way of projections and knobs and cracks for his fingers and toes, and no water ran down the groove itself. Hand over hand, he went up, like a spider in a corner, and never once was he at a more than momentary loss as to his next move. That is, till he reached the point where buttress and rock-face parted company, where the pinnacle of the former began. Here, he was in something of a quandary, for the cliff proper started to slope back, at a noticeably lessened angle. This in itself would not have been unwelcome, but for the fact that its surface deteriorated immediately into mere grit and gravel. And while the angle of ascent was lessened, it was not so much so that climbing over such an unstable surface above the dizzy drop that he had just surmounted, presented an attractive prospect. But, nevertheless, he had no option, since to continue on up the buttress, which still remained good climbable stone, would merely take him up to the top of the pinnacle, skied between heaven and earth like a weather-cock on a steeple. And to go back whence he had come, without the aid of a rope, was just not to be considered. He had not looked down once, as yet, and he was not going to, if he could help it; he knew what was apt to happen to climbers who got preoccupied with the depths below.

There being nothing else for it, Alan did not waste time and resolution in precariously clinging there and considering. There were one or two knobs of granite projecting out of the rubble, here and there —at least, he prayed that they were knobs of granite and not merely loose larger stones—which seemed to indicate that the loose stuff was not thick. The nearest such, unfortunately, was about ten feet along on his left. Taking his decision with a gulp, he started to edge out along the cliff-face, fingers in visible lateral cracks, toes feeling for invisible ones, like a fly on a window-pane. He kept his eye and his mind, firmly on that hoped-for knob of granite above the pink rubbishy gravel. Probably he did not breathe once on that ten-foot traverse.

Beneath his objective, he found that it was just out of arm's-reach. Which meant that he had to heave himself up somehow above his present secure hand-holds, depending on his feet. If that knob was solid granite, it probably would be all right; if it wasn't, if it came away in his hands . . . He preferred not to contemplate that eventuality. He dare not even look down, to pick out sure toe-holds—one look down might well be enough. Unfortunately, there was no definite lip, either, where the granite cliff and the rubble slope met, on which he could have leaned, to use as a fulcrum. All his eggs were rather noticeably in the one basket.

He expended no time or effort in dithering. Feeling with the steel-shod toe of his left boot, he found a cavity perhaps eighteen inches higher than the last. Tested, it seemed to be firm. That should be enough. Transferring his weight to it, his heart in his mouth, he straightened his knees, and threw his torso up and forward, along the gravel slope, reaching out with one hand for his knob, and with the other clawing, scrabbling, as deeply into the grit and rubble as his fingers would go. For a detached moment time stood still, his mind, his every sense, his whole consciousness was in the clutching fingers of his right hand, as they grasped that knob. It did not move in his grip. Only just daring to, he shook at it, wrenched it. It held. Gasping out a long breath of thankfulness and relief, he heaved himself up by it, got both arms linked around it, and relaxed there, sinking body, face even, on the warm gravel, like an exhausted swimmer clinging lovingly to *terra firma*.

But not for long. His position still was precarious in the extreme. There was approximately a twenty-yard belt of this rubble slope to be covered before solid rock lifted out of it again, and there were precious few of these providential out-cropping bosses of granite. It was like the roof of a house, tiled only with loose gravel—and with no rone or gutter at the eaves to halt the slider. The traversing of that score of yards was going to be no joke. But to lie there, hugging his little outcrop, was not going to help much.

Intently the man surveyed his treacherous strip of terrain, placing each projection and bump and protrusion, however small. The difficulty was that there were a number of faint lumps that might be solid and might not, and even of these there were too few to take him straight up. Obviously, his ascent would have to be a zig-zag one.

With infinite care he got one knee, and then his foot, on to his lifebuoy of a knob, and pushed himself upward, reaching out for another projection to the right—and listening apprehensively to the rattle and slither of the small stones that he dislodged, and then their silence. Before his legs were fully extended, he was able to touch and try his target, and to find it solid. Encouraged, he dragged himself up to it. Another, still further to the right, took him higher, and then, actually, he had to move downwards a little, as the only route towards another couple of knobs. He did not like that retrograde step, or wriggle. All this movement, such as it was, had been trending towards the right, and now he was directly above his buttress again, but half-way up the slope. There were further projections up in front, but quite out of reach; by no amount of stretching could he reach the nearest of them, by fully a yard. And he was risking no unanchored venture out on to the gravel—the entire surface moved under him, and moved naturally, but so very ominously, downwards. But what was he to do? To retrace his steps—or rather, his writhings—would not help, as well as being highly dangerous, for he had been forced to the course that he had taken by sheer necessity, and with no alternative.

He tried scraping down into the grit with his fingers, not heeding his broken nails. But though he felt that he was reaching solid rock, it was more or less smooth, without feature or excrescence—there was nothing to hold on to. A crack or two he found, but nothing that he dare try to stick the toe of his boot into. If only he had a spike, of some sort . . .

And then he remembered the clasp-knife. It was a thing that Mrs. Macdonald had lent him when he admitted that he had lost his own penknife that first day on the hill, a clumsy thing and not over sharp, that he had accepted only under protest, for sharpening his pencils. It was about the size of a Boy Scout's gulley, and gratefully indeed Alan's hand closed over it in his pocket. Scraping with it, after one or two false starts, he uncovered a suitable crack in the underlying granite, and worked the blade in patiently, till only the handle projected. He tested it carefully, but with considerable pressure. It gave a little, sideways, but it seemed as though it would stand a lot of downward strain. It meant trusting his life to the blade of an old clasp-knife—but it was his only hope, that he could see.

Kinnear had been working with his last granite knob between the crutch of his legs. Now, cautiously, he edged himself up, first one leg and then the other, till only his feet were supported by the projection. Then, digging in as good a finger-hold as he could with his left hand, to keep his posture upright, he raised his right leg up and up towards his knife, till he had his knee crooked round the jutting handle. Taking the weight momentarily off his left foot, he tested it. It did not give. Then straining, stretching his muscles to their utmost, he pushed his knee up still further, till just as he felt cramp coming on, he got the sole of his boot against the knife. And, taking a quivering breath, and quickly, because of incipient cramp, he forced himself upwards, desperately pressing down against the buried stone rather than against that frail stop, clawing with his hands and digging in with his nails. And, by a mercy, the knife stood firm. Good old-fashioned Sheffield steel, and buried, of course, in the rock fissure to the very hilt, it took the pressure and held. As the man's desperate hands clutched the further granite outcrop, he uttered a heartfelt groan of thankfulness. Pulling himself up to it, he left Seana Macdonald's knife behind him.

Thereafter, with two more hauling operations and a traverse, he was clear of that evil belt of gravel, and on to honest rock. Trembling like an aspen-leaf, he dragged himself up between a jumble of jagged rocks, and presently blinked to find himself actually amongst clumps of heather. He was at the top of his cliff. He had made it. Only a little elementary scrambling remained. His knees shaking beneath him, he forced himself on, pulling himself up by the tough heather-stems. He would lie in that heather, presently, when he reached levelish ground, just lie and lie, and let his body draw back from the earth some of the strength that damnable precipice had drained out of him. He would so . . .

And then, gasping, he faltered, and stopped. Over the curve of the hill, still steep above him, three persons had appeared. And one was a woman.

" There he is ! " she cried. " He's up. Good Lord—the complete and utter idiot ! "

CHAPTER IX

It WAS the girl Fiona Macpherson, and of the two men with her, one was John Cameron the keeper. The other was dressed in the louder checks associated with the sporting gentry. None of them were looking at the conqueror of the Coire Ruadh precipices with favour or admiration.

Alan Kinnear stared at them with frowning concentration. He felt as weak as a kitten, his limbs, his whole body, in the reaction to his efforts, seeming as though it did not belong to him any more. An uncertain nod was the best that he could do in the way of the civilities.

Miss Macpherson was not greatly exercised about the civilities, either. "What on *earth* do you mean by it?" she demanded of him. "A more senseless, more irresponsible, exhibition, I have yet to see!"

That seemed to the climber to be a little strong, even a little lacking in appreciation. But for the life of him, he could not think of any really satisfactory response—any response at all, indeed. The strings of his tongue appeared to have become tied too, in the general excitement. "Not at all," he said, vaguely.

His vagueness, the ridiculous vacuity of his expression, incensed Fiona Macpherson still further —and she already was considerably overwrought. She had had a distinctly trying hour, in fact, over this impossible individual, and was in no state to bear with further idiocies. From the moment that

93

they had spied him stalking up to the entrance to the corrie, and trained their glasses upon him, she had been experiencing pangs of various kinds. She had been angry, indignant, outraged, then astonished, agitated, and affrighted. She had known the misery of utter helplessness, the urge to action, however futile, and the certainty of tragedy. And she had climbed fifteen-hundred feet of mountain in double-quick time, making plans for improvised rope-lowering and rescue operations on the way. And now, here was the lunatic, perfectly safe and sound apparently, nodding and mouthing inanities! Even the heavy silence of her two male companions was an affront. It was all too much.

"Look here," she went on, her voice quivering slightly—she was a little breathless still, what with one thing and another. "I want an answer. I want an explanation. You can't do this sort of thing, and just stand there and say, 'not at all'!"

Kinnear was making a great effort. "Why not?" he wondered.

"Why not!" The girl turned to her associates. "Listen to him! Why not, he says! He marches right across our forest, disturbing ten thousand acres of stalking with his wind, he strides blithely right into the sanctuary and clears every beast out of it, ruining the place for goodness knows how long . . ." She bit her lip, and glanced hastily at the be-checked gentleman. "At least, he cleared it temporarily—they'll come back, of course, before long." That was not a very successful amendment. In consequence, her ire by no means decreased towards the cause of all the trouble, and her voice rose a further degree. "He goes headlong at a piece of cliff that even experts leave severely alone, thereby endangering his silly life, and laying up any amount of trouble for everybody else likely to be concerned, and when half-way up changes to the very worse possible route, thereby practically ensuring disaster. And now, now, by some crazy miracle . . . ! '' Almost, she charged him with having the nerve to come crawling safely out of the jaws of certain death, and further upsetting her with the reaction of her relief. She swallowed, instead. '' And he asks why not ! '' she ended, exasperatedly.

'' Quite,'' the gentleman said, since obviously something was expected of him. '' Er . . . quite.''

And John Cameron shook his grizzled head. '' Bad, it is,'' he declared heavily. '' Bad, yes.''

Alan had listened to all this with the knitted brows of concentration, but his attention had centred on one word of it. '' Sanctuary . . . ? '' he questioned.

'' Yes—sanctuary ! '' That was shot back at him. '' This corrie, Coire Ruadh, is the deer-sanctuary for the forest. The place where the deer are safe, where they are never followed or stalked or disturbed. And you went marching through the middle of it ! ''

Alan shook his head. It was his turn to be helpless. '' I'm sorry. I had no idea, of course. But they'll come back, won't they—the deer ? If this place is their headquarters, as you might say, they're surely not going to desert it just because a man walks through it, once ? ''

The girl opened her mouth to speak—and no doubt to speak to some effect. But the calm deliberate voice of her gamekeeper forestalled her. '' Och, they'll be back, yes,'' he said. '' In a day or two, they'll be back, right enough, and no harm done.'' And it was at the fourth member of the party that he looked, the tight-lipped frozen-faced individual in the gun-club checks, with only a swift glance at his employer in the passing. '' Och, yes.''

'' I hope so,'' the gentleman said, evenly, without

trace of any emotion. "The forest is totally unfenced, I think you said, Cameron?"

"That is so, yes, Sir Henry. But, och, this time
of the year, the beasts'll not go that far. Drifting
down towards the trees they are, these days—the
hinds that is, and the stags'll follow . . ."

"There are trees on your neighbours' forests, also,
though, aren't there?" Sir Henry intervened,
smoothly. "On Glenardoch, Invereshie, Glenfeshie,
and especially, Rothiemurchus? Aren't they just as
likely to drift there?"

"No, I wouldn't say that, just," Cameron
demurred. "The beasts have got their own habits,
see you, unless they're real badly disturbed. Och,
they'll be back in a day or so, sir."

"The problem seems to hinge then, on how badly
disturbed they are, have been, or are likely to be,
doesn't it?" Sir Henry, for his part seemed to prefer
to address his remarks to the young woman. "It
strikes me, that with all these hikers prancing about,
the deer are likely to be continuously disturbed."

Fiona Macpherson had been biting her red lip.
"We don't have many hikers really, Sir Henry,"
she assured. "This area is rather off their general
route, you see—it doesn't lead to any of the well-
known climbs." She looked at Alan. "This . . .
this man, is not really a hiker, at all, I understand.
At least, he's not just what we usually call a
hiker . . ."

"You are very kind," Kinnear acknowledged
elaborately.

Her eyes flashed at him. "I imagine that he's
just a holiday-maker . . . and that his holiday in the
district may not be lasting very much longer!"

"On the contrary, Ma'am, I find the neighbourhood suits me ideally," he returned politely.
"Scenery, air, inhabitants—especially the latter.

Such quaint local customs, such a unique outlook on life! And so friendly! To one such as myself, it is all quite enthralling." Alan was feeling much more like himself now, obviously. "I may well prolong my stay for quite a time, actually."

Fiona Macpherson glared. "Then I must insist that you keep off this deer-forest!"

Kinnear inclined his bare head. "I will do all that the law requires of me, in that respect," he observed.

The sound of her indrawn breath was eloquent indeed. He had her there, and they both knew it. Apparently the titled gentleman did not; he sounded English by his voice, of course, and English law is not Scots law, especially where the land is concerned.

"No use talking to this sort of fellow," he advised. "The police is the only answer."

Alan saw the young woman and Cameron exchange swift glances. "Oh, I don't think the police need to come into this," the former said, hurriedly. "It is hardly a matter for the police . . ."

"That is so," the keeper concurred.

Sir Henry raised his eyebrows. "Indeed? You know best, of course . . ."

And suddenly, Alan Kinnear was sorry for that girl. As has been said, he was not an unsympathetic character, at heart. The position was quite clear to him, now. She had brought this titled icicle up here to show him over the forest, with a view to renting it to him, even thus late in the season—presumably the man Crosbie had fulfilled his threat to back-out—as a sort of last hope. And he—Alan Kinnear—had rather queered her pitch, however unwittingly. She was mad at him, and wanted to show the fellow that she was—but at the same time, she didn't want too

G

serious a view taken of the incident, lest her bird took fright entirely, and decided that the place was too vulnerable altogether. She was in a difficult position, admittedly. She had to indicate to the culprit the enormity of his crime, and to convince the prospective tenant that she took a firm hand with hikers and trespassers generally, while at the same time she had to play down any damage done to the stalking prospects, and to gloss over the fact that Scots law gave her little or no assistance in the matter. If Alan's heart did not exactly melt for her, at least he recognised something of her point of view—which, in the circumstances, might be accounted to him for grace.

So, without being in any way ingratiating or even apologetic, it might be said that his tone was mildly conciliatory, when he spoke, " In my future walks, I'll endeavour as far as possible, Miss Macpherson, to avoid inflaming the susceptibilities of your so highly susceptible deer ! "

She did not seem to be as grateful as might have been expected. " That would be best achieved by keeping off the forest altogether, Mr. Kinnear," she said tartly.

So she knew his name ! Perhaps she knew other things, too. For certain she knew, anyway, that she could not keep him off the hill, without taking out an interdict against him to prevent him from doing material damage—which would be extremely difficult to obtain, there being no law of trespass, as such. " Unfortunately, I am extremely fond of walking," he told her, easily, " And I get quickly tired of walking on roads. And, strange as it may seem, I like a little climbing too ! "

The young woman seized on that swiftly—the more so, no doubt, in that she knew that the first part of his remark was unanswerable. " Then I strongly

advise you to learn something about it, before you
go endangering your neck another time ! ''

'' I appreciate your thoughtfulness on my behalf,''
Alan gave back, '' But I would point out that my
neck is my own, as yet, Heaven be thanked ! ''

'' May be— but the job of cleaning up the mess
would be *ours* ! '' That came vigorously. ''It's always
the same. Irresponsibles come up here from the
South, venture gaily into places no experienced
person would dream of attempting, get lost, break
bones, or kill themselves, and it is the local people
who have to turn out to form search-parties, in the
middle of the night, in all weathers, to go combing
the hills for them, in mist and storm and darkness
and snow.'' Finely worked up she was, and eloquent.
'' We it is who have to do the rescuing, and don't
you forget it ! There should be a law against irresponsible climbers ! ''

'' H'r'mmm,'' the man said. There was an answer
to all this, of course, but at the moment, he just could
not think of it. '' I have climbed before—even in
Switzerland,'' was the poor best that he could do,
somehow.

'' Then the more fool you for attempting Coire
Ruadh ! '' she flung back at him. '' You'd think
anyone could see that it's a death-trap.'' Then,
without warning, she swung round, and started to
stride off along the way that they had come, parallel
with the top of the cliff, her dark hair blowing bravely
in the breeze.

The man, Sir Henry, shrugged ever so slightly, and
followed after. John Cameron looked at Kinnear,
one eyebrow raised thoughtfully. '' Uh-huh,'' he
said, '' Just so,'' and turning, he too moved after the
others.

She had gone perhaps thirty yards when Fiona
Macpherson lifted up her voice again. '' Next time

you want to go walking on Glencoraig, I suggest that you consult John Cameron first," she cried back.

And the man left alone on the hill-top lifted his voice likewise. "Like hell I will!" he declared simply, forcibly.

And that was that.

CHAPTER X

FOR all the finality and vehemence of that last word of his on the blowy summit of Beinn Dearg that day, Alan Kinnear was not too happy about this latest upset and clash of interests. Inclined to obstinacy as he might be, he by no means enjoyed or made a practise of going through life in a state of war with his neighbours. Moreover, hadn't he come up here specifically to find peace and quiet to write his masterpiece? All this bickering and squabbling was irritating, off-putting, and far from conducive to concentrated thought and fertile composition. In fact, his book hung fire most lamentably—all he could think about was this confounded young woman and all her prejudices, arrogancies, and insufferability generally.

The fact that she had, not exactly some right or reason on her side, but some claim to sympathy, some slight appeal as a lone female fighting against odds, made it only the worse, the more difficult to dismiss her from his mind as she deserved. That the odds that she fought against were in reality no more than inevitable present-day conditions, and that she herself, therefore, was nothing more than an anachronism, a relic of an age and dispensation that was dead and gone—however unrelic-like and youthful she might appear personally, for there was no blinking her good looks—all that was beside the point. The faint stirrings of that outmoded and debunked complex that used to be known as chivalry, had their way with man—which indicated himself as something of a relic likewise, surely ! He remained ill-at-ease, unsettled, and just a little sorry for himself. But though he considered the matter many times, he made no attempt to leave the district.

Though Seana Macdonald got precious few details of his rock-climbing exploit and its consequences, from him, she seemed to have no difficulty in obtaining them from elsewhere—and in making the necessary comments. What she thought of rock-climbers in general, he already knew, and what she thought of his latest activity in particular, she left him in little doubt. But by refusing to take her seriously, the man avoided any actual crisis in their relations— or perhaps, that was her doing as much as his, for indeed, her attitude was a strange mixture of criticism and appreciation. Undoubtedly things would have to get considerably worse before she felt compelled to turn a genuine detective-thriller-writer out of her house. She was in the middle of *Inspector Hake's Last Case,* which Alan had presented to her, and was much impressed. She tried to make her lodger promise, by threats and cajolery—never by pleas—that he would engage in no more of this wicked Providence-tempting clambering, only to be put off with the flippant assertion that he could never do that till he had got her back her clasp-knife, at least. A state of watchful non-belligerence was maintained at Balnahard of the woods.

The day following the Coire Ruadh incident was wet again, and though the weather cleared up in the late afternoon, it was too late for any harvesting. But the next morning dawned bright, after a touch of ground-frost, and with the mist wraiths lifting in white streamers out of every valley and corrie and chasm at the behest of the stripling sun, Alan Kinnear took the sandy road through the forest to Dalnamuick.

The clack and rattle of the old-fashioned reaping-machine met him before ever he won clear of the trees, and Jean Fraser greeted him kindly. Och, he shouldn't have troubled to come again, she told him, and him on his holiday. It was far too good of him, whatever. She had been after telling Archie about him yesterday—yes, she had gone over to K'ussie by the bus, with wee Kirsteen too, and taken Archie some scones and an egg. Och, he was fine, yes, and getting right fat with nothing to do, at all. There was to be no bail in it—something to do with the keeper being killed at Dalinblair. The police were being real nice to him, but he was fretting himself for something to do, only. The trial was to be on Thursday, at Inverness—soon, they were making it, not giving the bail . . .

Alan knew that, for he had been cited to appear as witness. He was not very happy about the whole business, he admitted, and he could assure her, for what it was worth, that he would be as mild and inconclusive about his evidence as was possible, without actually committing perjury.

That was kind of him, she said, very kind. And Archie was grateful to him for giving a hand with the harvest, too . . .

Alan Kinnear, unable to stand any more, if he was to keep any self-esteem at all, cut her short almost rudely, and hurried for the harvest-field.

Old Callum had already cut almost one third of the first field, and the swathes of corn lay neatly in long lines, yellow patched with unripe green here and there, the stalks almost as short as hay, pathetically thin about the heads by southern standards, and loose too—for the reaper, alas, was no binder. Alan's job today, therefore, was precisely

the same as formerly—that of gathering armfuls of
corn, making a rope of stalks, tying it up into sheaves,
and building the results into stooks. And that back-
breaking task he applied himself to with a will that
was the more urgent for Jean Fraser's so galling
gratitude.

But labour as he would, it was slow work, and
even with the many breaks-down of the ancient
reaping-machine and the unhurried and contemp-
lative habits of both driver and horse—it was the
self-same grey carron that Alan had helped to lead
home from the hill that night, burdened with ill-
gotten venison—the sheafer and stooker was left
far behind. But Callum showed no inclination to
exchange his seat on the machine for a stance beside
the solitary gleaner—which made his leer and
chuckle, each time he passed, the more offensive.
The shirt-sleeved, perspiring, aching-backed volunteer developed a sudden violent and unreasonable
antipathy to all so-called workers who lolled back on
seats and failed to anoint their labours with the salt
sweat of their brows.

After a lunch of milk, sandwiches, and hard-
boiled eggs, taken on the site of their activities, Jean
Fraser came to assist again, and things immediately
began to improve—also, with Callum started on the
cutting of the second field, the sight of his easeful
perambulations was removed, to the peculiar satisfaction of Alan, at least.

Presently, John Cameron came stalking down
through the heather and birch-scrub to join them, to
greet the woman warmly and the man with cautious
civility and an elaborate summing-up of the weather-
prospects, and to hurry off forthwith to the second
field, in the wake of the reaper.

Another elderly man, unknown to Kinnear but
who gave no impression of being similarly handi-

capped, by his hurried climatic-commentary, arrived
and went to work, but at the other end of the field.
And when, half-an-hour later, Sandy Cattanach
rode up on his bicycle, and, mentioning to Alan only
that it was a fine day, stripped off his blue tunic,
and followed John Cameron to the other field, it
seemed that things were looking up. Only, Alan
Kinnear felt himself progressively to be more like
something drawn eloquently by Mr. Bateman, in a
meteorological bureau. Only Jean Fraser found it
convenient to work along-side of him.

It would be about three o'clock that the rattle of
the reaper was challenged by another rattle, as an
old car lurched along the rutted track and drew up
at the field gate. Straightening up, his hands going
involuntarily to the small of his back, Alan was
startled to perceive Fiona Macpherson alight there-
from. Obeying an impulse that he might not like to
have to justify later, the man stooped again quickly
to his corn-gathering, and kept on stooping.

" Well, Jean," her voice said, presently, from very
near at hand. " You seem to have collected quite a
mixed bag of helpers, today ! "

" Och, yess indeed, Miss Fiona—very kind they
are, whatever."

Alan looked up. She was standing looking directly
at him, her hands on her hips, a business-like figure
in a short-sleeved navy-blue jumper and tartan skirt.

" You have found something rather more useful
to do today, Mr. Kinnear, than some of your other
activities," she observed, " I congratulate you."

The man, with a sheaf under each arm, strode over
to where the next stook was to be. Only from there
did he speak. " I like harvesting," he said briefly.

" Mr. Kinnear has been very good," Jean Fraser
declared, looking from one to the other. " Och, just
kindness itself."

"That, of course, is nonsense," he said, almost irritably.

"I am inclined to agree," the other young woman commented cold-voiced. She picked up a few stalks of corn, parted them into two, and began to twist their heads together, expertly enough. "Though even Mr. Kinnear must have a change, sometimes!"

Alan frowned, but said nothing, as he returned to the swathes of cut corn, to gather up another bundle.

Jean Fraser looked a little unhappy. "It is kind you all are, indeed," she maintained, but uncertainly.

"How is Archie?" Fiona demanded. She bent, in her turn, to collect an armful of the oats, and to twist her rope round it. "I hear that you went to see him, yesterday."

"He is fine, then, thank you, and the police very good to him. Fat, he is getting, I was telling Mr. Kinnear. Och, it's himself will be the lazy one, after this." That had the gallant attempt at a laugh behind it.

Neither of her busy hearers laughed in turn, however.

"The case is to be heard on Thursday, I'm told," the other girl went on. "You realise, don't you, Jean, that I am not prosecuting—or, I should say, my brother is not, the estate is not. The prosecution is at the instance of the Procurator-Fiscal. That's the worst of the police having been brought in to catch Archie in the act, as it were. It was most . . . annoying, most unfortunate."

Alan twisted at his oat-stalks in silence.

"Och, it was just the way things had to be," Jean Fraser said, hurriedly. "And how is your mother, at all, Miss Fiona?"

"She is as well as she ever is." Miss Macpherson dismissed her mother's state of health summarily.

" I rang up Mr. Robertson, the lawyer, to see if there was anything that I could do, Jean—but it's difficult. I'd have testified, as a witness for the defence, as to Archie's character, and that he was a valuable tenant to the estate, and so on—but I'm tied, rather, by the difficulty of letting the stalking. You see, the Press have got hold of this already, and you can just imagine how they'd play up a story of the estate siding with a poacher caught red-handed. It would get endless publicity, and Glencoraig would get the name of positively encouraging poaching—and, Heaven knows, it's hard enough to let the place as it is, with the poaching it's got already . . . and the general disturbance of the deer ! '' There was nothing sidelong or veiled about the glance in the man's direction as she said that last.

Alan had neither material nor inclination to reply to that—besides, he was very busy indeed.

" Och, you mustn't think of anything of the sort, whatever.'' Jean Fraser declared. " That wouldn't do, at all. No, no . . .''

" I have sent a written testimonal as to Archie's good character, to Mr. Robertson, to use as he thinks best,'' the other went on. " I suggested that he pass it on to the Sheriff, though I don't know whether that is allowed or not. I know Sheriff Gordon a little, and I proposed having a word with him privately but Mr. Robertson wouldn't hear of it— said that was against the law, or something . . .''

" Mercy me, you shouldn't have done that, even— you are far too good, Miss Fiona. You are all too good, too kind. I . . . I don't know what to say, at all . . .'' The woman's voice broke, and she turned away hurriedly. " Och, I'll have to be away up to see to the tea, now,'' she mumbled. " Time, it is . . .''

And as she hastened, almost ran, across the golden stubble towards the fence and the house, the other girl straightened up from her labours, and turned to the man deliberately. " I wonder you have the nerve to come here, of all places, to do your Good Samaritan act ! " she said.

Alan Kinnear shook his sheaves down securely, to form the end of the stook, and, still leaning forward, hands on knees, eyed her levelly. " Miss Macpherson," he said wearily, almost, his voice as level as his glance. " You are determined to see no good in me, aren't you ? In your eyes I am damned beyond hope of redemption. I may say, that doesn't worry me in the least. To use the current phrase, I couldn't care less ! But I *am* concerned for these young Frasers, especially for Mrs. Fraser, who is the one redeeming example of much-vaunted Highland kindliness that I have come across so far in these parts ! " Perhaps he knew that that was not strictly true, but he did not give her time to formulate the vigorous retort that undoubtedly was bubbling up. " Mrs. Fraser obviously needed help in the unfortunate circumstances in which she found herself— circumstances for which I was partly, if unwittingly, responsible. It seemed equally obvious that I should try and be of what help I could . . ."

" *Partly* responsible ! " the girl took him up, strongly. " You underestimate your, your prowess, Mr. Kinnear ! It appears to me that you were wholly responsible for the unfortunate circumstances, as you so aptly put it ! "

Alan raised his brows. " Then it doesn't seem to have occurred to you, or to most of your neighbours, that if Fraser hadn't been shooting deer illegally and most furtively—in fact, poaching—there would have been no trouble ? The prime responsibility surely, must lie at his own door, for what he did."

" Rubbish," Fiona Macpherson said. " Non-

sense." She was back at her work, with commendable industry.

" Do you too deny that he was poaching, then? "

" Of course he wasn't *poaching*. Archie isn't a
poacher."

" He had your—or at least, the estate's—full
authority to take that stag, then? He was acting
under your instructions? Strange that he said nothing about that to the police, when he was arrested! "

" He wasn't acting under instructions, no—not on
this occasion . . ."

" But he had your permission? "

" Not exactly—no. But he'd know I wouldn't
mind—not so long as he did it . . . well,
discreetly . . ."

" I see! " Alan's voice rose. " So the Glencoraig
estate, having let the stalking for the season, to Major
Crosbie, or other tenant, ' doesn't mind ' if local
people stalk the place on their own, take stags if
they want them—so long as it's done discreetly, of
course! " The man even pointed an accusing finger
at her. " Speaking as a mere Lowlander, a mere
outsider, I should have thought that that was verg-
ing on the criminal! And I don't mean only Fraser's
share of it! Technically, I imagine, those stags,
during the season, are the property of the tenant. He
and he only has the right to shoot them, or to say
who shall shoot them. The estate has disposed of its
rights in the matter. You have no right ' not to
mind '! Isn't that so, Miss Macpherson? "

That young woman was not working, any more,
nor stooping either. Flushed and flashing-eyed, she
was glaring at him. " Stop pointing at me! " she
commanded. " I won't be cross-examined, like this!
What right have you to be asking all these questions?
What right have you to talk this way, at all? What
do you know about it all, anyway! I don't require a

summer-visitor to come and tell me how to run this
property—I can assure you of that!" Than the
generic term 'summer-visitor', from her tone of
voice, no deeper depths could be plumbed.

"It looks to me as though that's just what you *do*
require!" Kinnear retorted, warmly. "Some
understanding of a sane and business-like way of
doing things—I won't add, an *honest* way—seems
badly overdue, up here! It seems to me that the
'summer-visitor' you're trying to hire the stalking
to, definitely requires to have his interests looked
after."

"My Goodness—this from you! And after your
day-before-yesterday's exploit!"

"My day-before-yesterday's exploit appears to me
to be far less harmful to your prospective stalking-
tenant's interests than does the attitude of the people
round here—including, apparently, the estate itself.
It would almost seem that the reputation for poaching on Glencoraig, that you were mentioning a while
back, is peculiarly well-deserved. I don't wonder
you have difficulty in letting the place!"

"Mr. Kinnear—will you kindly mind your own
business!" the girl flared. And casting down the
armful of oats that she had been hugging, she
marched off, to start a new line of stooks on her own,
from the other side of the field.

Alan did not even trouble to follow her with his
eyes. Bending down, he attacked his corn
vehemently.

And so they worked, not together but so very
separately, in that small field, and by the very nature
of things, seek as they would to arrange it otherwise,
their labours inevitably brought them closer and
closer again, as the area of cut swathes, eaten up and
stooked, was steadily reduced. The girl worked ably,

deftly, a lissome, vital, eye-catching figure—eye-catching even to Alan, whose eye sought quite definitely not to be caught. It was no dainty lady-like pretence of work that she made, but a sustained adequate effort. She was no weakling, with a fine sweep to her bronzed bare arms, and plenty of strength to her long legs, equally and sensibly bare beneath her kilted skirt. And after every stoop, she tossed her errant hair back from her face with a curiously proud virile gesture. It was that tossing that so continuously drew the man's eye, however carefully he made a point of keeping his back to her as he worked. And Jean Fraser was an unconscionable time about fetching that tea.

Eventually, by a sheer process of elimination, the handling of the remaining swathes of cut corn brought them within twenty yards of each other, in the centre of the small field. They both maintained a strictly down-bent gaze until precisely the same moment—presumably their resistance to the strain of being ridiculous was fairly evenly balanced.

"It was your interests, your estate's interests, I was concerned for . . ." Alan began.

"Archie wasn't just taking *any* stag, off the hill . . ." Fiona began.

They both stopped, he frowning, she biting her lip. Stiffly, quite elaborately for a harvest-field, the man bowed.

"Yes . . . ?" he said.

The girl looked down, almost as though she had changed her mind. Then, the absurdity of that too, seemed to strike her. "I was pointing out that Archie Fraser didn't just go on to the hill to get a stag, *any* stag," she went on, frigidly. "That beast shot was a switch. It was a nuisance—we all knew of it, and I have tried to grass it myself, more than once. It was a good thing he did—and a very difficult thing to do, too. He actually was doing the estate a good turn, by getting rid of a switch.''

'' A pity, then, that he chose to do it so guiltily. I never saw anything done more surreptitiously.''

'' That could well be in the estate's interests, too—naturally he wouldn't shout it aloud from the hill-tops, at this season of the year. That, unfortunately, was left to other people ! ''

Alan shrugged. '' And yet I too was only trying to act in your estate's interest, trying to do you a good turn. I thought I was laying one of these poaching gangs by the heels. I was wrong—but my intentions were excellent.'' He smiled, but without mirth. '' I wouldn't have tried, needless to say, had I known a little more, not only about Fraser, but about the management of the Coraig estate ! ''

'' Then I am right, I trust, in imagining that we will be spared any more of your good turns, Mr. Kinnear ? '' That was acid-sharp.

'' You are, indeed,'' he returned, trenchantly. '' I can assure you of that, quite definitely ! ''

'' Good,'' she said.

'' Exactly.''

They built the last half dozen stooks in presumably satisfactory silence. The fact that the last one of all required the remaining sheaves of both of them to complete it, and so was, as it were, a mutual effort, was got over by the girl tossing her contributions approximately a yard from the man's feet, before striding off to the second field. And though Jean Fraser, coming down with the jugs of tea, called beckoningly, her laird's sister did not appear to hear her, but continued on her way to further labours, in determined fashion. Alan Kinnear, therefore, consumed his tea in solitary state, leaning against that last stook, and, deciding that there was almost a plethora of assistance in the other smaller field, waved goodbye to his hostess, and slinging his jacket over his arm, set off down the road to Balnahard.

And despite the loveliness of the afternoon, and all the panorama of the sun-bathed hills, he frowned as he went.

CHAPTER XI

COULD there be any truth, Alan Kinnear wondered, in the stories of the Great Grey Man of Ben MacDhui, the Ferlas Mor as the locals called it, this spectre of high Cairngorm, that climbers talked about around camp-fires, and shepherds and keepers preferred not to mention? The Brocken of the Hartz Mountains and elsewhere could be explained away by the sun throwing the beholder's own shadow on to a screen of mist, for it was only seen in daylight. But this Grey Man was a different proposition by all accounts; he was to be seen in the mist admittedly, but mainly at night, when there was no light to cast any shadow. And he was to be *heard*, as well, both by night and day. And by reputable people, so it seemed; many were the tales told, and the experiences vouched for —very many of them by men who had never so much as heard of the thing previously—and by sober unimaginative folk, or folk who thought that they were sober and unimaginative, or ought to be, as lawyers and doctors and the like.

It was said that solid professional men had run all the way down from the high wilderness of MacDhui and the Larig Ghru to the first houses of Rothiemurchus in the forest almost without stopping, over seven of the roughest miles in all Scotland, to get away from that giant striding thing. It was said that climbers mounting MacDhui had heard footsteps that kept pace with theirs, only, they were not in rhythm but occuring but once for every three of the men's, so that they were no echo. It was said that mountaineers on the top of MacDhui, second highest peak in our islands, had frequently seen a tremendous shadowy creature, usually at night, anything from ten to forty feet in height—and had seldom stayed to investigate further. Was Ferlas Mor any sort of reality? Alan Kinnear, glancing about him into the dusk a shade uneasily, decided that it was just possible.

He had had a good day, walking to the station at Corriebeg and boarding there the morning bus from Kingussie to Grantown, that had set him down at the bonny place of Coylum Bridge, where the amber Druie and Luineag meet beneath the trees. From there he had walked for hours south-eastwards, through the vast forest of Rothiemurchus, all tall heather and scattered ancient pines, by a track well marked by iron-shod boots, that rose gradually but steadily, till at last it brought him out above the treeline into the very jaws of the frowning Larig Ghru, greatest and highest pass in Scotland, with the huge mountain masses of Braeriach and Cairn Lochan and all their satellites guarding it on either flank. Perhaps a mile up that long gut in the hills, he had started really to climb, clambering up its left and eastern side till eventually he had come out on the beetling ridge above, and followed it along and round, by rock and scree and moss, till it had brought him, wondering, to the wind-blown top of the tremendous cliffs of Cairn Lochan, where he had sat and calculated and assessed, and eventually admitted defeat—and thought about that confounded woman Macpherson. And from there he had worked back on the high plateau round the dizzy black trough of Loch Avon, and on to the lofty tableland of great MacDhui itself. He had not thought about Ferlas Mor up there, either; it was only now, on his way

back in the arms of the night, that it had come to
him.

He had climbed and slithered down into the Larig
again, and back up and over the heaped boulders of
the summit, past the Pools of Dee, black unwinking
eyes staring at the narrow strip of sky above, and so
down half-way to the tree-level again, where, climbing out of the pass once more, westwards, he had
skirted round the stony flank of the tall pyramid of
Carn Elrig and so into Glen Einich—where he had
to wade the turbulent Beanaidh almost up to his
waist over a devilish causeway of water-polished
granite spheres. In the mounting up to the long ridge
beyond, through heavy peat-hags and high old
heather, he had felt his weariness growing upon him
—but it was the pleasant weariness of achievement.
It had been his biggest day, so far, and he had not
done so badly. Now, three tough miles further still,
with the long ridge of Creag Dubh conquered, and
the horrible peat-bogs between Meall na Corrie and
Creag Follais, where the dusk had overtaken him,
behind him, he was not so concerned with achievement. He was concerned now with rest, and the
cessation of effort, and supper . . . and the feeling
that he was not alone on those night-bound hills.

He was not so far from home, though—not as that
day's distances went. He was back on Glencoraig,
at least, with only another four or five miles to go,
perhaps, most of it walking down a road. Indeed, he
was not so very far from where, on that night of
ill memory, he had waited with the police for the
return of Archie Fraser. He was making now, down
through the open birchwood, for the bridge below
the waterfall on the Coraig River, to which the same
Archie had directed them.

Not abruptly, but gradually, almost reluctantly,
Alan stopped and turned to stare behind him. He

could have sworn that there was somebody, something, following behind him, there. He had heard
nothing, and peer as he would amongst the shadowy
slopes and looming scattered trees, he could see
nothing. But the impression was there, and strongly.
He went on, and weariness or none, his stride had
quickened.

He was a long way from Ben MacDhui now—
though perhaps not for Ferlas Mor and his seven-
league boots ! Not that he had ever heard of the
apparition hurting anybody, doing more than
frighten them—not that he believed in the story at all,
for that matter. But he wouldn't be sorry to be on
the road again, just the same. Probably tiredness
and an empty stomach were at the bottom of his
imaginings.

The man found, not ungratefully, that he was
closer to the river than he had assumed. The noise
of the waterfall it was, that gave him his warning,
and picking his way down through denser woodland,
he came out at the water's edge just below the bridge
—which was not bad navigation for only his second
time in the vicinity, and the twilight to contend with.
It was just as he was approaching the bridge-end that
he stopped again, suddenly this time, and whirled
round. The crack of a stick somewhere behind him
was definite and undeniable, even above the distant
roar of the falls.

Stepping back against a tree-trunk, Alan stared,
for perhaps a minute. But there was no further
sound, no sign of life, no hint of movement, amongst
the shadows. It was a quiet night, with no wind
down here to stir the trees. But other things besides
a man—or a spectre—might snap a piece of dead
wood. The forest was alive with roe-deer, and even
woodland stags. Capercailzie and blackcock could
blunder noisily. Even the squirrels could break a

twig. All the same, Alan felt that the sooner that his
feet were on the gravel of that road, the better. It
was only something like a quarter-of-a-mile beyond
the bridge. Forthwith he set about making it still less.

Perhaps it was his hunger that was responsible.
Perhaps it was that his perceptions were heightened
by the circumstances. But always he had had a good
nose, that man—too keen, on occasion. And just as
he was stepping off that pine-log bridge into the
shadows of the birch scrub and junipers beyond, his
nose gave him pause. Stopping, he sniffed. There
was no doubt about it. Blood, he was smelling, raw
and throat-catching and very close at hand. Swallow-
ing, he tested the air, and unhesitantly yet far from
enthusiastically, his flaring nostrils led his reluctant
feet towards a large juniper bush half-a-dozen yards
from his path.

It was with a flooding sense of relief that he
stooped down over that juniper, and made out what
was hidden therein. It was the white gleaming teeth
that he saw first, and then, as his eyes focused into
the dark interior of the bush, he picked out the paler
insides of the great ears, and even the dull glimmer
of the glassy eye. It was the remains of a deer, in
there, as he might have guessed—the unprofitable
remains, head and neck, legs below the knee, and all
the entrails. He could sense the steam of these last,
rising up to him—that was what had caught his
nostrils. There were no antlers, which indicated that
it was a hind, and therefore shot only for the meat—
and since the entrails still were steaming, gralloched
only very recently. More poaching, obviously.

Alan Kinnear's comment on that discovery was
almost a snort. Poachers, was it, that he was amongst
again ! Well, they were safe from him, at anyrate—
local or otherwise. He'd had his lesson. As far as he

was concerned, they could poach to their heart's content. There would be no urgent messages to police, or keepers, or anybody else, this time! Once bitten twice shy, was as good a motto as any. Alan Kinnear was not interfering again.

Nevertheless, before he left that bush, the man stooped and picked up the hind's lower foreleg. It was just conceivable that he might make some play, have some fun with the thing, sometime. There were people to whom he might be pleased to show it . . .

He moved on up towards the road.

Alan had barely set foot on the sand and grit of the track, and turned his face northwards, down towards Coraigmore and Balnahard, when once again his nose spoke to him. Only, it was petrol that he smelt, this time, quite distinctly. That was not so surprising either, perhaps, in the circumstances—but that did not prevent him from following his nose once more. And tucked into the bushes at the roadside, he discovered a large motor-van, such as a country grocer might use for his rounds, but nameless, and with even the registration plates removed. Within the open doors at the back of it, Kinnear counted the headless, footless carcases of no fewer than four gory deer.

Pensively, the man was considering the implications of activities carried out on this scale, when from quite near at hand, a whistle sounded, no night-bird's call, that was repeated and then answered from down the road somewhere.

Alan thought quickly. If some of these people were along the road, and presumably coming back to their van, he would have to pass them. And it was just conceivable that, desperate specimens as they were said to be, they might resent the presence of a stranger amongst them, at this stage in the proceedings, in such a place and at such a time. He was no craven, but on the other hand, he certainly was not looking for trouble—especially not on the .Coraig estate's behalf. A little discretion might be indicated—also a little quiet observation might be interesting and could do no harm. Without more ado, he slipped into the bushes at the other side of the road, and a little down from the hidden van, prepared to watch and wait.

He had not long to do either. Just as footsteps sounded on the road, together with a strange scuffling, and he craned forward the better to observe the two men that walked curiously dragging something heavy between them, a noise directly at his back twisted him round swiftly. Another man crouched behind him, only a yard or two off, beside a tree-trunk, one hand upraised.

" What the devil . . . ? " he began.

" Damn you, you spyin' bastud—that for you ! " the fellow cried, and his hand crashed down.

Alan Kinnear knew an ineffable surprise and sheerest resentment, saw a blinding light, was aware of a stunning jolt—and nothing more.

He pitched towards the verge of the road, one hand outflung.

CHAPTER XII

It was in the neighbourhood of twelve-thirty that night, that Seana Macdonald came to the back door of the tall house of Coraigmore, gaunt and huge in the dark, and rang the jangling echoing bell. It was some little time, and the old woman was considering a second ring, before a small scullery window was pushed open, and a pale face peered out.

"What is it, at all? Who's there?" a voice demanded.

"Is that yourself, Jessie? Me, it is—Seana. It's that man that does be stopping with me—Mr. Kinnear. He's away and lost himself on the hill. Will you be telling herself—Miss Fiona?"

"I will, yes. Och, this is bad, Seana. Wait you."

"Don't you be waking Mrs. Macpherson, now, Jessie—just Miss Fiona, see you . . ."

In a couple of minutes Fiona, in her dressing-gown and pyjamas had unlocked the heavy door. "What's all this, Seana?" she wondered. "What's the trouble?"

"Och, it's that Mr. Kinnear, Miss Fiona—sorry I am to be troubling you. But he's gone and lost himself, or killed himself, even, on the hill. I had to be doing something . . ."

"Mr. Kinnear is an utter and complete nuisance!" the girl said, with entire conviction. "What on earth will it be, next! But come away in to the kitchen, Seana—it'll be warm there." She raised her voice. " Jessie—see if you can get some water boiling for a cup of tea, will you."

" He's a nuisance, yes—but, och, he's not such a bad one," Mrs. Macdonald declared, unhappily. " Headstrong, he is, just. He means well . . ."

" I'll take your word for it," Fiona interrupted, tersely, yawning frankly. " Now—what's happened ? "

" Och, he's been away since nine this morning— up on the hills. He said he'd be back about seven, whatever, and him with only a bit sandwich in his pocket. I waited till midnight, see you, and then I couldn't wait any more, and him maybe lying up there with the bones of him broken, somewhere."

" Much more likely he's just lost himself. It's easily enough done—especially for someone so clever at doing the wrong thing as your Mr. Kinnear ! " Fiona Macpherson did not sound particularly sympathetic. Perhaps the hour and the circumstances were not of the most propitious. She scratched a bare instep against a tussore pyjama-ed calf.

" Aye, maybe—but I have just the notion he was away to those rocks again. Och, dearie me—those rocks ! I've been after trying to make him promise not to go back to them, but he laughs at me, just. He's been talking about getting back my knife for me, the man . . ."

" Knife ? What knife ? "

" Och, my man's old knife, he carried. I lent it to Mr. Kinnear yon day, the day he was after climbing the Red Corrie, there. He was after leaving it stuck in the rock, half-ways up, he was telling me. He had to use it to get his foot on, some way, he was saying. Two-three times he's said he'd have to be getting it back for me—like as if I cared about the bit old knife ! "

" Good Lord ! " Fiona exclaimed. " Not Coire
Ruadh, again ! Even that idiot couldn't be quite
such a fool, surely ? "

" Och, I don't know, at all. Always, he was
smiling when he said it—maybe he was not just
serious. I do not know. But he had a bit rope tied
round his middle, see you—after yon day, he was
saying he'd not be after taking the hill again, without
a bit rope."

" But this is crazy—maddening ! " the girl
declared. " Why must we be saddled with
lunatics, like this ? What have we done to have to
put up with these utter nit-wits, coming up here and
getting themselves into trouble ? Why should *we* have
to get them out of it ? " But while she was declaim-
ing, the single eyebrow raised, seemed to indicate
that that was not all that she was doing. " Which
way did he go, d'you know ? " she ended, abruptly.

" I couldn't say, at all—he didn't tell me. But he
was asking yesterday just where your march was—
the Glencoraig march—and whether the deer would
be back in the sanctuary, yet."

" Damn ! " Fiona said, baldly. She tapped the
kitchen-table with urgent fingers. " Look here—
there's no good any of us starting out to search for
the creature until we're sure he's not just having a
late night, an extra long day . . ."

" Och, he'd have been back by this, Miss Fiona,
for sure," the old woman said. " It's been black dark
four hours and more. He was out late yon time with
the police, right enough—but I'm not thinking he'd
be doing the likes of that, again ! "

" I wouldn't even put *that* past him," the other
observed, caustically. " But it's an idea—we might
ring up the police-station at Kingussie, and enquire
if he's been at them again."

" Maybe, then. I left a bit note on the table, by

his food, to say I had come along here to you, and if he was coming in before I got back, to be coming along himself to let us know."

"That was sensible, at anyrate," the girl commended, grudgingly. "Well, you wait here, Seana, and I'll go and phone."

She was back in a few minutes, pulling her dressing-gown more tightly around her, for the night air was chill. "They've heard nothing," she reported. "I rang up Sandy Cattanach, too. He has no news, either." Faintly, she smiled. "I don't think Sandy was any keener at getting out of his bed than I was. But he deserves it more than I do—Mr. Kinnear's largely his fault, isn't he? He sent him to you!"

"That is so, yes. But what is to be done, at all?"

"Well, I'm going upstairs to get dressed, first of all," Fiona said. She looked at the old clock on the mantelshelf. "It's nearly ten to one, now. If there's no sign of your wretched lodger by quarter-past, Seana, it looks as though we'll have to go out and search for him. I told Sandy not to go back to bed till I rang him again. He's telling Andrew MacBean and Colin Fraser to be ready, too. Will you go and tell Willie Maclean, the Sawmill, while I dress, Seana? Say if we need him, I'll be along for him with the car, in just over half-an-hour."

"I will, yes."

"Jessie—is that tea not ready, yet?"

Twenty minutes later, Seana Macdonald was back from the nearby sawmill-house at Druim, and Fiona dressed in jumper, skirt, leather-jerkin and stout shoes, was downstairs again, and helping Jessie to butter a large number of scones. She turned this task over to the old woman.

"Looks as though the prodigal isn't returning," she commented. "Nothing for it, I'm afraid, but a

search. I'll go and phone Sandy again. He'll be
delighted ! "

In a surprisingly short time the policeman, with
three other men, was knocking at the back door of
Coraigmore. He had seen from his window a light
in the hotel, and had telephoned to Alec Macphail,
the stalwart host thereof, who had not yet retired for
the night. He had agreed to collect Cattanach in his
car, and they had picked up MacBean and Fraser on
the way. The latter was the local butcher, and the
former a small farmer. They made an adequate-
seeming quartette, even if none of them were very
youthful, with their lean stringiness, their big boots,
and their oily-scented and hairy homespuns.

Fiona Macpherson explained the position briefly,
and with reasonable restraint. " We can't go searching all the Caingorms for this fat-head," she pointed
out. " But I think we ought to have a look at Coire
Ruadh—which is just too bad for the sanctuary,
again; You heard the creature climbed that cliff the
other day, completely clearing out the deer, of
course ? It seems that somewhere on the way up, he
had to use a knife Seana here had lent him, presumably to make a foothold, and evidently he left it
behind. Seana thinks he may have gone back for
it—apparently the idiot has threatened to, more than
once."

" That's right, yes," Mrs. Macdonald concurred.
" But, och, I couldn't just be sure that he wasn't
making a joke of it, the man."

" But he did go off with a rope wrapped round
him, didn't he, Seana ? "

" Yes, he did. A bit of my clothes-line, it was."

" My Goodness—he is an awful man, that," Sandy
Cattanach bewailed. " Och, just a holy terror he is,
yes, and him right pleasant and sensible-like to speak
to, whatever."

"You have been more fortunate than me, Sandy," the young woman said, dryly. "Now— d'you all agree with me that we ought to have a look at Coire Ruadh?"

"That would be best, yes," Alec Macphail agreed. "We can't just be letting the man be, and him maybe stuck half-ways up yon—or lying at the bottom, indeed."

There was a rumble of agreement.

"That's how I feel, myself." Fiona nodded. "However much he's asked for it, we can't just go back to our beds and forget about him. It may well be just a wild-goose-chase, of course—he may well be nowhere near Coire Ruadh. But it's the only clue that we have—this knife and the rope. And apparently he was asking Seana yesterday whether the deer would be back there yet—in the sanctuary."

"Nothing else we can do, I'm thinking," Cattanach acceded. "It'll not take us that long to be getting to the Red Corrie, with the cars?"

"An hour-and-a-half, I'd say, even allowing for the darkness," the girl considered. "We've warned Willie Maclean, and he'll be ready. Then, I think, we'd better go up for John Cameron. It'll take a little longer, but he knows the hill better than anybody else. That'll make seven of us. That should be enough, even if we have to make up two parties. Take some of these scones in your pockets, will you —we'll be glad of them, I dare say. There's some tea left in that pot—a bit tarry by now, maybe, but better than nothing . . ."

"I've brought a droppie of the real stuff with me," the hotel-keeper mentioned, patting his capacious pocket. "Useful, it could be—and for more than the casualty!"

That was not contested. "Alec, will you go along to Balnahard, with your car, just to make sure our

bird's not returned meantime, and gone cheerfully to
bed?'' Fiona suggested. '' You could give Seana a
lift back, too. I'll pick up Willie at the sawmill, and
then go up for John Cameron. Say we meet up at
the old bothy on the track up the glen? Give us half-
an-hour—John won't take long. Is that all right? If
you find Mr. Kinnear beforehand, of course, come
right after us to Cameron's cottage. And bring the
wretch along with you, too—I've got something to
say to that individual that I'd be the better of getting
out of my system just as soon as possible!''

'' We will that, Miss Fiona.''

'' Yes, indeed.''

'' Thank God it is not my own self, at all!'' That
was Macphail piously.

Drawing up behind the other car, Fiona switched
off her headlights, and got out, her two passengers
behind her. It was dark there amongst the trees,
after the brilliant yellow fairyland that the lights had
made for them—though, actually, it was not a black
night. John Cameron and Willie Maclean the Sawmill, greeted the others with the cheerful grumbling
that the occasion called for.

'' What's the ploy, then, Miss Fiona?'' Alec
Macphail questioned. But it was at the keeper that
he looked. John Cameron, obviously, would be the
leader of the party, though the civilities had to be
observed.

'' Och, we'll go back down a wee thing, and cross
the river by the wire-bridge,'' he directed. '' Then
up the burnside beyond, keeping well to the east,
there. With the wind that's in it, from the west, we'll
no' be disturbing the beasts more than we can help,
at all. That'll be best, wouldn't you say, Miss
Fiona?''

'' Whatever *you* say, John. But it seems to me,

that if we're going into Coire Ruadh, we're going to disturb the deer pretty thoroughly whether we give them our wind or not.''

"That is so, yes—but in fine weather the like of this, a lot of the beasts'll be lying out below the corrie, there—the stags especially. That is, if they've come back at all, after yon last ploy. Of course, if this Mr. Kinnear's been climbing up there again, the corrie and the whole hill will be empty, anyhow.''

"Quite.''

"But if he's not, see you, I'm thinking we can maybe save disturbing all the ground below the corrie. Coming from the east, in the dark, and entering the corrie from maybe half-way up, I'm thinking I could maybe search the foot of the cliffs, without clearing the whole place.''

"M'mmm,'' the girl doubted. "Perhaps, John. But if he's not at the foot, he might be stuck somewhere up the cliff-face. We wouldn't be able to see that, in the dark. We'd have to shout. And if there's going to be a lot of shouting, you're going to have the hill cleared, anyway.''

"My God, you are, if there's to be shouting in it!'' the keeper agreed grimly. "We'll not have a beast left on Beinn Dearg, if we start that.''

"Perhaps not,'' the other admitted, level-voiced. "But if a man's life is at stake, that can't be helped.''

John Cameron said something under his breath, something brief but heartfelt.

"Amen to that, John.'' Fiona concurred, with just the shadow of a smile. "Lead the way, then.''

They walked down the road, back the way that they had come, for perhaps quarter-of-a-mile, and then Cameron turned off right-handed, on to a tiny path through the trees, practically indistinguishable in the dark. In single file, and unspeaking, they followed on, the girl first and Sandy Cattanach bringing up the rear. It was quiet and still there in the forest, and the seven walkers did surprisingly little to outrage the hush of it.

They crossed the alarmingly-swaying suspension-bridge of wire and planks above the seething rushing river, breaking step heedfully to minimise the vibration. Beyond, the keeper turned downstream again to follow the bank, now at the water's edge, now high above it, till a boisterous burn came in a series of white-gleaming falls. On the farther side of this, he led them upwards.

There was no visible path, though Cameron seemed to know exactly where they were going, and set them a fairly stiff pace on that long ascent between the scattered pines amongst the long heather. Nor did he once look round, to assure himself that he was not going too fast for the young woman; presumably he knew her capabilities on the hill. And though, before long, she was breathing fairly deeply, and not infrequently she stumbled over hidden snags, stones and outcropping tree-roots masked by the heather, never once did she fall more than a couple of yards behind the iron-shod heels of her leader. The others followed steadily, stolidly, behind her. Only Sandy Cattanach dropped back a little; police-station stools have to be paid for one way or another. By the time that they reached the tree-level, he was some hundreds of yards to the rear.

They found themselves just below the entrance to a high valley between two steep hills, a valley out of which tumbled the stream that had been their intermittent companion, and whose farther end appeared to be blocked by the vast black mass of a much larger hill, the flat-topped Beinn Dearg, out of the swelling flank of which the Coire Ruadh was scooped. It was surprising how light it seemed, now, after the constriction of the trees, scattered open woodland as it

I

had been, with their eyes accustomed to the gloom. While there was no certainty to the view, they could see for fair distances.

Once through the bealach between the two smaller hills, Cameron led them away left-handed in a wide circuit, over very wet and unpleasant ground indeed, old heather, black and broken peat-hag, and out-cropping granite. And he was very explicit that they should not kick nor rasp their feet against the stone; in a great hollow of the hills like this, on a still night, a sharp sound would carry a long way. The joke about policemen's feet was inevitable.

With their semi-circling almost completed, they began to climb in earnest, and though the work was harder the going improved steadily, as the ground firmed up and the heather dwindled beneath their feet. There was no talking now, only the sound of heavy breathing and the crunch of gravel underfoot —and, as far as the girl was concerned, the thudding of her own heart—to counter the absolute silence of the night-bound hills.

Once, John Cameron held up his hand, and they stopped, thankfully enough, while the keeper bent down, wormed forward, and seemed to disappear into the dark body of the hill. After a blessed breath-ing-space, he was with them once more, and, unspeaking, led the way back, on the same level but farther to the east again, before once more turning uphill. They guessed that they had been nearly into deer.

Sometime, with time only to be reckoned in terms of toil and effort, heaving lungs and aching muscles, they reached the lip of the great basin of Coire Ruadh, something under half-way up its eastern side. With the dark pit of it yawning before them, Cameron signed to them to sit down.

"Wait here," he whispered. "I'll away down

along the foot of the cliffs, and have a bit look. I've got this torch, and if I'm wanting you to come, I'll wink the light two-three times. If you come, watch how you go—there's a lot of scree about here. I'll be a while, likely.''

'' Hadn't some of us better come with you, John? '' Fiona suggested. '' It's a big job for one man to do.''

The keeper shook his head. '' One makes less noise than a number,'' he said. '' We've not disturbed the beasts yet, I'm thinking, and I want to be saving this hill if I can, at all. If he's fallen, there's only the two bits he can be—or, maybe two lines of places, as you might say. Either amongst the big tumbled rocks at the foot of the screes, or, if he hasn't just rolled that far, at the top of the screes below the cliff-face. I'll go along the bottom, and back along up above—and one man can do that as well as many, whatever. We'd have to be in single-file, anyway, see you. Right, then? Watch for the light.''

And quietly, he rose to his feet, was silhouetted for a moment against the wan glimmer of the star-hung sky, and then swallowed up in the black gulf below. Hearken as they would, none of them heard his going. Only the eddying night wind of the high places whispering amongst the short heather and blaeberries, made any sound for them to listen to.

Though the girl had been warm enough from her exertions when first she lay down on her front in the heather, to stare into the murky void before her, she was being racked by recurrent great shivers before, something over half-an-hour later, John Cameron materialised once again, coming down to them from a little higher on the braeside.

They all were prepared, of course, for the news that he brought. '' Devil the thing,'' he reported briefly.

"We were afraid not," Fiona said, and then breathed a half-laugh. "Though I suppose, that's hardly the way to put it! We should be thankful, no doubt." She did not sound altogether sure of that. "Well . . . there's nothing for it but to shout, I'm afraid."

"Tst—tst," John Cameron complained. "Must you be doing a thing like that, Miss Fiona?"

"Do you see any alternative?"

The keeper scratched his chin, and they could hear the rasp of his nails on the bristles of it. "Well, now," he said, doubtfully.

The girl went on. "You know as well as I do, John, that if the man went climbing up that cliff-face, there are a dozen places where he might have got stuck, unable to move either up or down. He may be up there this minute, clinging on for dear life. And we've been so quiet, in our efforts not to disturb the deer, that he wouldn't know that we're here."

"If he had a rope with him, he'd not be that likely to be stuck, maybe?" Macphail put in.

"Nonsense." The young woman dismissed Alec Macphail and the rope together. "What good would a few feet of rope be on a cliff nearly a thousand feet high? Even if he had positively wrapped himself up in rope, he wouldn't have enough with him to take him half-way down. And Seana said it was only a bit of her clothes-line . . . !"

"Depends on where he'd left this knife, I'm thinking." Cattanach observed, "You didn't see that, when you were after watching him through your glasses, yon time, Miss Fiona?"

"No—we weren't close enough for that. He had a bad time about three-quarters of the way up, though—probably it was there. There's a belt of loose stuff there, like a small scree but very steep, with nothing to hang on to. If he'd tied his rope to a rock at the top, and let himself down, it *might* have reached that far. But without knowing the length of rope he has . . . But all this is beside the point, anyway. He *may* be up there. We just don't know—but we can't merely walk away, without giving him a chance to *let* us know, deer or none."

"That is so, yes."

"We can not, as you say."

"We could try the light," Cameron suggested. " If we were to shine my torch up at the cliff-face, there, anybody up there would be seeing it, likely. And if we sort of shielded it at the side, with a coat maybe, the deer wouldn't be noticing it."

" M'mmm. It's worth trying, anyway," the girl acceded. " But it's not a sure test, by any means. He might be dozing, and so not see it. Or he might be in a position where the light wouldn't show— behind one of those buttresses, for instance. But try it, by all means."

So John Cameron, shielding the torch on the right within his jacket, switched on the light. Its beam seemed entirely feeble and inadequate in the vast blue vault of the night, but while it did not illuminate the rocky backcloth of the corrie undoubtedly it would be visible from there. The keeper winked it off and on for fully a minute. There was no response.

" If he was there, and saw it, he'd shout—and then your stags would be off anyway," the farmer MacBean pointed out.

" If he's up there, at all, the sanctuary will be cleared, as *it* is," Macphail amplified.

" Exactly." Fiona agreed, " We're just wasting time. If you won't shout, John—I will ! " And cupping hands to her lips, she called in high-pitched ululation. " Cooo—eee ! Cooo—eee ! Are you thae—er ? Cooo—eee ! "

"Och, my Goodness!" muttered John Cameron.

Tensely they listened, while the echoes mocked them. Startling and ghostly, that last Cooo—ee came back to them, from hillsides near and far, time and again, till it faded into the affronted night, a strange forlorn sound, that sent another shiver down the back of even the girl who initiated it. But it was only her echo that they heard, indubitably.

"No sound of anything . . ." she began, when her keeper interrupted her, rudely for that mannerly man.

"H'ssst!" he said, "Quiet, you." He was listening, like the rest of them, but differently, lying forward with his ear to the ground. For almost a minute he lay there, while the others barely breathed.

"Hear anything?" the girl whispered, at last.

With a sigh, the man straightened up. "Aye," he said, heavily. "Plenty. They're running. Hundreds of them."

Fiona swallowed. "Oh, blow the deer, John!" She turned away. "Sandy—you've got lungs of brass. Try a shout."

And so, perhaps deeper, louder, but no more penetrating, the constable's voice boomed out into the mirk, and was thrown back in its turn by the encircling hills, their only response.

With one accord, all seven listeners got to their feet.

"Well, that's that, then," Macphail commented.

"There's nobody in it, to be sure."

"Aye, then."

"And we've cleared the sanctuary, and the best beat on Glencoraig besides, for nothing, just nothing at all," John Cameron lamented. "Damn all Sassenachs, I say!"

Fiona Macpherson said nothing.

"What's the way of it now, then?" Maclean

from the sawmill wondered. They all looked from
the young woman to the gamekeeper.

She shrugged. "I don't see that there's anything
else we *can* do. We can't go round all the cliffs and
corries of the Cairngorms, shouting. Since apparently
he's not here, we haven't a clue as to where he may
be—confound the stupid idiot!"

Nobody gainsayed that.

"We'll just have to get back down to the cars,
I suppose. Unless anybody has any bright
suggestions?"

Only Cameron had, it seemed. "You do just
that," he agreed, nodding at them. "Myself, I'm
thinking I'll take a bit daunder round the back of
this hill, here, and over the big moss yonder, and on
to the side of Meall na Corrie—that's the hill to the
west, there." And he pointed towards its dark ridge,
black against deep blue. "That'll bring me down to
the road, maybe a mile or so up from the cars."

"Why would you do that, John?" the girl wondered. "What makes you think Mr. Kinnear might
be over that way?"

"Och, it's not your Mr. Kinnear I'm thinking
about, at all, ma'am," the keeper said, very definitely
—and it was seldom indeed that she had known him
call her that. "It's your brother's stags, you see,
that's my responsibility—not half-witted summer-
visitors that do not be taking a telling! As I see it,
these beasts you've put up with your bawling will be
moving westwards off this hill, with the wind that's
in it. That means they'll have to be crossing the big
moss, there. But they'll be doing that slowly, I'm
thinking—they'll just be sort of drifting, by then.
In fact, it might be they'll stay in the moss till daylight, even."

"That's right, John, aye," MacBean, who was
something of a stalker, agreed.

"Aye. So I'm thinking if I was to be going round that way, crossing to the west of the moss, and just giving them a bit whiffle of my mind, I'd likely be sending them back this way. You see, they won't have scented us yet—it's just the noise they'll have got, and the echoes will have confused them, maybe. Och, it's just a chance, whatever—we're not wanting them away off the ground, and into Glenardoch."

"Well, if you think it's worth it," Fiona allowed. "Don't you want someone else with you, to give you a hand?"

"I do not, then. This will have to be done gently, see you—one's plenty. It's just a gliff I'm wanting them to get, or they'll be worse upset than ever. Deer are kittle cattle."

"Very well. How long will you be, at it?"

"Och, not that long at all. As far as the distance that's in it, it's not much more than the road you'll be going your own selves. I shouldn't wonder if I'm not down at the road about as soon as you are, whatever. If you'll be coming with a car for me, to the bit where the path goes down to yon bridge the soldiers built in the war, I'll not be keeping you waiting long."

"All right, John. We'll just go back the same way we came?"

"That's right, yes—just that. And let there be no more bawling in it, Miss Fiona, for the good Lord's sake!"

And so they set off down hill, a somewhat subdued party, while the keeper stalked on upwards, long-strided, a tireless man. And right down to the peat-hags, and through the bealach, and on till all the trees received them, they went unspeaking, save for a muttered imprecation or two from the young woman, when she stumbled over projecting stone or clutching

heather. She was feeling like that. But she led them
safely back down to the Coraig River, to the suspension-bridge, and up to the road.

At the cars, it was agreed that there was no point in
Macphail's car either going further up the glen to
pick up Cameron, or waiting there for him. It was
three forty-five, and no time for needless hanging
about. Amidst a quiet chorus of goodnights, the
hotel-keeper turned his vehicle, and lurched off down
the narrow road towards home. With only Willie
Maclean the Sawmill for passenger, Fiona moved on
further into the huddle of the great hills, her headlights making almost an indecent display after the
dimness to which they had become accustomed.

It was that yellow glare which, a few minutes later,
picked out the figure of John Cameron kneeling at
the roadside, over something dark, ominous, and
asprawl.

" Aye, it's himself, all right," the keeper informed,
as the girl climbed out. " A nasty knock he's taken,
too. Concussion, I'd say."

"But how on earth could he do that? Here, I
mean? Or has he just sort of struggled this far, and
got no farther?" Despite her enquiries, she got
straight down on her knees besides the recumbent
Kinnear.

Alan's eyes were open, and his lips were moving
very slightly, but he was unconscious, obviously.
That curious impersonal unseeing stare, revealed in
the car's headlights, was rather horrible.

" No—he hasn't moved, I'm thinking," Cameron
declared. " I found him just here, but lying on his
face. He's taken an almighty dinger, the lad."

" Yes—obviously. It's concussion, all right.
Willie—get me the first-aid box. It's on the floor at
the back." Fiona Macpherson had been a V.A.D.

in the not so distant past. "He's got a frightful swelling here, and the scalp's a bit broken. When you turned him over, did there seem as though there was anything else wrong, John? No bones broken?"

"No, I wouldn't think so. I'm thinking he's just been hit on the head—and hit almighty hard."

"Hit? You mean . . .?"

"Aye, then—just that. Attacked. There's been queer on-goings here, I'm telling you. Look you at what he's got in that hand, there."

"Yes—what is it? Good gracious—it's a leg, a stag's foreleg!"

"It is so. He's not giving it up, either. I'm thinking our Mr. Kinnear isn't maybe such an eediot as we were naming him, back there. D'you smell anything, at all?"

She sniffed. "I can't say I do—except this disinfectant I'm using."

"Aye—and your car, too. But before you came, there was a right strong smell of petrol about here. It was coming from across the road, there. A car has been standing there—there's oil in it, too. And blood —och, lots of blood. The grass is thick with it."

"Blood!"

"Och, not *his* blood, no. He's not bleeding that badly. It's deer's blood, I'm thinking. It looks like our Sassenach came on a gang of these damned poachers, and took what was coming to him."

"Poachers, yes!" The word on her lips was spoken strangely, her voice rising, high-pitched. "Oh, dear." That was almost a laugh, incipient hysteria. She had had a trying night, she was tired, and this was an unpleasant thing to find at the end of it. Fiercely, desperately, she mastered it. "Poor Mr. Kinnear—he's as good as a magnet for poachers!"

"Aye, he is that . . . Now, I'm wondering how he comes to have that bit leg in his hand . . . ?"

"Look—he's coming round. He tried to say something there . . ."

"Och, no—it's just kind of deleerious he is," the keeper asserted. "He's been doing that same since I got here. Just nonsense he's been talking—och, about Ferlas Mor being after him, and the likes of that."

"Ferlas Mor! The Grey Man, you mean? What on earth . . . ?"

"Just wandering, he is. A right nasty dunt he must have got, whatever."

The girl finished tying the bandage round that damaged head, and heedfully flexed neck and limbs to assure herself that Cameron was right about no bones being broken. "Seems all right, otherwise," she conceded, "Now—to get him into the car. John —I think you'd better drive. We'll get him on the back seat, with his head on my lap. Take the whole back seat out, Willie—it'll serve as a sort of stretcher. Now, carefully does it . . ."

And so, Alan Kinnear, eased cautiously into the old car, and with his head pillowed where he never would have expected it to be, went back to Balnahard at last.

"Drive slowly, John," the girl commanded. "And when you've dropped us at Seana's, I think you'd better go straight on to Blairard for Doctor Forbes. Concussion's a thing we don't want to take any chances with. Now, watch these bumps, for Heaven's sake!"

CHAPTER XIII

ALAN KINNEAR'S recollections and impressions of the
pattern of his life after his hurtling descent into deep
and unrelieved blackness, remained incoherent, fleet-
ing, unreal, and quite puzzling, to this day. There
was no sense of time about it all, no order and
sequence, no outline or clarity—though certain very
strong perceptions remained with him. The trouble
was, to ascertain how much of it was dream, mental
miasma, and reality.

For instance, Ferlas Mor presumably was not a
reality—though he had seemed substantial enough in
all conscience, and Alan spent aeons of time striving
to escape from his terrifying clutches. Then there
was an enormous stag, that had the ability to change
without warning into a grey garron with flashing eyes
and gleaming teeth, that took turn-about with the
Grey Man at chasing him into a stony trap, cynically
called a sanctuary, out of which the only escape was
up an endless cliff of sliding scree, which, for every
step that he took forward dragged him an equal
distance back. Again, the girl Fiona Macpherson
kept coming into things, a changed and improbable
character this, who looked on him kindly and
soothed him with soft words and gentle touches.
When she was there, he could escape from both
Ferlas Mor and the stag, but they were always waiting for him when she went. Seana Macdonald, too,
intervened frequently on his behalf, but the Grey
Man was not so frightened for her—as who can blame

him?—even though she went for him with a great clasp-knife.

But these varying apparitions were the high-lights, the certainties, of his dark uneasy journeyings; in between and all around them, were the black depths, the swirling mists, the eddying fathomless tides and boundless plains of an empty chaotic world, wherein was neither time nor sequence nor dimension.

He could not even set in order in his mind the first occasion on which he managed to struggle feebly to the surface of that dismal flood, only momentarily as it was, and saw blessed sunlight filtering through golden birch-leaves, the red roses in their serried ranks, that was his wall-paper, and the kindly-smiling apple-cheeked face that came near and swam away and came again. He would have liked to stay with Seana Macdonald, then, but could not; the tide was strong, and nameless potent things were dragging him down. But he came back again, presently, and though no smiling face was waiting for him this time, the sun was there, and the swaying leaves and the dependable ranks of the roses. Another time, Seana was there again, and another face, a man's face that he knew not, with bushy eyebrows that frowned on him, but not unkindly, before fading away and leaving only the infallible roses. Those roses, so sure and steadfast in their regular lines, became increasingly his standby and support, as his surfacings became more frequent. And once, he listened, listened intently, desperately, to a voice in the darkness, a voice that he knew but could by no means place, soft, kindly, reassuring. But none of these manifestations could he set in any order of arrangement, then or any time.

But one day, in all that eternity of time, he knew lucidity, tremulous, swimming, but certain, undeniable. Seana Macdonald was standing above his bed, smiling. And she was speaking.

"Well, now—isn't that just fine, now. Och, more like it you are, whatever, Mr. Kinnear. Yes, then. My, oh my—aren't you the boy!"

Alan had something to say. He tried hard, very hard, to find the words, but could not. But he managed just the shadow of a smile.

"There, there—grand, that is," the old woman nodded, smoothing and tucking-in the sheet under his chin. "Just grand. You're doing fine. We'll be having you on your feet in no time, at all."

The man made a great effort. His lips moved, but no sound came. He frowned, and closed his eyes. But the urgency was still there, inescapable. He drew a ling quivering breath, and moistened his lips. And words came. "Tell her," he besought, in a whisper, "There was five of them . . ."

"Surely, surely," Seana said, soothingly. "Just that. Hush you, now. Do not be fretting yourself at all . . ."

Feebly, Alan shook his head—at least, that is what he meant to do. "Five," he insisted. "No heads and legs. In a van." His weakness made him feel light, unsubstantial as the air, yet his tongue was as heavy as lead. "Tell her . . ."

"Och, now—wheesht you," he was commanded. "Everything is fine, just. Don't you be worrying about a thing, see you. Not a word out of you, whatever."

He tried to fix her with his eye, to let her see that this was important. "She must be told," he breathed, "Miss Macpherson . . . Up the road, they were . . ."

"Yes, yes. All right, then. Herself will be here, surely. Och, she comes every day, indeed. You'll see. Now, away to sleep with you . . ."

" Every day . . . ? " he muttered.

" That is right, yes—every day. Now, there is to be no more talking in it. I'm away, see you. Sleep, now. But I'll be back. And Miss Fiona will be back . . ."

She would be back. And every day . . . Desperately, he tried to think what that meant, what were the implications of that. But he could not. He was tired. He could not think, just now. The roses were there . . . and the sunshine. There was a lot of roses, hundreds of roses . . .

He slept, and woke, and looked for the girl to tell her about it all, and slept again. And woke, and slept—but if she was not there, neither was Ferlas Mor or the stag, any more. And she would come.

She did come, too, presently—as she had come each day since she had brought him home to Balnahard with his head on her lap—which might well be considered as a strange development for that young woman. But it was not so strange as it might seem. Fiona Macpherson, if she could be a severe critic of meddlesome and feckless young men, could be an equally severe critic of herself rather more so, on occasion. In the present connection, her self-criticism was pointed and keen. She felt that she had misjudged the man, if not entirely, at least in regard to the night in question, when, while she was miscalling him for disobeying her injunctions, for criminal foolhardiness and self-centred obstinacy, he was not only innocent of all this but was actually lying unconscious, struck down by brutal hands. And, in some measure, she felt responsible for his misfortune; after all, these ruffians were *her* enemies, not his, and it was on the estate's behalf, presumably, that he had interfered, and suffered this calamity. The least that she could do, was to use what little skill and knowledge she possessed, in aiding his return to the *status quo*.

It might be, too, perhaps, that there was another side to it all, less obvious, but none the less potent in its influence. That man, however she had misjudged him, had been strong, unyielding, stubborn, sure of himself—almost insufferably so. Now he was weak, helpless, disarmed, and child-like in his need. She would have been less than a woman if she had not reacted positively to these so changed circumstances, if she had not derived a certain satisfaction from tending and supporting this self-sufficient disputant laid so utterly low. It was no unpleasant sensation, perhaps, to be thoroughly and so practically sorry for him.

Not that she felt any different about him, personally, of course. He was still an obstinate, overbearing, cock-a-hoop young man, who badly needed to be taken down a peg—even if not quite such a large peg as this!

So she had come, and so she came.

He heard the voice, knew it now, most definitely, and struggled up out of the heavy mists. She was standing there beside Seana, and looking at him.

"So-ho—look who we have here." She smiled down at him. "You know, Mr. Kinnear, you look much more like a genuine author, with a beard!"

He did not quite get that. He was listening not to what she said, but only to her voice. That was the voice that had reached him sometimes, in that curious incoherent past, that he had known and yet not recognised. He knew why, now; it was the tone that was different, kindly, warm, sympathetic—not at all what he had known previously. He could not have been expected to recognise it.

"Och, he's looking more like himself—he is so." Seana put in, "Dr. Forbes will be right pleased."

Alan was going through the business of finding
words, again—though it came a little more easily,
this time. "Miss Macpherson," he said, earnestly,
"Poachers. I saw them."

"Yes, I know." Fiona agreed, gently. "But
never mind about them now, Mr. Kinnear. Just
forget the poachers . . ."

"No." He even interrupted her, had the strength
to do it. "I saw them. They had five deer . . . in a
van. Up the glen. You must stop them . . ."

"We will, yes—never fear. We'll get them, yet.
But not just now, you see . . ."

"Yes—you must get the police. They got the
wrong man, you see, the police. They got, they
got . . ." For the life of him he, could not remember
the man's name. "They got it all mixed up. He
wasn't a real poacher, at all. These are the real ones.
They have a van . . . They followed me, through the
hills and the woods, them and the Grey Man . . .
You'll have to catch them right away, or it will be
too late." The man was panting with his effort.

Fiona Macpherson laid a cool hand on his brow,
and stroked it gently upwards, backwards, into his
hair. "It's all right, Mr. Kinnear—quite all right.
Don't you worry about them, any more. The police
will look after them, fine. And Archie's all right, too.
They've gone now, anyway, you see. It is five days
since you saw them—all that. Now, you must be
quiet, and don't worry about anything."

"Five days . . . !" the man said, and his mind, as
it were, peered back into the swirling abyss out of
which he had so lately struggled. "Five days."

"Yes. But it is all right, now. Look—Seana has
something for you to drink, here. In this cup. Try
and take it, will you? Here's a spoonful."

"I'm not hungry," he objected, frowning.
"These poachers . . . !"

K

"Open your mouth, now. You will like it, once you try it. Just forget the poachers." She laughed, softly. "Now, look what you've done—you've spilt some of it on your new beard! Come on—another spoonful . . . That's better. A man must eat, you know—especially a terrible man like you, that's growing a beard. It takes it out of you, you know. No—no talking till you've finished your gruel."

When it was done, he said, "Five days, I have been here? Five days since I saw the poachers? A man came behind me—he struck me . . ."

"Yes. You have had concussion. But you're getting on all right, now. You just need rest and quiet. So you mustn't talk any more, today."

Almost, he had to blink back tears of indignation. "But you said . . . after the gruel . . . !"

"Women were deceivers ever." Fiona Macpherson smiled. "No talking—or I go away, at once, and Seana too."

As at a straw, he grasped. "If I do not talk, you will not go?"

"No. Not if you want me to stay. If you promise not to talk, that is. But it's got to be a genuine promise, you know."

"Yes," he nodded.

As Seana Macdonald, smiling her conspirator's smile, tip-toed out of the room, the girl sat down on a chair beside the bed, and reached for her bag.

"Archie . . .?" he began. "That's it—Archie. You said Archie was all right, now . . . ?"

She half-rose from her chair. "Is that how you keep your promises, Mr. Alan Kinnear! One more word out of you, and I'm off. And that *is* a promise!" She raised her brows at him, and just the corners of her mouth, as well. "But I'll tell you just this—Archie's all right. He's back home, indeed—arrived this morning. Now—go to sleep."

Alan shook his head. "No," he said, very definitely.

In three minutes his eyes were closed, and he was puffing with quiet regularity through pursed lips above that incipient beard.

The young woman sat still. She was reading a scarlet-backed book. Every now and again, she glanced up from its pages, to consider the sleeper, and more than once she smiled, faintly, secretly, as only women can smile. The book was entitled *Inspector Hake's Last Case*.

CHAPTER XIV

THE next day, the doctor came, and seemed to be pleased with his patient. But unfortunately the interview, and all the questioning he put to Doctor Forbes, tired Alan so much that he fell asleep very promptly thereafter—or, maybe, it was something in the dose out of the bottle that the bushy-browed old fellow made him take. At all events, he was asleep when Fiona Macpherson made her daily visit, and still asleep when she left. He was most annoyed when he found out about it later, and told Seana Macdonald so. There was a positive conspiracy of silence, amongst them all, a plot to keep him in the dark.

But the day following, Monday, and apparently a week after his adventures up the glen, the young woman arrived in mid-forenoon, just after he had wakened up and was feeling at his brightest. In fact, he was feeling a great deal better, in every way, and showed it. Fiona, sitting down, had no excuse for refusing either to talk or listen a little.

"I want to hear what happened?" he insisted. "How I got back here, and when, and everything."

"You got here in the back of my car, about five o'clock the next morning, after John Cameron had found you lying at the roadside, up the glen," she informed. "We'd been out searching the hills for you. When you weren't home by midnight, Seana got worried and came round to Coraigmore, and we organised a search-party." The girl smiled. "I must admit we were none of us very enthusiastic—we thought you'd been back at Coire Ruadh, at the sanctuary, you know—climbing the cliffs again. We thought we'd probably find you at the bottom of them—or what was left of you.''

'' But why? What made you think that? I wouldn't do a thing like that, after . . . after what you told me . . .''

'' Seana said you'd talked about going back for some knife or other. And you had a rope with you. It was the only clue we had, you see. If you weren't there, where were you, all day? ''

'' I was up on high tops—the Cairngorms,'' he told her. '' That was only a joke I was having with Mrs. Macdonald about the knife. I climbed Cairn Lochan and Ben MacDhui and came back across the Larig and Glen Einich, and Meall na Corrie. It was there that . . . it was there I began to think that I was being followed.''

She had looked up when he had mentioned Ben MacDhui. '' You talked a lot about Ferlas Mor, when you were unconscious, Mr. Kinnear,'' she said, a little hesitantly. '' I was wondering why? ''

The man drew a hand across his brow. '' I don't rightly know,'' he admitted, '' I had been thinking about it—the stories, you know—when I felt that I wasn't alone, in those hills, that I was being followed. I suppose I must have got it into my head . . .''

'' Then you didn't actually see anything—or hear anything? ''

'' Oh, no—not then.'' He smiled, wanly. '' It was only *after* I got my knock on the head that I began to take the Grey Man seriously . . . ! ''

'' I think I understand,'' she smiled, gently. '' Shall we send him back, where he belongs—to Ben MacDhui? ''

'' With all my heart.'' Alan agreed. '' He and I

never got along too well together, I'm afraid." He changed the subject. "How did you come to find me, then?"

"It was John Cameron. After we'd inspected Coire Ruadh, and found no sign of you, we all came down the way we'd gone—that's down to the road by the suspension-bridge. But John went away round westwards, and came down by Meall na Corrie—the same way that you came yourself—to the Soldiers' Bridge. That was quite fortunate, wasn't it?"

"Why did he do that—go round that way?"

"Something to do with the deer, I think," Fiona said lightly.

"Yes—the deer," the man nodded, and not lightly at all. "That's what I was thinking. If you all went to this Coire Ruadh, searching for me, that means that the sanctuary must have been disturbed again? You were prepared to do that for me, on the off-chance of my being injured there, Miss Macpherson?"

Fiona was looking out of the window, to the tree-tops. "One man's life—even that of a Lowland visitor—is worth many deer, Mr. Kinnear." She produced the beginnings of a laugh. "Though I will admit that there was a certain amount of argument about it!"

"I can believe that," the patient said, unsmiling. "I thank you, anyway, for the decision you made. It couldn't have been an easy one."

"Just as easy as the one *you* made, I think," the girl returned, serious in her turn.

"Me? What decision was that?"

"When, despite all that I'd said, all the discouragement, all that had happened to you after your previous attempt at apprehending poachers on Glencoraig, you still were prepared to tackle these ruffians, on my behalf."

Alan frowned. "I wish I could accept that, Miss Macpherson—I do indeed. But it's not a fact. I didn't tackle them—they tackled me. I did nothing more gallant than get in their road. I wasn't so magnanimous as you, you see, when it came to the bit—I was prepared to wash my hands of all poachers. The fact that they weren't disposed to wash their hands of me, so easily, is scarcely to my credit . . ."

"And yet you were found lying directly across the road from where their van was hidden—and clutching a stag's foreleg in your hand! John Cameron says you obviously had been hiding there, watching them, and with the evidence of their guilt in your hand. You will forgive me, Mr. Kinnear, if I prefer to accept the evidence of my common-sense, rather than your modest disclaimers?"

That man was weak, yet. Also he was much aware of his indebtedness to this young woman. She was undoubtedly highly attractive, too—when she was not being autocratic. Perhaps he may be excused if he did not press his contention in the matter so obstinately as sometimes he was apt to do. He changed his ground, instead. "I have more to thank you for, than the deer business, too," he said. "All your visits here—and I understand that you've been nursing me . . . I can't begin to say how grateful I am . . ."

She shook her head. "Then don't—for it's quite uncalled for. I have done very little, believe me. It's Seana you've to thank, if anybody. She's done all the hard work. I only took a hand now and again . . . because I was nursing in the war, you see, and knew a little about it. I've seen concussion cases before." She nodded significantly. "Which brings me to the point, young man. And that is, for a concussion convalescent, you've talked quite enough for one day.

You see? In other words, silence reigns, from now on." Cunning, she was.

"Oh, I say—but that's not fair!" he protested. "That's a rotten trick. I feel fine. I'm much better today. And there's lots I want to hear yet . . ."

"Next fine day, perhaps. We were very good at sick-room discipline in the V.A.D.!"

"I bet you were." He rubbed his chin, scraped thoughtfully amongst the wiry growth, and then his eye lit up. "Look, Miss Macpherson—I want a shave. I must get rid of this ghastly stuff. But I need help."

"Oh, you're not going to cut it off, Mr. Kinnear?" She looked shocked. "It's most . . . impressive, I assure you. It's quite an asset. It makes you *look* like a member of the intelligentsia . . . and you *are* a member of the intelligentsia, I understand . . . ?"

"It is the first time I've been accused of *that*, at anyrate!" the man said, with surprising vigour. "That clinches the matter, at all events! It comes off, right now. All I need is some hot water in a mug, and a pair of scissors. My shaving things are over in the dressing-table drawer, there. And if you'd hold the mirror for me . . . ?"

"Anything else, sir?"

"Yes. You can tell me all about Archie Fraser, while I shave. I promise I won't open my mouth, once."

"You had better not," she said. "For I will be holding the shaving-brush!"

So, while he clipped and lathered and shaved, and the girl held and twisted and tipped the mirror this way and that with fair success, Alan heard the outcome of the Archie Fraser affair.

It seemed that his, Alan Kinnear's, plunge into unconsciousness, had simplified matters for all con-

cerned with the case, most fortunately—instead of
complicating things as he had feared. With the trial
scheduled to take place in Inverness on the Thursday, the information that the principal—indeed, the
only—witness on the poaching charge was suffering
from concussion, was something of a blow for the
prosecution. An urgent medical report was called
for, by the Procurator-Fiscal's office, a report which
Dr. Forbes, with the assistance and advice
undoubtedly of the volunteer nurse, compiled and
despatched with commendable promptitude. If this
report took a rather gloomy view of the patient's
condition and when he was likely to be restored to
sufficient mental stability to give trustworthy
evidence, and this prognostication subsequently had
been proved to be unduly cautious, nobody was more
happy than its compilers, it seemed. But medical
opinion disapproved of wild optimism, and most
rightly, and Dr. Forbes had had many factors to take
into account. Fiona Macpherson was very explicit
about that, even if she avoided the shaver's eye in
the process of making it plain—and even if she
omitted to mention the doctor's rider of the
possibility of subsequent loss of memory.

At anyrate, the Fiscal, with this report in his hands,
had been confronted with two alternatives. Either
to apply for an indefinite postponement of the hearing, or to desert the charge of poaching altogether.
That he took the latter course indicates his good
sense, and undoubtedly some knowledge of local
conditions.

So when the Thursday came round, and the name
of Archibald Fraser, tenant in Dalnamuick, Coraigbeg, was read out in Inverness Sheriff's court, it was
to face only the one charge—that of being in illegal
possession of game, on the night of Tuesday 6th of
September, on the property of Ewan Macpherson,

Esquire, of Coraig—a charge to which the three
police witnessess could testify. To this the prisoner
had wisely pleaded guilty, and the Sheriff, hot
against poaching as he might be, but faced with no
specific charge of such—as well as the absence of a
charge by the actual owners of the property, plus a
sheaf of testimonials to the good character of the
accused—found himself somewhat trammelled and
restricted. Consulting the records of Kingussie Police
Station, and after some humphing and nose-blowing
and a brief but acidulated homily on the evils and
prevalence of deer-poaching, he decided that the ends
of justice might be served by sentencing Archibald
Fraser to fourteen days imprisonment on the charge
libelled—which, that being the fourteenth day since
his arrest on the side of Meall na Corrie, meant his
immediate release.

So Archie had returned home to Dalnamuick and
the bosom of his family, if not in triumph, at least in
some satisfaction—a satisfaction that seemed to be
shared by all concerned. And it was to be hoped, by
Mr. Kinnear, also. For, of course, however involuntarily, he was responsible for Fraser's release. But
then, his responsibility for the arrest, too, had been
involuntary, he had claimed? Could anything have
been more suitable?

Alan Kinnear rubbed his new-shaven chin over
this interesting account, while he considered the
reporter through narrowed eyes—possibly in an
attempt to read between rather evident if metaphorical
lines. But obediently—and wisely—he held his peace.
He was learning fast, undoubtedly.

As Fiona Macpherson cleared away his shaving-
kit, and prepared to take her leave, she pointed to his
pillow. "Down you get, and shut your eyes," she
ordered, "You've just time for a little snooze before
lunch."

"I don't want a little snooze," the man declared. "I've done far too much snoozing, recently. I'm practically fit again, now. You heard what the doctor said yesterday? You can't go on treating me as an invalid, you know."

"M'mm," the girl said, "Perhaps you're right. Certainly, you look much more like your previous self, without your beard—though whether that is a matter for congratulation, is another question!" She paused. "I shouldn't think there'll be any need for me to come back, then after this. Seana will be able to cope, quite easily."

"Oh—but, I say . . . !" the convalescent objected, "That's a bit thick. I mean . . . well, I'll still need a certain *amount* of attention, you know . . ."

"Quite," she nodded, "And Seana Macdonald will be able to give you just that, I'm sure. Goodbye, Mr. Kinnear—and a quick recovery!"

"But, hang it—look here!" he cried, "This isn't good enough . . ."

But she was gone, and as the door closed behind her, he thought that he heard just the hint of laughter, soft but mocking. Indignantly, he punched his pillow, and threw his handkerchief as far from him as possible—a feeble gesture, but it was all that he had to throw.

Women, he decided, not for the first time, but with refreshed conviction, were utterly and completely deplorable.

CHAPTER XV

ALAN KINNEAR did make a quick recovery, for all the neglect of him—for Fiona Macpherson kept her word, and came no more errands of mercy to Balnahard; if on her lawful occasions and essential perambulations about the property, she paid an occasional call on Seana Macdonald, of course, that was a different matter. Asking graciously after the convalescent was no substitute for honest-to-goodness attention, and the man left her in no doubt of the fact, or of his disappointment in her. His sustained and rapid improvement, therefore, was just a little bit galling, though he made the best of the situation by indicating that it was his robust masculine constitution triumphing *despite* feminine neglect.

For his normal health was excellent, of course, and this general fitness was not long in throwing off the effects of so sudden and extraneous an infirmity. Though he found himself subject to splitting headaches, and bouts of dizziness when he got up and began to move about, these quite quickly faded. In a week from the day he shaved off his beard, he was, if not wholly himself again, at least a passable reproduction.

In that week, however much neglect by Fiona Macpherson he might plead, he could not complain of lack of visitors. Considering how unpopular locally he had been before, and how little he had done personally to merit any change of opinion, it was surprising how they came—and, in view of the depopulated state of the countryside, where they came from. John Cameron called, discoursed gravely on the weather, and enquired searchingly regarding the poachers. Sandy Cattanach came twice, a mine of affability and encouragement. Jean Fraser arrived, shyly, one afternoon, with a new-baked scone and a comb of heather-honey, and was almost in tears again because Alan wanted to walk at least half-way home with her. A Mr. Macphail, said to be from the local hotel, turned up, and with a bottle whose tonic properties undoubtedly were just the thing for the recently-concussed. Somebody from the sawmill came, in company with a farmer called Maclean—or it may have been Macbean. And even the parson called, though he had to travel seven miles on a bicycle to do so. It was all most astonishing.

And then, one wet evening, when Alan was chewing his pencil over the uninspired affairs of Detective-Sergeant Paul Pryor, Seana Macdonald announced another visitor. Archie Fraser, Dalnamuick, to see Mr. Kinnear.

For a few moments the two men eyed each other in silence, Fraser turning his cap in his hands, Alan standing still by the table. The visitor it was who spoke first.

" Wet, it is," he mentioned, heavily.

" Yes," Kinnear allowed, " It is." He coughed. " This is a surprise, you know—quite a surprise." He waited, a trifle warily, for the other to give a lead.

Fraser nodded. " Yes, then. I would have come before this, but I was thinking maybe you'd not be well enough. I wouldn't want to be troubling you, and you sick."

" That was thoughtful of you," Alan returned, carefully. " But I am pretty nearly well again now, thank you—well enough to take what's coming to me, at anyrate ! But won't you sit down ? "

" Och, I'm fine standing—it isn't that I've that much to be saying, at all." He turned his cap over, frowning.

" Er . . . quite," the other acceded. " You don't mind if *I* sit down, do you ? Less, h'm, formal, you know."

" Aye." A pause. " It's not that easy to be saying what I want to say, Mr. Kinnear, see you. It's maybe not a thing you'll be glad to have me saying . . ."

Alan nodded. " I can well believe that, Mr. Fraser. But I assure you, I'm ready for it—ready for the worst you can say. You couldn't regret all that happened any more than I do myself, I may say. But I realise how you feel. I suggest that you get it off your chest. Shoot ! "

" Och, it's not just as bad as all that, see you—no, no," the other disclaimed. " It's just not a subject easy to put words to . . ."

Alan was frowning, now. Perhaps his evening's frustrations with insufficiently intriguing fictional crime had left him impatient. Or perhaps it could be ascribed to the after-effects of concussion. " Oh, cut it out, man ! " he pleaded, urgently. " Get a jag on. You hate my guts—and I don't blame you ! Out with it, and let's get it over ! "

The other looked surprised, shocked. " Och, it's not that way, at all," he declared, " Nothing like that, my goodness—no. What for would I be talking that way . . . ? "

" I got you into plenty of trouble, didn't I ? " Kinnear interrupted, almost accusingly, " I got you arrested, and into gaol for a fortnight—and at harvest time . . ."

" Och, that," Archie Fraser dismissed a fortnight in gaol with a wave of his hand. " Yon was a holiday, just. Man, I was near three years in Jerry prison-camps in the war—after yon, K'ussie polis-station

was as good as Alec Macphail's hotel, whatever!
Och, it was a right picnic, yon." More seriously, he
continued. "But about the harvest, right enough—
that was real good of you, Mr. Kinnear. Och, you
shouldn't have done it . . ."

"Good Lord!" Alan cried, "Don't say *that's*
what you came to say—to say thank-you for giving
a bit of a hand with your corn! Damn it—wasn't
that the very least I could do, in the circumstances?
Your neighbours all did infinitely more. Anyway,
I enjoyed every minute of it. Don't tell me that's
what you're having so much difficulty in getting
out!"

"Well . . . maybe not just that, itself," the visitor
admitted, "Though Jean was telling me I was to
thank you, right enough. It was something else,
see you, Mr. Kinnear." He examined his cap again,
for guidance and support. "It was . . . well, just
about Ferlas Mor, Mr. Kinnear. Yon one!"

"Well, I'm damned," Alan exclaimed, floundering.

"Och, if you'd rather not be speaking about it,
that's all right," Fraser assured, hurriedly. "It is
a difficult thing to be talking about—fine I know it.
Just say you the word . . ."

The other shook his head, "No—it's not that. I
was just surprised, that's all. I hadn't expected that."
Curiously he looked at his caller. "What makes
you interested in that subject, I wonder?"

"John Cameron it was that was telling me
yourself had been after talking about Ferlas
when he found you, yon time. He was saying you
had it right on your mind, as you might say, Mr.
Kinnear."

"I see. Perhaps I had—but when you're delirious,
you're apt to talk a lot of rubbish, I'm told. It's not
usual to take it all seriously, I would say—such a
subject as Ferlas Mor, especially."

"That is so, yes," the visitor agreed, "But yon one is not that often mentioned, at all—and it could be that he should be taken seriously, too, in a manner of speaking." Fraser looked at the other with sudden directness. "Did you *see* him, Mr. Kinnear?"

"No," Alan said. And after a tiny pause. "What makes you ask?"

"Just that I have seen him, my own self," Archie Fraser returned. "It makes me interested, as you might say."

Kinnear swallowed, "I think you should sit down," he suggested, quietly. "Tell me, will you?"

"I will, yes," the other nodded, taking his chair at last. He drew it in, towards the cheerful blaze of the birch-logs. "But I'd be glad if you were to be telling me, first, what you know about yon one, your own self. You see," he smiled faintly, significantly, "it is not just the sort of story to be telling to a man who is going to be after laughing at what you say. It is not everybody's story, at all."

"I understand," Alan nodded in his turn, gravely. "You want to test my probable reactions? Well—you need have no fear of me laughing, at anyrate. I haven't seen Ferlas Mor, and I haven't heard him—but the effect of his name on me doesn't produce any desire to laugh, believe me! My Ferlas may not be your Ferlas, but I had my bellyful of him—while I was supposed to be unconscious. It predisposes me to listen to what you have to say without whoops of mirth."

"Aye, then. But I was hoping maybe you'd seen him—that was what made you talk that way when John Cameron found you . . .?"

"No. I have heard one or two stories, read an odd mention of the thing, here and there—that's all. I had been up MacDhui, that day, and was coming back across Glen Einich and over this way, when I began to think about it—just vaguely, generally, you know. And then, in the half-dark, I got the feeling that I wasn't alone, any more—that I was being followed. Actually, I know now, it was the poachers —or one of them. Once I got down amongst the trees, I even heard one of them crack a twig behind me. But I didn't know about the poachers at the time . . . and I must confess to a certain uneasiness. Then, I suppose, in my delirium, these more or less unformed fears came back and took shape. That's all there was to it, really, as far as I am concerned. But I'd be more than interested to hear your story, just the same.''

Archie Fraser accepted that. It was on a day of October, just under the year ago, he said, when it happened. He was acting as gillie for the gentleman that had taken Glencoraig last season—a Colonel Mallinson, and a right queer bird at that. But this day, stalking on the beat around Meall Odhar—that is, at the extreme eastern end of the forest—he shot and wounded a stag, a good beast. As Mr. Kinnear would know, it is the custom on the hill to follow up a wounded beast. Always it is done—part of the game, it is. But the Colonel would have none of it. He was tired and disgusted, and was for back to his hotel, right away. John Cameron didn't like it, but could not be making him follow up, of course, and could not be leaving him, to follow the brute himself. But down at the ponies, he told him, Archie, to go after it, with the spare rifle, saying the way it had gone, and how hard he thought it was hit.

That was in the early afternoon, and he was glad enough to do the job. With his glasses, he soon found the beast, up on the next hill to Meall Odhar eastwards—actually off Glencoraig land altogether. But in following up a wounded stag, the marches of

L

unfenced forests were not to be considered—that was the thing understood. And so he had started on his trail.

And it was a long trail the brute led him, too, for though it was hard enough hit—shot through the belly, it was—it still had a lot of life to it, though it had to rest frequently. That enabled him to keep it in view, to keep not too far behind. It was bleeding, too, but not very heavily, and every now and then he came on a splash of blood on stone or gravel.

Back on to the side of the Sgoran it took him, and over the ridge between it and Càrn Bàn More, and down into the big moss above the head of Einich, Crossing the bogs and peat-hags of that had been a bad business, but at least he'd got a shot at the brute there, and hit it too, but with the stag moving, he hadn't killed. And up between Braeriach and Cairntoul that traveller had led him, and now there was more blood and the beast had to rest oftener. But the light was failing, and somewhere in yon long Garbh Choire that leads down towards Corrour Bothy, he lost him again.

Alan Kinnear gently reminded him that it was Ferlas Mor that the story was about.

But the Highlander was not to be hurried. His story it was, and he would tell it his own way. He had found his stag again, after a bit, well ahead—in fact across the Glen of Dee, and away up on the side of Ben MacDhui; only it crossing a bit of the snow-field had shown it to him in the poor light, and he had got the glasses on it. And on a patch of heather between two great banks of snow, the brute had lain down. He saw how he could get up near to it, by using a burn channel, without it maybe seeing him nor scenting him. He did not want to have to follow that beast any further; it had led him eight desperate miles already.

And he had got up near to it, too, near enough for a shot. But the light was nearly gone now, and he could barely see his foresight—nor could he see where deer ended and heather began. He had just to judge by the position of the antlers sticking up, and aim below and back. At his shot the stag had leaped up again, and run off across the snow, but this time it was dead on its feet, he knew, by its shambling run. He didn't actually see it fall, as he picked himself up to follow it; one moment it was running, the next it had dropped. But it was in the snow somewhere, not far ahead, and he knew that he could find the tracks.

But he didn't find it, for all that—not that night, at anyrate. As he hurried forward along the steeply sloping braeside, his foot plunged through a hole below frozen snow, he lost his balance, and pitching forward he struck his head on rock, and knew no more.

Another concussion patient, Kinnear commented.

Archie did not know about that. He was stunned, just. When he came to, it was practically dark— probably he hadn't been unconscious for more than quarter-of-an-hour. He had a headache, and was slightly dizzy, but otherwise little the worse, as he set off again to get that stag.

He hadn't gone more than a few yards when he heard the footsteps behind him, slow heavy steps, crunching on the frozen snow, dragging a little, and nothing like in pace with his own. He peered back into the dark, but could see nothing—though, with the glimmer off the snow it was possible to see some distance. It was an unlikely place and time to meet up with anybody, but he was not so very far from the bothy at Corrour, and it was just possible that it might be a be-nighted climber. But the footsteps were plain, and not far away at all—he could see, actually, where they should be coming from. But

there was nothing there. He stopped, and the footsteps stopped. That convinced him they were his
own echo, despite the unequal timing. But he wasn't
convinced for long. When he moved on, the steps
resumed, but when he stopped once again, they
didn't. They came on towards him.

Alan Kinnear was leaning forward, watching the
other intently. Fraser wiped his hands on his knees.
There was no use denying it, he said, he did not like
it, at all. He had heard about the Grey Man, of
course—who hadn't in that country? But he had
never taken it seriously, and it wasn't till that moment
that the thought of it crossed his mind. He began to
hurry on—och, he would admit it, he began to run.
But the footsteps behind did not run—they just came
on slowly, heavily, as before. Only, they were making up on him, fast. By heaven, but he didn't like
that, at all—he did not. He ran till he fell again, and
by that time the footsteps were almost on top of him.
And there was nothing to see.

He lay in the snow where he fell, and maybe he
said a prayer or two. It could be that he shut his
eyes, too. And then, it dawned on him that the steps
were passing, had passed. He might have felt a cold
breath, but he could not be sure. But it was past.
And in his relief, he turned to follow with his eyes the
line those steps were taking.

And that was when he saw it. Striding away from
him, was a great shadowy figure, tall—och, maybe
twelve or fifteen feet or more—and crouching,
stooping, with long arms hanging. He was surer of
the long arms, than of anything else. It wasn't clear,
at all—it was dark, mind—but there was no mis-
taking that it was in the shape of a man, or maybe one
of those gorilla-things. It was just the outline that
he saw—but that was plenty, whatever! He would
have got up and run from that spot, there and then,

had he had any strength in him to run anywhere. But he was fixed, planted just . . .

Alan said nothing. He was staring at the man. There were tiny beads of sweat glistening in the lamplight, on Fraser's brow, as he continued.

It went on, walking, just walking away—he could hear the crunch of that snow, yet. And gradually the thing faded into the dark. He wanted to run, but didn't want to make the noise of running. He didn't know which he was more scared to do—to stay there or to run away. He was not a brave man, at all, Mr. Kinnear would understand. He decided that he wouldn't move till he couldn't hear the thing as well as not see it. And he still could hear it, fine. He was listening, plenty.

And then, there was a difference—something had changed. There was a different sound, a scraping, scuffling sound, as well as the footsteps. He could hear the crunch-crunch of the steps through it. And suddenly, he knew—the thing was coming back. He wanted to run, then, as he never had wanted anything in his life before, at all—but he could not. He couldn't move, whatever. He could wait, only.

And then, then he saw it again—about where it had faded before. It was just the same, only coming towards him now—and dragging something. That was what was making the scraping. It was something big and heavy and dark—darker than the thing that dragged it. Then he saw the antler, outlined against the snow. It was the stag. The thing was dragging the stag back to him, dragging it not as a man would try to do, by the hind legs, but by the head, by one horn. And at the sight of that, something sort of gave way inside of him, and he was up on his feet and running away back the way he had come. He didn't remember anything about that running, except that he did not pause however often he fell, nor did he look round once. But some time or other, he found himself down at the door of the bit bothy at Corrour, and bursting in he slammed the door behind him. He would have locked and barred it if he could. And there he spent the night, frightened even to light a bit of fire—a worse night he never spent in his life before, and not a wink of sleep in it. And in the morning he was away back through the Larig for home, just as fast as his legs would carry him—for though he'd dropped the Colonel's rifle when he made a bolt for it, he wasn't going back for it, alone, for all the tea in China.

Kinnear took a long breath. There was no point in asking if he really believed that all this had actually happened—the man was most obviously speaking in all sincerity, and out of no little emotion. And ex-Sergeant Archie Fraser of the Lovat Scouts, who had won the Military Medal at Alamein for bravery, and then served three years in German prison-camps, was not the type to go in for fairy stories . . . Alan spoke, and had to clear his throat to do so. He had only seen this thing, the Grey Man, to one side of him, hadn't he said? That was queer, wasn't it? Was there a moon that night, by any chance?

It was queer, right enough, Archie agreed—and there was no moon. When the footsteps had been coming to him, from the south that was, he had seen no thing. But when they had passed, and he turned to look after them, then he saw the thing. But it could be no sort of shadow of himself, anyway, moon or none, because he was lying down in the snow, and the thing was walking. Yes, that seemed to dispose of that, Kinnear allowed. This dragging of the dead stag was amazing—the whole thing was amazing, of course, but that struck him as strangest of all. It seemed to come into a different category, from the other, er, manifestation. But that stag would be on his mind, at the time . . . and he had just had a knock on the head ! A knock on the head could be responsible for queer things, as didn't he know ! A hallucination, now . . . ?

The other accepted that, reasonably. It was the thing that had occurred to himself, when he had thought about it all afterwards, quietly. Fine he'd have liked to think it was all something like that. But that wasn't so easy to believe, either. For the next day, himself and John Cameron had gone away back to collect the rifle, and to get the stag's head for the Colonel—the only beast he'd managed to hit, that far. He hadn't been that keen on going back, either, but they couldn't just leave the rifle—and having John with him made a difference. And back on the side of MacDhui, they had found the rifle all right, and other things besides. The story was there for them in the snow. But not the whole story. His tracks and the stag's tracks, and its blood. But there were no tracks for Ferlas Mor.

Alan began to speak, but the other held up his hand. Aye, but wait you, he said. Where his tracks stopped, before turning back, and the rifle lay, the stag's tracks led on for about another two hundred yards, and then they too ended in a trampling of snow and a lot of bloodstains. But that was all that was there. No stag. And back from there, south again, was the trail of where it had been dragged, clear in the snow, with smears of blood here and there. Back that trail they went, with no tracks for the dragger, mind, and och, for maybe quarter-of-a-mile they followed it, along the slope of the hill. And it led them to a deep crevice, a sort of narrow crack in the braeside, with a bit burn sounding away at the foot of it, out of sight. And there, at the edge of it, their track ended. That was all they ever found of the Colonel's stag, whatever !

Alan stared. Did he mean to say that the beast wasn't there—had disappeared.

Fraser shrugged. He couldn't say but what it was down at the foot of that crevice. But if it was, they couldn't see it, though they peered for long enough.

Kinnear had one last query. Could the brute, being not quite dead, have dragged itself there, and then fallen in?

That was what John Cameron said, Archie nodded. So they had followed back the dragging trail again. And not one hoof-mark was there to the length of it. And that stag would weigh sixteen stone, if it weighed a pound.

And after that, silence settled down on that pleasant lamplit room, for some considerable time.

It was Seana Macdonald who came in and chased Archie Fraser away that night, demanding to know if he was wanting Mr. Kinnear on his back again, and him a sick man yet. He should have been back in his bed an hour ago, and that was a fact. Hurriedly, the two men combined to placate her with their assurances, as they made for the door, the invalid hastily hiding Alec Macphail's whisky bottle behind a chair, in the by-going.

Out in the porch, at the edge of the dripping night, they stood for a moment. Then Kinnear thrust out his hand. " I'm glad you came—it was good of you to come, Fraser," he said, " Whatever the answer is to your story, I wouldn't have missed it for anything—I'm just sorry I couldn't add anything to it."

" Och, that is all right, Mr. Kinnear—never heed. But it's done me good to be getting it off my chest, as you might say—for there's only just John Cameron and my wife that I've told the whole story to, before, see you. Och, it's not just everybody that wouldn't be laughing at the likes of yon. And it wasn't just a laughing matter to me."

" I believe you," Alan nodded. " I know one or two experts on psychic phenomena, down in the south. I might have a talk with them on the subject, one day. I'll let you know their reactions, if you like ? "

" Aye, then. I'd be interested to hear that."

" And thank you for the other thing, too—for not holding your arrest and imprisonment against me. I'm more than grateful for that."

" Och, never think of it, at all," the other cried. " Damn, no. Man, it wasn't your fault, whatever— it was the fault of those bloody poachers ! "

Alan smiled, but only faintly. " That is true, in a way," he agreed. " So we've both got something against them."

" We have that—I'll say we have ! And, man, Mr. Kinnear, I don't know just what way you feel about it, but for my own self, I'm not just thinking of taking it lying down—I am not ! "

" You're not ! Fraser—neither am I, then. I've got a score to settle with these blackguards—a score that throbs damnably. You know, I think you and I might just conceivably join forces ? "

" Damn't man—just the job ! I'm with you there, right enough."

" Good. I'm not sure just what we can do—but we'll think of something."

" We will so. We'll see if we can give these borachs something to . . ."

"Archie Fraser ! " That, though it came from the kitchen was clear, high, and ominous. " If you're not out of my house in half of one minute . . . ! "

" Lord save's all ! " Archie cried, " Good night to you, Mr. Kinnear. And keep her, will you, till I get round yon bend ! "

CHAPTER XVI

THERE were a number of reasons for the two men
keeping to themselves their decision to try to do
something about the poachers. For one thing, they
had a shrewd idea that they might meet with a
certain amount of cramping restriction and embargo
from well-meaning but over-cautious females. Then
again, it was possible if not probable, that this gang
had some local contact, someone in the district who
could supply them with information, unpleasant a
conception as that might be in a sparsely populated
area where everyone knew everyone else; and since
anything they did must be done cunningly and
without warning, complete secrecy was indicated.
But most potent reasons of all were the conflicting
interests of the Coraig estate itself; while this gang
poaching was long-term ruination for it and for its
impoverished owners, there was the short-term con-
sideration to be taken into account, also. The position
at the moment, despite all Alan Kinnear's indis-
cretions, was that Sir Henry Mortman was nibbling.
He had agreed to take the stalking on Glencoraig for
that season, at a much-reduced rent, more or less as
an experiment; if he was satisfied with his bargain
at the end of the season, he would consider taking an
extended lease. And once he took the lease, he was
prepared to spend something on the place—and since
he was a motor-car manufacturer, he presumably
had the wherewithal to do it. He had indicated,
without any excessive tenderness towards suscep-

tibilities which nobody there was in a position to afford, that the forest was deplorably under-keepered, understaffed altogether, the Lodge was all but unhabitable for people with any standards at all, the roads and tracks were a tragedy, the heather-burning wickedly neglected—in fact, the whole place was shockingly uncared-for, altogether. Inferentially, if Sir Henry took a lease of it, something would be done about much of this, a development which the estate could by no means allow to be prejudiced.

Sir Henry, presumably, had heard nothing about the organised poaching, and all that it entailed—and, obviously, it was vitally important that he should not do so, at least, not at this stage. So there must be no public outcry, no hullabaloo, either about the poachers' activities or about any steps taken to frustrate them. The police must not be brought into it—officially at anyrate—for once they were involved, the Press was apt to become interested. Anything that was done must be done quietly, with the minimum of upset and publicity—like the poaching itself. It was all very difficult—a vicious circle. If the poaching continued unchecked, Sir Henry's sport was going to be affected, and he would be scared-off; on the other hand, if any adequate steps were taken to stop the menace, he would be certain to hear about it, become wise to the situation, and be scared-off likewise.

What were the two men to do about it, whatever scores they had to pay back?

That problem was presented to them in practical form, rather sooner that either of them expected, or was ready for it. Alan Kinnear it was, again, who was confronted with the situation—not to be won-dered at, perhaps, considering that he was the one man locally who had little else to do but wander about, as it were looking for trouble, since as everybody knows book-writing is not to be classed as any arduous or genuine form of occupation. Idle hands, in this instance, were certainly found employment, and the Devil was probably implicated too, though whether agreeably or not, is a matter of opinion.

Only three mornings after Fraser's evening visit to Balnahard, Alan was making his way, notebook in hand, to Coraigbeg to purchase stamps, tobacco, and other necessities of life, from Aeneas Mackay's General Store, when, on the road, as he emerged from the short-cut through the wood, he came on a group of hikers. Four husky-looking young men there were, two of them rather older than the usual run of such, and with them a couple of girls. The men were dressed unexceptionably, largely in the ex-Army battle-dress that has been so widely adopted as uniform amongst their type, hatless, with open-necked shirts and heavy boots, and packs on their backs. Two carried long sticks of the alpenstock variety beloved of greenhorn mountaineers of all classes. The girls were not quite so suitably got up, either, in clothing, footgear, or make-up, and their hard crinkled permanent waves, the thin scimitars of their plucked eyebrows, and the vivid scarlet slashes of lip-stick, shouted aloud their species and origin. Also, they smoked cigarettes as they walked along that road to the hills, and their voices, as they passed him, were coarse and strident. Altogether, they seemed a long way from home. Obviously they had come off the ten-forty train.

It was the aspect of those two young women that made Alan turn and look after them. Though he had seen many hikers in his day, some of them memorable enough, these two did not look the part, not the Cairngorm class of hiker, anyway—they did not even look like the kind of woman any sort of hikers would be apt to take along with them. They seemed to him much more like Sauchiehall Street or perhaps Shaftesbury Avenue. Whereas the men looked the real thing; tough enough to be more than hikers— real mountaineers. And looking after them, Kinnear's glance lighted on the pack one of the men was carrying on his back, lighted and clamped.

It was the gleam of sun on bright metal that caught his eye, first, up at the right-hand top corner, where it projected just a little beyond the khaki webbing of the flap. But it was not on that point that his regard lingered. Down from it, stretching diagonally across the front of the pack, the remainder of the gleaming article was outlined beneath the webbing material. And, picked out by the slanting forenoon sun, there was no question in the beholder's mind as to what that article was. He had been an infantry officer recently enough to know the unmistakeable stocky shape of a Thompson sub-machine gun when he saw it.

For a few moments, his mind seethed. Questions, speculations, doubts, chased themselves. And then they crystallised into disciplined thinking and decision. No normal hikers loaded themselves up with tommy-guns, just for the fun of the thing—they weighed too much, apart from other considerations. And the use of automatic weapons by these modern deer-poachers was notorious. Anyway, they weren't normal hikers; the women made that evident— though what their rôle could be, was not very clear. And if they weren't genuine hikers, and yet were endeavouring to appear as though they were, it must be for some cogent reason. They might not be poachers, *the* poachers, but they were up to no good, that seemed obvious.

What to do about it? He could follow them, at a distance—but one man wouldn't be much use against

four toughs like that, if it came to trouble. He had
better go for Archie Fraser . . . but not till he had
ascertained what route these people were going to
take. He'd shadow them, meantime, then, and cut
off for Archie just as soon as possible.

Keeping within the cover of the dark trees, Alan
followed the party on the road, at an interval of
about three hundred yards. They looked behind
them once or twice, but fortunately the bend at the
bridge, just below the outcome of his short cut, would
hide from them the fact that the man that they had
passed was in fact not proceeding up the road towards
the station. He did not have to try to walk with
absolute silence; the people in front were making no
attempt to go quietly, and the girls' high-pitched
laughter came back to him with monotonous
regularity.

About half-a-mile up, the road forked, the left
branch going on towards Glencoraig Lodge and
Cameron's cottage, the right being the route that led
past the drive to Coraigmore House, past Balnahard,
and Dalnamuick, and ultimately right up the glen—
the road for which his track through the pine plantation was the short-cut. That this party should turn
right-handed along this way was convenient for him,
and significant, too; for the other route was the usual
one for hikers and climbers, leading directly towards
the Cairngorm massif and the high-tops, whereas the
one that they had taken gave access, in the first
instance, to the Glencoraig deer forest only. Feeling
that his suspicions were suitably confirmed, Kinnear
followed on, still within the pines. It was dead easy
country for following people unseen.

Approximately a mile up the road—that is,
between Balnahard and Dalnamuick—they turned
off to the left to take a side track through the forest,

eastwards. That meant that they were going to follow the valley of the Allt Bàn, which would bring them up on to the hillsides between Beinn Dearg and Creag Follais—it led nowhere else. Which, he thought, permitted him to leave them fairly safely, and hurry up the remaining mile to the farm-place at Dalnamuick. He only hoped that Archie was not out on the hill with his sheep, or something of the sort, and inaccessible.

But he was in luck. As, panting a little—for he was not yet entirely fit again—he mounted the rutted track to the Fraser's steading, he saw Archie and Old Callum building a stack out of the sheaves that he had so laboriously stooked in those days that seemed so long ago. He shouted, and waved.

Archie, tossing the sheaves up from the cart to Callum, who stood on the top of the forming stack, laid by his fork, and got down, to come and meet his visitor, reaching into a pocket for his pipe in the process. Like every good Highlander, he rated sociability above any mere sordid industriousness. "Good it is, to see you on the road again, Mr. Kinnear," he greeted.

"I look like being on more than the road, Fraser," Alan declared. "I've just come from following a bunch of rather unusual hikers—they've cut up that track back there that leads up the Allt Bàn way. Four men and two women, the men tough and the women flashy—and one of them with a tommy-gun in his pack!"

"Whe-e-ew!" the other whistled. "A tommy-gun, you say? Man, d'you tell me that!"

"I do. And what's more—I tell you that though the men look the real thing, the women don't. I can't think what they're there for, but they're not hikers, those two."

"So-o-o-o! And they're away up the Allt Bàn?"

"That's right. I followed them, out of sight, from the bridge at the head of the loch, and left them to hurry on here, when they turned off the road. I thought it best to let you know—we ought to be able to pick them up again, up there?"

"Sure—och, yes. That's right. Uh-huh." Archie pondered, but not for long. "Och, we'll soon find them again, up yonder. But are you fit for the hill, yet, Mr. Kinnear?"

"Yes, yes. I'm fine. I don't say I'm for the top of MacDhui, but anything within reason."

"Right, then. If you'll wait a wee, while I tell the wife . . . no, better you be going on, and I'll make up on you. See, if you keep up behind the house there, and over yon bit between the wee hills, where the trees were cut—that's right, yes. Over there, and down beyond, brings you to the Allt Bàn track again. There's a bit path most of the way. Och—but I'll be up with you long before you get that far."

"Right-ho. My apologies to Mrs. Fraser for whisking you away . . ."

Alan was perhaps half-way to the summit of the little pass indicated, when Archie came up with him, long-striding. He had a stalker's-glass slung over his shoulder, and the pockets of his shapeless tweed jacket bulged rather noticeably. From one of them, he brought out a paper-bag, and handed it to his companion.

"Just a bit piece, from the wife," he explained. "Och, she says it's gey rough, but it'll keep you going, maybe."

"That was kindly thought of," Alan acknow-ledged. But his eyes were still on the other's pocket, where, in his efforts to extricate the sandwich-bag, Fraser had revealed something of its further contents. "What's that you've got there?" he wondered.

The Highlandman laughed shortly, and drew out

a square-stocked automatic pistol of particularly pugnacious design. " It's just a Luger I took from a Jerry, one time," he explained. " If these borachs have got tommy-guns, damn't we're entitled to something ! "

" H'mmm," said Alan Kinnear.

Over the gap between the small hills, the land sloped down before them through open birch-woods to a green valley wherein a stream ran amidst alder-lined banks, the Allt Bàn, a valley that lifted and shallowed steadily towards the right, south-east-wards, till presently it tailed away into a wide corrie high up between two tall hills. Archie got his glass out of its leather case, and leaning against a birch trunk, scanned all that spread of country systemati-cally, starting at the high ground and working down. " I don't see any sign of them," he reported, after a couple of minutes. " But, och, there's lots of bits where we wouldn't be seeing them, from here."

" How far would they have got, presuming that they hadn't stopped ? " Alan queried. " They were walking at a normal sort of speed, and it must be all of three-quarters of an hour since I left them."

" They should be three miles up, then—nearly to the end of the trees, there. We can wait up there, to watch for them with the glass, or we . . . Damn't —there they are ! Down below—half-right. Aye, four men and two lassies. Och, they're away behind trees again—we'll not be seeing them for a bittie, now. Let's away down then, Mr. Kinnear."

" Surely. But I do think we can dispense with this Mister-business. Kinnear's good enough—or Alan to my friends, and such folks as I've had flung into gaol ! "

" Fine, then," the other grinned, " Alan it is. Och, I've never called a man by his last name just, in my

M

life—except in the Army. A coarse business, the Army. You were in that, your own self . . . ? ''

'' Royal Scots.'' Alan nodded, '' Not like the Lovat Scouts—just P.B.I.—but not bad of its class. We had some fun, too . . .''

They were still on military reminiscences, and down in the floor of the valley beside the swift-flowing Allt Bàn, when Archie stopped short abruptly, in both in his talk and his stride, and his hand shot out to grip his companion's arm. '' Sssst ! '' he said.

And listening, they heard, presently, above the prattle and murmur of the burn, that high-pitched and irritating laughter that Alan had listened to earlier in the forenoon. Raising his brows, Fraser beckoned with his head, and led the way, up off the path, and round in a sweep to the right, amongst the bracken and birch-scrub. They were practically at the end of the trees, now.

'' Having a rest, before the climb,'' Alan whispered, as they worked their way round.

'' Aye, maybe. Yon women'll be needing plenty rests, I'm thinking . . .''

But at the crest of a little rise, where they halted and threw themselves down amongst the yellow bracken fronds, and peered over, they found that they were wrong. The men were not resting—they were not there, at all. Only the two girls lay on their backs in a hollow, hidden from the path, smoking. And littered around them were, amongst other things, four empty webbing packs and two alpenstocks. And those young women, their shoes off, looked in their sprawling ease, as though they were there to stay.

'' So that's it,'' Alan breathed. '' Camouflage— nothing else ! ''

'' Eh? What was that you said? ''

'' Camouflage. That's all those women were—like

the alpenstocks and the packs. Just camouflage, to
be discarded once they were past the haunts of men.
The men have gone on, leaving all the unnecessaries
behind.''

'' I'm thinking you're right, too,'' Archie agreed.
'' These lassies were just to make them look the
part.'' Already his glance had left that hollow, and
was scanning all the high ground in front. '' I
wonder, now . . . ? ''

'' This is a new technique, surely ? '' the other suggested, '' I thought these people usually worked from
cars or vans ? ''

'' Aye, they do—they have to, at the end of it, to
be getting the meat away. But the beasts have got to
be shot first, see you, and coming on foot this way,
will be saving the risk of the cars being seen by day.
Och, another of them'll just be able to bring the car
up to some bit they've fixed on, in the dark, and
away they'll go. A better scheme it is, than leaving
the van hidden at the side of the road, all day, and
it maybe being seen.''

'' But they couldn't get cars up here—up to these
girls ? That path's impossible . . .''

'' No, no. The lassies likely'll have to go back
down to the road-end, on their own, when it begins
to get dark, and be picked up there. That'll be the
way of it. These borachs may not be after coming
back down here, at all. If they've deer to get down,
they'll be wanting to get their car up nearer them
than this, whatever.''

'' I dare say. I wonder where they are ? ''

'' Och, they'll still be in the glen, there, ahead.
There's another mile of it, we can't see from this.
We'd best be on our way, I'm thinking.''

Completing their detour, they came back to the
path by the burnside, well above where the girls were
hidden, and proceeded on up the shelving valley at

a pace that soon had Alan panting. But after about twenty minutes of it, Archie's fear that they might lose touch with the quartet ahead, was relieved. From a bend in the glen, now little more than a shallow trough of green in the prevailing purple and brown of the heather, they caught sight of their quarry, up on the open hillside in front. Squatting down, Fraser had his glass on them, swiftly.

" Och," he said, after a moment, " *One* tommy-gun, did you say ? Man, Alan—they've all got them. Slung on their backs—four of them. And they're going hard. They're making for the bealach, there, up between the two hills. And we'll not can be after them till they're over it, too—they'd be seeing us right away if we were after them now. We'll have to let them over the top, and then up after them at the double ! "

" M'mmm," Alan commented, without enthusiasm. " I'll look forward to that ! "

The other smiled. " Och, no need to be troubling yourself, and you not just that fit, yet. I'll away up, in a hurry, so's to be able to keep them in view, and you can be coming up in your own time. It's not that far, anyway."

Alan considered the long face of the mountain ahead, heather and stone and scree, with a jaundiced eye. " Quite," he said.

It was over an hour later before, breathless and dizzy and sweating profusely, Alan Kinnear reached the summit of the bealach, or saddle, between Beinn Damh and Creag Follais, and cast himself down beside his outstretched companion. Archie removed his eye momentarily from his telescope, to glance at him. " You made it then, right enough ? " he commented, cheerfully.

Alan, hugging the ground, and feeling sick as a

dog, merely grunted—and even that was an effort. His heart, thudding on the earth, all but choked him, and the pulse in his temples and ears was like a sledge-hammer.

But Fraser had his mind on other things. "They're the boys, these ones," he cried. "I'm telling you, they know their stuff. I've been watching them, this half-hour—this is as good as a grandstand here, whatever. I'm thinking I've got the hang of their ploy. There's deer on the side of that hill, yonder—Cnoc Breac. A fair herd, mainly hinds and calves. But there's precious little cover to stalk them, at all—bare as an egg, it is, as you can see." Alan could not see, was not looking indeed, but the other had his eye glued to the telescope again, and went on without pause. "The only side there's any sort of cover in it is to the west there—to windward. And you'll not be stalking deer to windward, whatever. But they've sent one of them round that way, just the same—going nice and quiet, he is. I can see him with the glass, just down amongst those peat-hags. The other three are away round to the east. I'm thinking I see their game. They're making for yon broken ground on the far side of the hill, there. If I'm not mistaken, they're going to lie-up there, and this brave boy here's going to be after moving the deer over to them. A tricky business that, but just possible, if they know what they're doing. A hit or a miss, right enough. Are you wanting a bit look, through the glass?"

"Lord—no," Kinnear groaned.

"Is it blown you are, still?" Archie wondered, sympathetically, but with only half his attention. "Och, you'll be right in no time, just—no time, at all. The boy on his own has stopped, now—waiting for the others to be getting into position, he'll be. Och, I'll keep you wise to the way it works out, Alan."

Archie Fraser, for all the lack of encouragement that he got from his companion, did that ably, his glass ranging from one end of the long hog-backed hill of Cnoc Breac to the other, across the peat-pocked low ground in front. He reported, in the next half-hour, how the party of three had worked down left-handed, amongst the peat-hags, in dead ground to the deer opposite, and how they were making their way up the valley of a burn beyond, off the side of Beinn Damh now, altogether, and on the extreme northern spur of Cnoc Breac. How the lone individual was on the move again, uphill too, a mile away from his colleagues, making skilful use of sparse cover to work up to windward of the deer, and perhaps six hundred yards from them. And of how he'd lost the three of them, now—they must have got out of that burn channel while he was watching the other boy. They'd be getting amongst the broken ground, though, that he'd said they'd be making for, and they'd lie-up there, likely—that was the place for them. The brave lad to the west must be nearly into the beasts' wind, now. This was going to be interesting to watch—och, moving deer by giving them a whiffle of your wind was no joke, at all . . .

By this time Alan was sitting up and taking some little notice, though still he was feeling sick and dizzy. He again refused the offer of the telescope, claiming that he would not be able to hold it steady. He hoped that they weren't going to have to climb any more hills that day, or he was not going to be a great deal of use. He wasn't the man he had been a week or so ago. . . .

Fraser interrupted with an exclamation. The deer were moving, now. They weren't running, bolting— maybe Alan could see them with his bare eyes? They were just walking, drifting, uneasy, downwind and

westwards. That was good work—the man wasn't
showing himself, just giving the beasts enough of his
wind to unsettle them. They weren't even looking
round, yet—except an old grey hind, all nose and
ears. But they'd half-a-mile to go. If he could keep
them going, like that . . .

Archie Fraser sounded almost as though he was
cheering for the enemy; as a stalker himself, he
appreciated good stalking when he saw it. Alan,
instead of admiring, was more concerned with wondering what they could do to stop it all. He said so.

" If we were to get up, and walk straight in front
there, downhill, we'd spoil their little game, wouldn't
we—scare those deer right off the map ? "

" We would, yes," the other acceded. " But what
would be the good of that ? These boys would see
us, as well as the deer, and they'd maybe be right
annoyed. Rough caterans they are, mind—are you
wanting another dunt on the head, or a burst of lead
between your oxters ? Och, if we're for doing something, it'll have to be cleverer than that, whatever.
Besides—it's no good unless we have something
against them," Archie pointed out. " What they're
after doing just now is no offence against the law—
except maybe the carrying of fire arms. And they
could dump them in the heather, before anybody
came up with them, if they wanted. Just taking a
bit walk, they'd be." He smiled. " Och, man, it's
red-handed you've got to catch a poacher—with his
kill. Man—I'd never have thought I'd have to be
reminding *yourself* of that same ! "

Alan coughed. " Quite," he said. " But what are
we to do, then ? Just lie here and watch them do their
stuff ? It seems very feeble . . ."

The Highlandman shrugged. " What else ? " he
demanded. " You need bait in any trap, see you.
And anyway, the best time to be doing anything

about these borachs is when they're at a disadvantage when they're laden down with their venison, I'm thinking. Not on the open hill, and them free, with guns in their hands.''

" There's something in that,'' Kinnear admitted. " Oh—I can see the deer, now. Moving slowly, still, aren't they ? ''

" Aye, they're doing fine. Most of them are a bittie low, for yon broken ground, though—scattered they are, and just feeding as they drift. There's two-three up at the top, though, that'll come within range of where I think the tommy-guns'll be waiting. Another four hundred yards, and they'll be in range —if they don't take fright, first.'' He switched his glass back. " I can't see yon lad that's moving them, at all—but man, he's making a good job of it ! John Cameron should see this ! I'm just wondering where he was after learning his stalking.''

" A renegade keeper, perhaps ? ''

" Maybe, aye. But, och, there was a lot of people quartered up here in the war—soldiers, lumberjacks, Newfoundlanders, Poles, and the like—even Darkies. They had a free run of the forests, lots of them, and some of them learned plenty, whatever. And a few of them stayed on, when the rest went home. There's some right queer folk living about the likes of Inverness and Aberdeen, these days. . . . Look—that old hind at the back's getting suspicious ! She'll have the whole lot of them away out of it, in a minute, if he isn't careful. Always the old hinds, it is . . .''

" Can you see the waiting guns ? ''

" I can not, no. I haven't seen them the once, since they were in yon burn-channel. Och, but they'll be in the broken stuff, there, amongst the outcrops. Nowhere else for them, at all. And the nearest beast's only two hundred yards off. But it's not proper rifles they've got, mind, with a decent long range. These tommy-guns aren't accurate beyond fifty yards, maybe. Gosh, Maggie—they've had it! There goes the old hind!"

It was true enough. Alan, without glasses, could see the grey streak that was the hind, away at the back of the herd, suddenly bound forward. And in a split second all the deer, scattered over the sunny flank of that dark hill, were on the move, flitting like brown shadows, with an ease and grace that deceived the eye as to its speed. Eastwards they bolted, and except for one or two, well below the area of broken ground where the marksmen would be waiting. Still, two of them, at least, in a few seconds would be within range—they were heading straight for it. Useless with a rifle, of course, at that speed—but with automatic weapons . . .

And then Archie Fraser gasped. "The fool!" he cried. "Look at that! Och, the daft eediot . . . !"

Right in front of the advancing deer, a man had arisen out of the outcropping rocks, and now was dancing about before them, waving his arms. They could even hear his shouts, drifting across the valley to them. A more crazy, extraordinary, and undignified performance would have been hard to imagine. And if they had waited another few seconds . . . !

The deer reacted immediately. Blocked in front and slightly uphill, and alarmed behind, they swung off left-handed and down, almost at right-angles, bunching together largely in the process, and their pace increased. Going like the wind now, they swept over the boggy floor of the shallow valley, and upwards beyond. In a few moments they were hidden from the watchers, by a shoulder of their own hill of Beinn Damh. They would not stop running for a long time, obviously.

"The bealach, they'll be for," Archie declared. "That bit spur of Cnoc Breac curves round in a sort of crescent, and where it meets the end of this hill, Beinn Damh, there's a bealach, a bit pass in between. The deer aye make for a bealach. Man— have you ever seen such damn foolishness? I'll bet the boy at the back, that was after moving them, will be having something to say to this! Of all the . . ."

His words were cut short. Harsh, vicious, murderous, amongst those quiet hills, like the sharp tearing of fabric, repeated half-a-dozen times, came the evil noise of bursts of automatic fire. For as many seconds, the air vibrated to it, and the echoes repeated it. Then the silence returned.

The two watchers stared at each other. " My God! " Archie cried. " The bealach! They weren't so daft—two of them were up in the bealach! They'd enfilade the brutes as they came through—like damn sheep to the slaughter. whatever! Ambushed they'd be, just. Man, Alan, they're right devils, these! " His eyes widened. " And, Losh—I see it, now. That bealach's just up above the bit road that leads from the Lodge to the Black Corrie beat. They'll get their cars up there, to just about a mile below it. Man, they're fly—they're after making their venison carry itself on its own feet, most of the road to their cars! Can you beat it! "

" I don't think I can! " Alan Kinnear agreed, grimly.

CHAPTER XVII

RETRACING their steps a little distance, the two men made their cautious way round the north face of Beinn Damh—since to have continued on the southern face would have revealed them at once to the two members of the poaching gang still on Cnoc Breac, and who both now were heading north-eastwards to join their fellows in the bealach.

In the meantime, there was no risk of the watchers being seen, with the bulk of the hill between them and the miscreants. But they went warily, just the same, out of an involuntary but none the less sincere respect for the forces that they were up against. They were not a little impressed by what they had just seen.

Alan Kinnear was scanning all the wide dark spread of the forest-lands below them almost wistfully, considering the tiny far-scattered dwellings of men, as though reinforcements could be conjured up from thence, to their aid. " Those shots ? " he enquired, " Wouldn't they be heard from some distance ? Don't you think they'd be noticed ? "

The other shook his head. " Not a hope in it. Too high, it was. The sound doesn't carry down, that much—and this hill gets in the way, too. Och, in the stalking season, I never hear a rifle-shot down at Dalnamuick, and I'm nearest to the hill. Besides, yon bursts were muffled, some way. Silencers they'd have."

Alan sighed. " I don't see what we're going to do, then—the two of us against these four. We seem to be rather noticeably outmatched. And out-armed, too ! ''

'' That is so,'' Fraser admitted. '' I don't just see the way of it, my own self. They seem to have it right well organised. But a bit look, we can be having, at anyrate.''

'' A look is as much as we'll have, I imagine.'' It is hard to be heroic on a heaving stomach and a splitting head.

In that spirit they worked discreetly round the flank of that hill.

Where the braeside began to steepen and curve in towards the little pass, Archie led the way upwards. He preferred to make their approach from above, he said; men, like deer, were never so apt to look upwards for danger. Soon Alan was panting again; a poor mountaineer these poachers had made of him.

Presently, with the hill trending away before them sharply, round and down, Fraser crept forward to investigate, while his companion was well content to await instructions in the heather. He would have been content to lie there indefinitely. The sun, though beginning to level already, was pleasant, and the hum of the bees an invitation. He glanced at his watch. Four-thirty . . .

A hiss from ahead revealed Archie beckoning. Picking himself up with a sigh, Alan moved up, crouching. Fraser pointed.

'' See you yon big outcrop—no, the lower one ? Get to that, on your belly, and you'll see them. You'll see plenty, I'm telling you ! ''

Worming his way over a further fifty yards of blaeberry and thin heather, Kinnear reached his granite outcrop, and lay puffing. Then, raising his head cautiously, he peered round the side of it.

The bealach lay open below them, a cleft between the swelling breasts of the hills, the summit of it no more than three hundred yards from them. In it, two men knelt, at work. And scattered around them in that narrow space were the sprawling carcases of no fewer than eight deer, hinds, calves, and a single stag. Four of them lay as they had fallen, in the ungainly attitudes that such graceful beasts only achieve in violent death, two were being worked upon, and two others were already dealt with—at least, it was probably two, though it was somewhat hard to tell. The men, with great knives in their red-stained hands, had been effectively if unconventionally busy.

Here was no normal gralloching, bleeding, or flaying. To all intents, the carcases had been cut in two, unskinned. The lower part of the back, and the hind legs, had been cut off in one piece, and with skilful butchery, leaving the belly unpunctured. It, and all the foreparts—the main bulk of the beast, indeed—was left on one side. The hind-quarters had the lower legs cut off. Even as they watched, another deer was finished, its rear part laid aside, and the pathetic remainder dragged over and dumped on the larger gory and indecent heap.

Archie worked round from his side of the outcrop. "The bloody murderers!" he breathed, "Have you ever seen the likes of that! A massacre, just . . . and calves in it! Damn it, I'd like fine to be getting my hands on those devils. And d'you see what they're after doing! They're only taking the haunches and the foot of the back. They've got that much meat, they can leave the rest. Only the best for these boys! They'll be easy carried, too . . ."

"You mean, they're going to waste all the rest? Just leave it?"

"Looks like it, yes, the way they're going about it. Och, man Alan—this is a dirty business, right enough."

Kinnear nodded, and pointed. A third man was coming into the mouth of the bealach, from the west —no doubt the individual from the broken ground who had made all the noise. He laughed, as he came up towards his colleagues, and they heard his raised voice quite clearly.

"Say—we ain't done so dusty, Bert," he called. "Strewth, we ain't." His accent had the twang of some five hundred miles south.

"Och, now—a damned Englishman!" Archie deplored. "Listen to that, will you."

But the voice that answered was not English, at all. "Hell—get a jag on wi' ye, man—whit wey're ye dawdlin' up there, like ye'd got 'oors tae play yersel'? Get yer knife steekit inti' these bluidy brits, pron'o." That accent came from no more than fifty miles south of the Highland Line.

But to Archie Fraser, there was no great significance in the difference. "Blasted Sassenach!" he muttered, in catholic disapproval.

They heard no more, as it was only when the poachers shouted that their voices carried thus far. The newcomer got busy with his knife on another carcase, and now there were only the two left untouched.

"If it was my rifle I had with me, instead of this bit pistol, we could hold them up from here," the Highlandman declared, "we'll not be getting another chance like this, with them busy, and their damned tommy-guns laid aside. But a pistol's no use at all at that range, and we couldn't be moving a couple of yards nearer without being seen. There's no sort of cover, in front . . ."

"Of course there isn't—it's quite impossible," Alan agreed, very promptly. "Besides, the fourth fellow will be turning up, any moment."

"Aye, then—we'll have to wait, just. But it's ill

work, waiting, and knowing we'll not likely get another chance like this . . ."

" Supposing one of us was to work back, away round the hill, and show himself to these blackguards at a distance—say over on that hillside,Cnoc Breac ? What d'you think they'd do ? Would they make a bolt for it ? "

Fraser pursed his lip, and then shrugged. " I'm thinking they'd do what I'd do my own self. Hide all that stuff in the heather—deer, guns and all—and then lie about, like as if they were having a bit picnic, just. Brazen it out, see you—knowing fine one man wouldn't be asking too many questions, with four tough boys to deal with."

" I'm afraid you're right," Alan conceded regretfully. " No hope that way. Honestly, I don't see what we're to do. It would take us two hours, at least, to get down for help. Even with luck, we couldn't expect to round up enough to be of any use in less than an hour—in fact, we wouldn't do it in that. And then, to get back . . . no use. It's almost five, now. It'll be sunset in two hours, dark in three."

" That is so. Anything we do, it's our own selves'll have to be doing it. We've no time to be going for help . . ."

" You're sure about this road, below here ? I don't know that part, at all. You say they'll get a car pretty well up—to just about a mile from here ? "

" That's right, yes. The hill slopes down steep on the north side, there—fine and easy to be getting their meat down. It's scree and thin heather all the way, and there's the trees below, with the road running through them—just a track, but good enough for a car, whatever. Och, the four of them, dragging those haunches, will be having them down to the road in half-an-hour from here."

"I see. And you think the car, or cars, will wait till dark before coming up for them?"

"They might, yes, likely. But maybe not—maybe they're there in it, now."

"I shouldn't think so, myself. Why would these people come on foot, then?"

"That's right enough—but we'll not can be just sure of it."

"We must take a chance on it. What I suggest is this. Though we haven't time to gather assistance in time to stop these beauties, we *have* time to get down there and block that road."

"Uh-huh. Aye. True for you. You mean, block it to keep the cars from coming up?"

"No—block it once they're up to keep them from getting back again. This track doesn't lead anywhere else, does it, but to this Black Corrie you were talking about?"

"That's right—it ends up at the bothy, just. Man, Alan—that's an idea. You mean, bottle them up?"

"Yes. There's no other track leading off it, no other way out—so that if they turned their cars, they could get out another way?"

"There is not. There's a bit track, about a mile up, that leads to where they had a sawmill during the war. But it stops there. It wouldn't help them."

"They couldn't get round, anywhere—cross-country?"

"God—no! In yon forest and bog! Man, the cars wouldn't get two yards off the road, anywhere."

"Good. A tree felled, would be best, wouldn't it? Or two trees. Big ones. Somewhere where they couldn't make any sort of detour to avoid it. Is there such a place, down there?"

"Och, plenty of them. Yon road runs along the hillside most of the way, with the ground going up

steep on one side, and dropping on the other. And
trees all the way."

Alan nodded. "Good enough. It's five now. We'd
need an axe, or a saw, or something. The nearest
place to get them, is your own house, I suppose?
Without me to hold you back, how quickly could you
get there, and then back to this road?"

"Och, I'd be home in an hour-and-a-half, maybe.
And back over yonder, in less than an hour—three
miles it'll be, no more."

"Yes—but rough going. Say two-and-a-half
hours then, till we can start our tree-felling, at the
earliest. Three hours, to be safe. It won't be really
dark till eight, anyway. We ought to have time
enough."

"Aye, but hang on a wee. We can't be sure, yet,
that these boys are *going* that way. It looks like it—
but we don't *know*. They maybe have some other
ploy, altogether. We'll have to wait here and see,
just."

"Damn it—I suppose you're right. I was assuming . . . That's a nuisance. We may be stuck here
for quite a time, yet, then."

"Maybe, yes. But they're getting on quick
enough. They're not wasting their time, I'll say that
for them."

That was true. The fourth poacher had come up,
while they were whispering, and now they were working on the last of the deer. One of the men was tying
up the hindquarters, so that a flap of skin was folded
over the raw meat, and also linking them together in
pairs with rope. Obviously, each man was going to
drag a pair. Even as they watched, the individual
with the Lowland Scots accent, that the Englishman
had hailed as Bert, got up, wiping his blood-stained
hands and arms with grass, and proceeded to the
northern end of the bealach, to stare out and down.

N

"Looks hopeful," Alan murmured. "Deciding their route."

But after a moment or two, he came back, passing his colleagues, and made his way to the other, southern, end of the col, the prospect from which he considered, in turn, and for slightly longer. Then he returned, and pointed, southwards.

"Well I'm scuppered!" Kinnear complained. "Of all the . . ."

Archie touched his arm . "See what it is they're taking, though," he pointed out.

It was the fore-ends of the deer, that they began to drag away, the heads and shoulders and bellies. Using ropes to aid them, they hauled off these sorry remains southwards, out of the bealach and downhill, the man Bert leading. He made for a peat-bog, perhaps four hundred yards down, and into the black maw of it dumped his burden. Two others followed suit, and then turned and came back for more. The fourth members of the party still worked on the last pair of haunches. Fraser cursed him. If they had all gone with the offal, the tommy-guns, lying there gleaming in the level rays of the westering sun, would have been unguarded. They might have nipped down, grabbed them, and had the caterans at their mercy.

Alan, not so enthusiastic about these fire-arm tactics, was less disappointed. After all, what would happen if these toughs refused to believe that they would shoot—as with good reason they might?

Three trips to the peat-bog, and a judicious pulling down of the overhanging cornices of peat-soil, completed the disposal of the evidence. Only a man hunting for them, and maybe provided with a dog, might stumble on the remains of those eight deer, and that with a deal of luck. No-one else was going to see anything, save only some blood on the grass, that the

rain of a night would wash away. These people knew
what they were doing.

The leader went back to the northern end of the
bealach, and lying down, scanned all the ground
below, near and far, with meticulous care. The
watchers above, fretting as they were with all this
delay, sighed with relief. It looked as though their
guess was right—if only the wretched specimens
would hurry up. It was quarter-to-six now, and the
sun was sinking low over the long black ridges of the
Monadh Liath. In two hours it would be dark.

"They're going that way, down to the road,
obviously," Alan whispered. "There's no need to
wait, any longer. You advise me to go back down
past where we passed those women, and then over the
ridge to the right?"

"I do, yes. About a mile down yon glen of the
Allt Bàn, you'll see a bit burn coming in on the right.
Follow yon up—there's a sort of path all the way up.
It brings you over to the Black Corrie road a couple
of miles from where it starts. Wait you there—it's the
way I'll be coming over, my own self. I'll meet you
there at quarter-past-eight—and I'm hoping we won't
be too late, whatever."

"I hope not. I wish we'd risked it earlier on. Off
you go, first. And good luck!"

Archie Fraser, turning, wriggled off through the
heather, back whence they had come.

It was a strange nerve-racking business, waiting
there in the benighted forest, listening, idle, helpless,
and yet with so much to do. Alan listened for
Fraser's hurrying footsteps, he listened for the sound
of motor-cars on that narrow difficult road, and in
between, he listened to the quiet persistent voices of
the night.

For the hundredth time he peered at his watch,

Eight-ten. He had been there almost three-quarters of an hour—though it seemed infinitely more. He had found his way over from the Allt Bàn valley easily enough—and there had been no sign of the women when he had passed their hiding-place. It had been only twilight when he arrived down at this road, but it was dark now—especially down here amongst the black trees. Tall gnarled and ancient pines they were, relics of the original Caledonian Forest that once had clothed all this land. The first thing that he had done was to hunt about amongst those trees, for what they wanted—for, as Archie had indicated, almost anywhere that road was apt for blocking, with the west bank rising steeply up and the east falling steeply down. And, quite close to where his path and the road joined, he found a suitable tree—a great massive pine overhanging the track, that, once felled, would take a lot of shifting. But the felling looked a tough proposition—possibly Archie would say it was too much, too thick. Probably they wouldn't have time to tackle anything so large. And yet, it must be hefty, if it wasn't to be cleared away by these husky ruffians. If only he could have got started on to it. Here he was, sitting twiddling his thumbs . . . But you can't fell a tree with your bare hands . . .

Anyway, the more he thought about it all, the more flaws there seemed to be in this plan he had concocted. That was the trouble—it wasn't a plan, at all; it was just a wild idea. It had seemed sound enough up there on the hill-top, but now, with quiet and time for thought—too much quiet and time—the thing didn't look so good. Assuming that they got their tree felled, and the road blocked, in time—what then? How were they going to deal with these customers . . .? Damnation!

Alan jumped up from the rock that he was using

for a seat, at the sound. A car—there was no doubt
about it. They were too late, then—they'd missed
their chance. He might have known . . .

And yet . . . ? He cocked his head. Praises be—
it was coming *up* the road, not down. That meant . . .
if it was the poachers' car—and what other would it
be in that place at that time?—then they hadn't con-
tacted their friends yet. There was still some time.
He'd been assuming that the cars were up there,
already. Unless, it was Archie? Maybe he'd met
somebody, and come round by car . . . ?

The snort and throb of the engine, and the creak
and rattle of sorely-tried springs and chassis, drew
nearer steadily, but not so very quickly. The driver
was taking his time, as well he might. Getting behind
a tree-trunk, Alan peered down the road. There was
no gleam of light. Whoever was coming, was dispensing with his headlights. That could be Archie,
too, of course . . .

And then, the man realised that the sounds that
were coming to him were being duplicated. There
were two cars coming up that road, one some distance
behind the other. That pretty well clinched the
matter; the possibility of Fraser finding *two* cars to
fetch along, at such a time, was too remote to consider. Kinnear crouched further down, out of
possible sight.

The first vehicle to lurch past was an old and heavy
saloon, a Humber it looked like. And though the
watcher could not see its occupants, he could hear
them; the two women were in the front with the
driver.

Their calculations hadn't been so far out,
after all. Then, perhaps quarter-of-a-mile behind,
came a plain closed-in van, which to that man looked
ominously familiar. The same gang it was then.
Involuntarily, Alan Kinnear touched the still angry

weal on his scalp. His misgiving tended to lessen in consequence.

The noise of the vehicles had barely faded when Archie Fraser arrived, breathless, a two-handled cross-cut saw under one arm and a woodsman's axe over his shoulder. He had heard the cars, feared the same as Alan, and then been reassured by their direction. He hadn't seen a soul but his wife, but she was away off on his bicycle to be telling Miss Fiona what they were at. What that one would do about it, he couldn't just be saying, at all . . .

Alan showed him the tree that he had selected. The Highlandman agreed that it was big—but then it had to be big. A small one would be no use. Och, but they'd have it down in time, if they put their backs into it. And with the cars just away up, they'd have a wee whilie—maybe half-an-hour, with the road that bad, and the venison to load. They mightn't be in a great hurry, the borachs—the later they were, the less they were likely to be noticed.

Throwing off his jacket, Archie got busy with the axe, breathless as he was with his hurrying, wielding it with a lusty and judicious swing that bit cleanly and economically into the wood with every stroke. Kinnear offered to spell him, but the other would not hear of it. Quicker this way, he insisted, and him accustomed to the axe. Alan's turn would come, with the saw.

It did, too. With a neat wedge cut in each of the two sides of that tree, that on the east or road side quite a few inches lower than the other, Archie tossed aside the axe, and picked up the saw. "Hold it this way," he directed, panting, "and stand you about there. You've used a cross-cut?"

"Just once or twice, on firewood," Alan admitted.

"You'll be finding it heavy-going, maybe, and you with the head you have on you. But, och, you'll

manage fine. Just guide your end, at the first, and
leave the pulling and pushing to me, till you get used
to it.''

" Damn that for a game ! '' Alan retorted, and got
down to it.

It was not long before he was complaining, at the
girth, bulk, and general stubbornness of that tree.
A monster, it was, and hard as iron, and the saw
puny and blunt as any butter-knife. He thought
pine-trees were known as softwoods ?

The other laughed. '' Och, it's the age, see you.
They're the tough old warriors, these—a shame it is
to be cutting it down. They do be saying this kind is
hundreds of years old.''

'' I can well believe it,'' Kinnear gasped. '' This
is . . . practically fossilised ! ''

After that he had no breath left for complaints.
The sweat was pouring off him, and his head was
throbbing fit to burst, in tune with the snoring vibration of the saw. Today, he was taking drastic treatment for a convalescent. Though Fraser had not
made the cuts too low on the trunk, for convenience
of felling, very soon his back was aching with the
stooping, as his arms ached to the pushing and pulling. He tried crouching down, as he tried changing
hands, but with scant and very temporary easement.
And still the saw seemed to make precious little
headway.

They changed sides after a bit, and Alan consulted
the watch on his trembling wrist. It was eight thirty-
five. They had been quarter-of-an-hour at it. At this
rate, could they possibly finish it in time. Lord, with
the head and the back and the arms he had, could
they finish it at all ? That Archie assured that they
could, they would, that they were doing fine, that
the second half was always the easier, that he was

just getting into his stride, did not completely dissipate his doubts.

But Archie was right, in his first contention, at anyrate. Possibly, even, the second half *was* easier if that was a term that in decency could be used; or it may have been merely that Alan was so preoccupied in listening, above that horrible saw's raucous plaint, for the sound of the cars coming back, that he had less attention to spare for his physical distress. At all events, his hand and arm, racked and practically numb now, was still going back and forth limply, little more than a passenger on that saw when his companion called out that he thought that would do it. Thankfully, Alan staggered back and sat down, head between his knees, too exhausted even to look up at the results of his efforts.

Fraser was pushing against the bole of the tree, in a series of rhythmic and steadily increasing thrusts, and though there seemed to be little effect down at the all-but sawn-through base, there was an ever-growing agitation up in the topmost branches. But a man's strength seemed to be insufficient to tip the balance. Archie reached for his axe. "Stand you right back," he ordered his drooping colleague. "Likely she'll fall the right way, but och, you never can be sure, just. There's no more than an inch, holding her."

Making certain that his own way of escape was clear behind him, Archie swung his axe at the lowermost cut, at the roadward side, opposite from the saw's incision. Four or five discriminating blows, and the tall tree shuddered. There was a groaning sound from straining fibre, a sighing amongst the swaying branches, and slowly, majestically, the great pine toppled, with a rending tearing cracking roar. Down across the road it fell, tons and tons of it, bringing down a small tree opposite, and the earth shook with the crash of its impact.

Hurrying down after it, Archie's voice came up into the silence that succeeded. "Beautiful!" he cried, "just beautiful, whatever!"

Surveying their handiwork, the Highlandman clapped his companion on his wilting back. "They'll not be getting by that this night," he chortled. "They will not. Man, Alan—is that not just the job!"

Kinnear nodded, but with less satisfaction. "It's *part* of the job, anyway," he agreed. "The point is —what now?"

"Aye. I'ph'mmm." Fraser rubbed his jowl. "Just that. We could maybe be felling another tree."

"God forbid!" That was heartfelt. "What on earth for? This is quite heavy enough, surely. They'll never shift this one, without cutting it up. You said yourself . . ."

"Och, no—but it's not this side I'm meaning. It's back a bit, there—up the road."

"*Up* the road . . . ? But, what's the good of that?"

"Well, when I'm saying fell a tree, I'm meaning not quite fell it just. If we could be having it just about down, see you, and let the cars pass, then down with it, we'd be having them bottled up, right enough. The way it is now, they'll not can get out, but they'll maybe can turn their cars round, and away back somewhere. This bit road goes three miles before it stops at the Black Corrie. If we're for after them, we'd have to be looking anywhere in the three miles. If we're after felling a tree behind them, as well as in front, we've got them cooped, whatever."

"M'mmm," the other said. He saw the point of that, of course, but he did not feel in the least like felling another tree. Cravenly, he hedged. "Probably we wouldn't have time."

"Maybe not, no—but we can be having a try, surely."

"I don't honestly think I can do it," Alan confessed. "That one nearly had me beat."

"Och, you'll be fine." Fraser declared, with engaging confidence, and started to walk up the road. "We'll be choosing not such a big tree, at all—just enough to sort of discourage them. And you'd just be having to guide your end, and leave the sawing to me. Man, you'd never notice it."

Wanly Kinnear smiled. "I'm in a noticing frame of mind," he mentioned, but went along, just the same. Almost, he prayed to hear the sound of those cars, now.

About four hundred yards up, and round a bend, Archie selected another pine, something much more modest, admittedly, but still a sizeable tree. This time, he put in rather more axe-work—to which his companion took no exception. Also, he made the inside cut fully four feet above the ground-level, so that little or no crouching and stooping was entailed. And still there was silence from up the road.

As Alan put his reluctant hand to the saw-handle, he observed. "We'll have to stop sawing pretty frequently, to listen, or we'll have them down on top of us . . ."

The other nodded. "Surely. Now, do you nothing but guide your end, and keep the saw level. Me it is that's sawing this tree."

And so the ghastly business began again—though it was not quite such a purgatory as before, undoubtedly. The tree, no veteran this time, was neither so thick nor so hard, the higher position was a definite help, and Alan, while doing more than the other had adjured, did not put so much into it as he had sought to do previously. Also, the break every score or so of strokes, to listen, was a boon; Kinnear counted each stroke between, as a weary tramp might count telegraph-poles between milestones. At what stage he began to hope that they *would* get the job finished before the cars arrived, it would be hard to say.

They did. Presumably, the poachers recognised what Archie had suggested—that delay only meant that their retiral would be the less conspicuous. Archie, peering and feeling, declared that they dare not cut further, and that a good push would bring the tree down. They must just wait, now.

Alan by no means contested that. But what were they going to do, once the cars were trapped? He was dead weary, his head was splitting and his brain muzzy, and he couldn't for the life of him see the next step.

Archie wasn't very clear about it all, either. Obviously they couldn't tackle these people openly, head-on. With the car-drivers, there presumably would be six of them, now, excluding the women, armed desperate men, and no doubt considerably annoyed. Maybe they couldn't do anything at all, more than they had done—but at least they would have deprived them of their transport. If these folk cleared out of the district, that night, they'd have to do so on foot. That is, unless they'd come provided with saws and axes . . .

"Which makes it pretty obvious that we shouldn't be sitting here with the axe and saw beside us," Alan interrupted. "We don't want them coming after us at all, of course, but it's on the boards that they will—especially if they hear this tree crash. And if we have to make a bolt for it, these things won't be any help. And if we drop them, or they catch us, they can saw their way out."

Fraser was picking up the tools before ever the

other had finished. "Man, you're right there," he acknowledged. "I'll away off and dump them some place, safe."

"I think you should." He paused. "But don't be too long?" That afterthought was distinctly significant.

"No, no. I'll not be two minutes, just."

He had not *been* two minutes, when Alan drew a sharp breath. The cars were coming. They were near at hand. There must be a bend in the road above, that had blanketed the sound. They were almost on him. Where in hell was Archie Fraser!

Fortunately, the car and the van were running close together this time, the van leading. They lurched and rattled past Alan's tree, with only perhaps thirty yards between them, unlighted as before. The second was barely past, before Kinnear was on his feet, pushing against that tree-trunk. The thing was as steady as a rock. He pushed and pushed, but apart from the merest whispering in the branches far above, without result. Desperately, he moved round to the roadward side, to try pulling instead, but with equal non-success. It was immovable. Infuriated with the tree, with his own puny weakness, with Archie Fraser, he cursed the latter, who should have been there, who'd said this thing could be pushed over, who probably hadn't cut through sufficiently far. Where on earth was he? But he couldn't wait for him—those cars must be practically at the block already. If only he'd had that rope of his . . .

He stared upwards. As with most pine-trees, the stumps of many broken-off branches projected on the lower trunk. But not far, perhaps ten feet, a fair-sized bough reached out towards the road. If he could get his weight on to that, using it as a lever . . .

Without hesitation, he started to climb, using those stumps as a step-ladder. As soon as he was within reach, he made a lunge for the projecting bough, and a moment later was hanging from it with both hands. And swinging along, hand over hand, he began to work outwards.

There was a crack like a rifle-shot, a sickening lurch, and the tree pitched over. But this one did not come down slowly, majestically, like its elder brother. As the trunk parted company with the stump, it did so with a vicious kick like a mule—the sort of kick that has killed many a lumberjack. That kick came just as the man was loosing hold of his bough, to drop to the ground and run. He dropped, but he was thrown off his balance by the thrust of it, and in his dizzy state fell headlong. And while he still was frantically struggling up, on his knees, something hit him hard on the back of his head.

And once again black oblivion descended on Alan Kinnear.

CHAPTER XVIII

ALAN considered for a few moments all the austere host of the pale unwinking stars, seen through the dark filigree-work of the birch-leaves, began to shake his head at its uncaring remoteness, abruptly discontinued any such activity, at the stunning pain in his head, and cautiously, on one elbow, proceeded to lever himself up into a sitting position. " Damn, blast, and confound it ! " he said, distinctly.

Something compounded of laugh, gasp, and sigh, very close at hand, caused him to turn his head, though extremely warily. " I must say, you are a glutton for punishment, Mr. Kinnear ! " a woman's voice declared, a little unsteadily.

Surprised, he studied the girl kneeling on the grass beside him, even in the gloom of the night-bound woods most evidently Fiona Macpherson. " How . . . how did *you* get here ? " he wondered.

" More orthodoxly than you did, I'd say—in a car ? " she announced. " But don't let's bother about that, just now. The point is, how are *you* ? "

He raised his eyebrows—and lowered them again promptly, wincing. " I have a sore head," he observed, objectively.

" I'm sure you have—but you feel all right, otherwise ? I mean—there's nothing serious come out of it . . . ? "

Alan Kinnear frowned—though it cost him dear. " Miss Macpherson," he said, slowly, deliberately.

" I feel sick, limp, dizzy, aching in every bone, and my head is split into three halves—otherwise I'm feeling just fine, splendid ! "

Her laugh at this was much more natural and unrestrained. " That's grand—that sounds much more like the old Alan Kinnear ! For a little you had us worried, you know. Having trees fall on your head is not the best treatment for concussion patients. But apparently, this time you were merely stunned . . ."

" Look here . . ." the man began to protest, but the effort was too great. Turning, not his head but his whole body, left and right, he peered about him. " Hang it, where am I now ? " he demanded querulously. " What's it all about ? How did I get here ? "

" You're about half-a-mile from where you had your argument with the tree," the girl informed him. " Down the track, nearer where it joins the road from the Lodge. We're just back from the roadside. Archie, here, carried you this far, and then came on for help. We met him, with the car . . ."

" Archie carried me . . . ? D'you mean, actually *carried* me ? Well, I'm damned ! What about him—where is Archie now ? "

" Och, just at the back of you, man Alan—I'm here," Fraser announced, moving into view. " Glad I am it's just stunned you were. I was thinking maybe you'd be taken bad, again. When I found you under yon tree, I was right scared. I got you over my back, and fetched you down here, keeping well into the wood, away from yon borachs at the cars."

Something of the magnitude of the task that Archie had had to accomplish was apparent to the patient, but for the moment the personal aspect took precedence. " Heavens—how long have I been out this time, then ? " he demanded.

" Och, not much more than half-an-hour, I'd say,"
the other assured, " I wasn't for wasting any time,
see you."

" And the poachers—what about them?"

Archie shrugged. " The last I was hearing of
them, they were making a right stramash up at yon
big tree. That was when I passed near them in the
wood carrying yourself. They hadn't tried to turn
their cars, then. But I was hearing an engine again,
before I got here, so maybe they'll be knowing about
the second tree by this, too."

" M'mmm," Alan said, holding his head, " So
you've had no contact with them, yet?"

" We have not, no."

The girl spoke, " I think you've done a marvellous
job, you two—I can't begin to say what I think about
it all. You've worked wonders, both of you."

" That is so," another voice said, gravely—John
Cameron's voice.

" Yes, yes, indeed," Sandy Cattanach concurred,
" Just that."

" So you're all here!" Alan commented, almost
sourly. " Even the police! And what are you going
to do about it, now?"

"That's the problem," the young woman admitted,
" We were just discussing that—though naturally
we were more concerned about you, than anything
else . . ."

Alan grunted at that. Undoubtedly he was in a
thoroughly bad temper. In some obscure fashion he
felt that he had bones to pick with them all. And his
head beat like a drum. " And did you come to any
conclusions?"

" Not exactly," Fiona shook her head. " It's
difficult, isn't it. Sandy wants just to go ahead and
challenge these people—arrest them, in a straight-
forward fashion."

"The more fool him, then," Kinnear snorted. "What does he think they're going to do while he's arresting them?"

"M'mm. You're like Archie, then—you think they'll fight?"

"Of course they'll fight. What d'you take them for? These are tough characters—they're the same people that knocked me on the head, the last time. I recognised the van. And they're armed—and pretty certainly angry."

"That's right, yes," Archie Fraser agreed. "And there are six men of them, at the least, and but the four of us, and Mr. Kinnear sick. And just the one Luger pistol amongst us . . ."

"Och, quiet you about your Luger pistol, Archie," the constable reproved, "We're wanting none of that, at all . . ."

"If we wait a while," the young woman intervened, "We'll probably get help. I sent Willie Maclean to collect Alec Macphail and one or two others. It would take him a while, though."

"What difference does it make?" Alan questioned. "You can have the whole district turned out—but what use are they against tommy-guns?"

"I know, I know—that's what I was telling them," the girl cried, "We just can't have any bloodshed. I'm not going to stand for it. I'd much rather we just let these poachers get away, than have anybody injured, or trouble of that sort. Mr. Kinnear, here, has suffered plenty already. After all, it looks as though we've got their cars—they can't get them away evidently. That will be a big blow to them. Probably they'll leave Glencoraig alone, after this . . ."

"That is all very well for yourself, Miss Fiona," Cattanach objected. "But the law comes into this, see you. I have my duty to do, whatever. I'm not

o

for just letting them go, at all, without making an attempt to arrest them. I am not."

" I don't see that's it's anything to do with you, Sandy, officially, at this stage," the girl declared. " After all, *I'm* the injured party. This is my property—or, at least, my family's. If I don't ask for the law's assistance . . ."

"Och, but the law's been broken, look, Miss Fiona. Apart from the poaching in it, these borachs do be carrying firearms—lethal weapons, itself— contrary to the Firearms Act, 1937 . . ."

"Firearms Act, my foot ! " That was Alan Kinnear again. " While you're arguing here about the Firearms Act of 1937, these gentry up the road won't be sitting still. They'll be getting to blazes out of it . . ."

" Just what I was thinking, my own self," Archie supported.

" And isn't that probably the best thing that could happen ? " Fiona suggested.

" And let the ruffians get off scot-free, after all our efforts ? "

" But I thought that was what you were advocating ? You said that we couldn't do anything against tommy-guns . . . ? "

Alan Kinnear, in his present state of mind, was prepared to wallow in the luxury of contrariness. " Not at all," he disclaimed, " What I was getting at, was that we couldn't just go for them bald-headed, like a bull at a gate. Anything we do had got to be more subtle than that."

" Such as . . . ? "

He raised his head from between his hands. " Well —it depends on what *they're* doing. But if they're clearing out, leaving the cars, I think we'd have the advantage. After all, you people must know this country infinitely better than they do—I mean, all

this forest land. It's pretty thick and pretty rough
stuff, and I imagine they're hardly likely to stick to
paths. We ought to be able to make that work for
us—head them off, get them lost, corner them,
ambush them even. In the darkness, in this forest,
they're going to be at a distinct disadvantage. If
they stick together, they've got to go at the speed of
the slowest, and choose the going for the feeblest,
and if they separate, we can pick them off one by
one . . ."

" Jungle warfare stuff ! " Archie Fraser exclaimed,
delightedly. " Man, Alan—that's the stuff."

Fiona Macpherson said nothing.

John Cameron spoke, " There's something in what
Mr. Kinnear says—but it's not going to be so easy,
with the few of us that's in it, and the dark. Anyway,
I'm thinking we'll not be getting the chance."

" Why not ? "

" Because of these women they've got in it. If
what Archie says about them is right, they're not the
kind to be getting through the trackless forest in the
dark, at all—even this sort of forest. I'm thinking
they'll not risk leaving the road, with them."

"Uh-huh. Aye. Maybe you're right, John,"
Fraser admitted, "That could be."

" They might leave them," Alan countered. " The
four men might well leave them, with the cars—and
with the drivers, too. After all, they've done nothing
illegal. If they got the meat out of the van, there's
nothing you could hold *them* for, is there, Cattanach ?
It's not a crime to drive a couple of cars up this road
at night, is it ? "

" That is so, Mr. Kinnear. Aye, they could be
doing that, right enough."

" It seems to me," Archie declared, " That we
can't be deciding anything, till we find out what
they're after doing. And we can't be finding out, till

we're up that road, and seeing what they're at. And
the longer we're waiting here, the less chance there is
of finding them, at all."

"Aye, then."

"That's right, Archie."

"Exactly." Alan Kinnear got to his feet, dispensing
with all proffered assistance.

"Are you all right?" the girl put to him
anxiously. And at his curt affirmative, " I don't like
this, you know—I don't like it, at all."

"It will be all right, Miss Fiona, never fear,"
Cameron said, soothingly. " But it is no work for a
lady, whatever. If you will just be waiting in the car,
there, and sending up Alec and the rest when they
come . . ."

"No . . ." she began.

"Yes ! " Alan said, harshly. " Use your common-
sense. At this sort of thing, a woman is a positive
handicap. You heard how the two in front will be
a trial to the poachers ? Well, you don't want to put
us in the same position, do you ? "

"Oh . . . ! " Fiona gasped, " Oh . . . ! " And then
she swallowed, bit her lip, and achieved a shrug.
"Very well," she said quietly, and turned about. As
she picked her way down to the road, she called
back, low-voiced, " I will be down in the car, if you
want me for anything."

The three men eyed Alan askance, and there was
a certain amount of uncomfortable throat-clearing
before they moved after her to the road, and then
turned off in the opposite direction. Kinnear stared
after the girl quite appreciably longer that the others,
from under down-drawn brows, before he followed
in their wake, unhappily.

The four men moved up, at the side of the road
within the shadow of the trees, in single file, Archie

leading. Alan, well to the rear, found himself a little unsteady on his feet, as in his head. Therefore he kept his eyes fixed firmly on the ground, lest anything got out of control. Thus it was that presently he bumped heavily into the back of the policeman, and so all but defeated his purpose.

The trio in front had stopped, and Archie was holding up an urgent hand for quiet. Unfortunately, Alan did not see it in time. " Sorry," he began, " My fault. Anything the matter . . . ? "

" H'ssst ! " Archie warned.

But it was too late. From ahead of them on the road, in the gloom of the trees, quick tense voices reached them. " Just in front . . . sure . . . Bloody keepers . . . Scram outa this . . . ! " they heard, and the beat of running feet, rapidly fading.

" B'damn—two of them ! " Archie muttered. Fifty yards away they were, no more."

" I'm sorry," Alan said again, sincerely. " I'm a blundering fool. I didn't see Cattanach . . ."

" Och, never heed, Alan—it's easy done," Fraser assured generously, " Likely they'd have seen us in a yard or two, anyway."

" Well, they know we're coming, now," Cameron said, " Will we go on ? "

" Why not, at all ? " Sandy Cattanach demanded.

" It shows they've not bolted yet, anyway," Alan pointed out.

" It's maybe ourselves that'll be doing the bolting, in two-three minutes ! " That was the keeper, grimly.

" I'm not so sure about that," Kinnear contended. " Maybe it's just as well that these two heard us coming up the road—heard rather than saw. They wouldn't know how many of us there were, for one thing. For another, they may get the idea that they're surrounded—at least, as far as the road goes. After all, they've had a tree felled behind them as well as in front. They'll be apt to think, won't they, that there's some of us *up* the road, as well as down? And they said ' bloody keepers ', you'd note—a reasonable enough conclusion. But they could expect keepers to be armed—with shot-guns, at least. I think they'll bolt."

" I shouldn't wonder if you're right," Archie Fraser nodded. " We're for on, then ? "

" Very well."

" Aye, then."

" I think so."

So they went on, keeping in to the side, and off the narrow road, as before. This time, Alan Kinnear watched the back of the man in front, rather than the ground at his feet.

In the darkness, they came on their fallen tree more quickly and suddenly than Alan, at least, expected. Archie's hand up, stopped them. " There it is," he pointed, " Not a hundred yards in it."

They stared into the dark, stared and listened. They could just make out the line of the great tree, sloping down from the high bank on the right. But that was all that they could make out. Nothing beyond it. And nothing was to be heard, save the whisper of the night-wind amongst the branches, and somewhere, the lonely hooting of an owl.

They crept further forward. Still there was nothing to see, nothing to hear. It was a strange and uneasy advance that they made, not knowing what was waiting for them. The thought of those four tommy-guns was undoubtedly in all their minds. Jungle-warfare was all very well in theory, but . . . !

John Cameron it was who spoke. " The car," he whispered, " I saw it, there. A sort of reflection on the windscreen. See—if you stand back here, you'll see it."

"Yes. That'll be the van," Kinnear acceded. " The

point is—are they still in it, or thereabouts? They're lying pretty low, if they are."

"Aye, they are. But we'll have to be finding out," Archie said. "Wait you here, just, and I'll take a bit creep forward."

They stood still, while Archie disappeared down into the low ground below the road. They neither heard him go, heard any hint of his passage, nor heard him come again, five minutes later. Even John Cameron was impressed. "You're no' a bad stalker, at all, Archie," he mentioned, "Are they in it?"

"They are not. They've gone. Both the cars are there—the big one turned the other way. I'm thinking it would turn and away up, get stuck at the tree above, yonder, and back down again. But the borachs have gone."

"And no sign which way, at all?"

"Och, I wasn't just looking that hard, for signs. I didn't hear a thing. But we can be having a bit look, now . . ."

"I'm afraid we won't have to," Alan Kinnear said, grimly. "Look there!"

Following the line of his outstretched arm, they stared. Over, eastwards a little, in the blackness of the forest, two or three orange points of light gleamed out. Even as the men watched, the points grew in number and in size, flickering, wavering lights that reddened ominously. Then one of them leapt up and up, and burst suddenly into flaming brilliance, and the evil crackle of it came to them clearly out of the night.

"My God!" John Cameron cried. "They've set the forest on fire! Come on!"

CHAPTER XIX

THERE was no question, any more, from that first moment of revelation, as to what they must do, strive to do, where lay their duty. The poachers could wait, could go. Indeed, after the first explosion of fury and indignation, they were as good as forgotten. The fire was the supreme enemy. The poacher could do Glencoraig injury, but the fire could destroy it entirely. A forest-fire, out of hand, could be the end of everything. The need to fight the fire over-rode all else.

Unhesitant, the four men ran, plunging through the heather that grew beneath the scattered pines, towards the blaze. Alan Kinnear's dizziness and weariness forgotten quite. The fires had been lit in a line, something over quarter-of-a-mile from the road, on the left-hand or eastward side. And they were doing wickedly well, in the light south-westerly wind, amongst the old heather and the resinous pines.

Before ever they got to the line of blazing trees, it was obvious that any attempt at mere extinguishment would be quite futile. A belt of old high heather, perhaps three hundred yards long and already quite fifty yards in depth, was alight, and creeping rapidly north-eastwards at the urge of the breeze, and out of it the scattered pines thrust up like flaming torches. No amount of beating, by ten times their number, could quench that crackling inferno. Momentarily appalled, the four of them stood and stared, shielding their faces against the fierce heat and glare of it.

"Hopeless!" Alan cried. He had to raise his voice to a shout, to penetrate the roar. "Hopeless, I say. A fire-break's the only thing."

"Yes," Archie bawled, "The swines!" Other things he said too.

"The Bruach . . .?" Cameron suggested. "How far from the Bruach?"

Too far, Archie thought—it would be half-a-mile east. If the fire had been further down, now, where the burn took a bend . . . Drawing back a little from the blaze, to where they could at least hear each other speak, the three local men held a hurried consultation. A burn like the Bruach would make a good base for a fire-break, but to sacrifice all the half-mile of forest in between was too much—also, who could tell how widely the blaze might have spread by then, possibly outflanking any break they made. What they wanted was an open area, a few hundred yards ahead of the fire, where they could burn a belt that the fire, when it came to it, could not leap across. The trouble was, to prevent their own precautionary fire going too far, itself. In that rolling expanse of scattered trees and heather, none of them could say for sure just how the land lay, relative to where they stood. There were open patches in it, and damp hollows, and bogs. But, just where . . . ? Archie had an idea that there might be one of these hollows not far in front, but it might be farther to the side, to the north. In hasty agreement with Alan Kinnear's fretting impatience, they decided that the only thing to do was to hurry on, ahead of the blaze, and take the first likely place that offered.

Thankful to be not standing still, at least, they plunged on, round the northern side of the advancing line of fire, scrambling through the knee-high heather

and cranberries, tripping over hidden windfalls and
the legion of the ant-hills, all in the eerie ruddy glow
from the leaping flames. But this stage of their
progress was a promenade, compared to the position
when once they had got round in front of the fire.
For now they were enveloped in dense rolling clouds
of smoke, drifting down wind, that set them coughing
and their eyes running, that not only obscured but
distorted their vision. Stumbling on, they strove
ineffectually to get ahead of its murky blanket. It
was as well that the flames did not travel so fast as
the smoke, at anyrate.

Once or twice Alan thought that they had come to
tree-less patches wide enough for them to attempt
their fire-break, but Archie objected that there was
nothing beyond to stop the new fire they would make.
And then, after one such suggestion, they found
themselves plunging over the ankles in clinging slime
and surface-water. They had reached one of the damp
hollows, that lay between the gentle folds of the forest,
soggy moss and reed-grown rifts, trending down
north-westwards, with the lie of the land. Fraser
shouted to turn back, and climbing out of the
quagmire again, they agreed that here was the
likeliest place to make their attempt.

They made a quick calculation, insofar as they
were able, of the fire's line of approach, realised that
they were too far down, northwards, and hurried
higher up the line. Then, spreading themselves out,
perhaps a hundred yards apart, they knelt to their
own fire-raising.

It was painfully easy to start their blaze. The old
heather had more wood to it than leaf or flower, and
the past two days had been dry. Alan's expenditure
of half a box of matches produced in a couple of
minutes a dozen well-doing little fires, that very soon
ran together and merged into a single wall of spurting

darting yellow flame, linking up presently with similar efforts by Archie on the right and Sandy Cattanach on the left. The breeze did the rest. In only a little longer than it takes to tell, their tide of flame was flooding strongly, alarmingly strongly, across and down towards the bog-lined depression.

But Archie Fraser was far from satisfied. They couldn't be sure that their cordon was wide enough, that the oncoming fire would hit it squarely. As far as they could judge, they were about three hundred yards ahead of the real fire. It could widen, change its course to some extent . . . With the wind that was in it, and the lie of the land, he thought that they'd be wise to extend their barrier eastwards . . . But *he'd* do that; the rest of them had better get round in front, right away, to keep their own fire under control.

So the three of them left Fraser, and hurried westward, round their heather-fire, back to the lip of the damp ground. Quickly, through bleary eyes and billowing smoke, they surveyed the line of it. For most of the way, probably, the stretch of bog and moss would be sufficient to check the rush of the flames, temporarily at least, and if they worked hard to assist it, green reeds, bog-myrtle and canna being not very inflammable. But there were one or two isolated trees on the edge of it, that would be a source of danger, and worse, the hollow did not extend far enough up, eastwards. Up there, it degenerated into a mere damp and grassy groove, only a yard or two wide, that the flames and sparks could leap in their stride. Here was where their real struggle with the fire would have to take place.

They had allowed for a belt of about fifty yards in width as being sufficient to halt the main fire, but already their own blaze had covered almost half of that. Anything that they did here, would have to be done very quickly. While Cameron and the constable

wrenched bushy branches from nearby pines for
beating with, Alan lit half-a-dozen more little fires a
few yards out in front of the narrow danger-spot at
the head of the hollow. These, at least, they could
keep under control.

Soon, bough in hand, he was in the thick of it,
standing actually in what was an incipient burn,
beating out the wriggling searching snakes of flame
that sought to cross, coughing, choking, his eyes
streaming. The other two were working on either
side of him, buffeting and stamping. It was hard
desperate work, while it lasted, but effective—and it
did not take long. In a few urgent minutes, their
latest conflagration had burned itself out, without
crossing the green margin, and a scorched area,
charred and smoking, black shot with twisting worms
of red, confronted the advancing heather-fire that
they had started, at the vulnerable stretch.

They were none too soon. The wall of flame was
almost on to them, only a foot or two high,
admittedly, but travelling fast and sending its blast
of heat in front of it. Seen through its curtain of
smoke, it looked sufficiently menacing. Leaving
Cattanach to see that it did not cross their charred
area, Alan and the keeper ran down along the edge
of the hollow. With more than two hundred yards
of it to deal with, between them, they were unlikely
to have time hanging heavily on their hands.

Perhaps half-way down the line, Alan took up his
stance, a puny figure indeed to stem that onrush of
flame. Peer as he would, out of his smarting watering
eyes, he could not see back beyond it, past the
nearer glow of it, to that greater conflagration in the
rear; but above the hiss and crackle and roar of the
burning heather, he could make out, with a pang at
the pit of his stomach, the deeper ominous rumble
that was the forest fire itself.

Retreating before the heat and sparks, he was soon standing almost up to the knees in the moss and water and slime. Here and there a clump of bog-myrtle or reeds, higher and perhaps drier than its fellows, flared alight, but quickly died out. A ripple of flame at one point seemed to cross the hollow, burning the tops of the bog-cotton and the rushes. But even as Kinnear hastened to counter it, the flames died away and came to nothing. It seemed as though their damp patch would do the trick, hold the tide. Then one of the trees on the edge of it went up, with a roar, crackling and exploding like small-arms fire, and sending out showers of sparks and burning fragments. There were trees directly across from it, on the other side of the hollow, only thirty or forty yards away, and Alan was wondering feverishly whether he ought to go and keep watch over them, when shouting from further up the line reached him, above the uproar. Cattanach was in trouble.

Plowtering up through the quagmire, he found the policeman all but overwhelmed. The fire had been checked by the charred ground, but was sweeping round above it. This would be the result of Archie Fraser's extended efforts. There was a front of something like twenty yards of fire, with nothing to stop it save a wildly flailing Sandy Cattanach and a wedge of green grass and moss no more than six feet wide. Desperately, Alan threw himself into the fray.

And now began the real battle. All that had gone before was merely preparatory, a warming-up. This was a fierce contest, a race between breeze-driven fire and human energy and muscles. Beating, slapping, belabouring, with their branches, the two men stood in the path of the creeping devouring flames striving amain to hold that pitifully narrow line. Singed, choking, all but suffocated and blinded by the heat and smoke, they fought, and did not prevail yet were not defeated. At some time in their warfare, Cameron joined them, and some time later somebody thrust a new branch into Alan's hand to replace the burnt and almost useless one he wielded. Also, Archie Fraser's voice was upraised somewhere nearby. These things he knew, without really noting them. He did note that the fire was gaining on them. There was a tree behind him, on the wrong side of the green ribbon, a tree towards which he was being forced back, a tree which, if it once caught fire, could set alight half-a-dozen others grouped nearby to the east, and their efforts would have been in vain— worse than useless, for was not this fire of their own starting? He fought for that tree as though his life depended on it.

But something else he had to note, presently. It was a plea, urgent, beseeching. Turning, he found Fiona Macpherson at his elbow, something pale held out in her hands—what, his streaming blood-shot eyes did not perceive.

" You ! " he gasped, croaked, hoarsely : " You shouldn't be here."

" Put this on," she ordered. " It will help."

He shook his head, but found that she was tying some sort of damped cloth over his nose and mouth. " You shouldn't be here," he repeated, mumbling.

" It is my wood," she said, simply.

He found it better, undoubtedly, with that thing round his face. He coughed and choked less, was able to breathe more easily. Still, he hardly thought about the difference that it made, so intent was he in what he was doing. There was little room in his consciousness for anything other than the task in hand. For all that, he did not fail to realise that the girl Fiona was labouring next to him. The realisation brought its own involuntary, unanalysed, and

strangely contradictory reactions, firstly, that it was
wrong, that this was no place for her, or any woman,
and secondly, despite all that, that it was
an excellent and a comforting thing that she should
be there at his side. Indubitably, he wrought the
more redoubtably therefore.

Nevertheless, the fire was gaining on them. Back-
ward glances proved that to be undeniable. He was
almost underneath his tree now, the tree that he took
to be the symbol of success or failure. In a minute
or two that tree must go up. And then . . . !
Suddenly, it seemed vitally important that he should
share his fears with Fiona Macpherson.

" That tree ! " he cried, " If it goes . . . ! "

She nodded, dumbly.

" We'll have to let this go . . . either side of it," he
gasped. " Concentrate on round the tree . . . only
hope."

" Yes," she gasped, " But don't strain yourself,
Alan—please ! You're not fit enough . . . it's not
worth it . . ."

He ignored that, of course.

" I'll take this side," he panted, " You, that.
Concentrate on keeping the fire . . . from under the
tree."

" Yes."

So together they battled for that gnarled and
twisted Scots pine, beating and stamping out every
kicking tongue of flame, every wriggling red feeler
of the fire, every flying spark and rocketing ember,
while on either side, the blaze crept up and past.
Soon, they were almost islanded with their tree. But
peering ahead through the eddying veil of smoke,
Alan could make out how the ground in front was
black now, and only veined with red. The heather
belt had burned itself out, and the danger from there
was almost past. From the immediate foreground,

that is; behind that, the great leaping pinnacles of fire, where the forest burned, seen ruddily through the murk, was best not to be considered.

And then, with a crackling and a hiss, the tree above them caught alight. Some shooting flaming fragment, flying backwards had lodged in a bushy clump of pine-needles, and all their efforts were nullified.

The man's groan and the girl's cry arose together. But Alan did more than groan. The burning bough was a lower one, and not large, projecting in some isolation, as is the way of Scots pines, and so far it had not ignited any of its fellows. With an almost superhuman leap, the man sprang for it, not for its thicker end near the trunk, but for its burning extremity. Eight feet, perhaps, it was above the ground, but his hands closed on it, and held. Sprawling, he fell, and with a tearing crack the branch broke and fell with him. Rolling and twisting, he got himself bodily on top of the burning leafage, smothering the flames under his own weight. The girl was stooping to assist, when Alan looked up, and a choking cry almost strangled him. A burning ember must have flown off his branch as it fell, and had lodged in the curls at the side of her head. Crazily the man grabbed her, and pulled her down beside him, snatching at the ember, beating at the sizzling hair, enfolding her whole head between his sleeve and jacket.

" My dear, my dear ! " he cried, " Your hair ! " Tree and bough and general conflagration were forgotten.

For a timeless moment she lay there, clinging to him, her head against his heaving side. And then, as though at last daring to look, he pushed her a little from him, though still he held her. Her hair was dark again, as always. Infinitely gently his hand

went out, to stroke over and down those singed
tresses.

"Your poor hair," he cried. "Fiona, my dear—
I love you!"

She did not speak. She only stared at him through
swimming smoke-smarting eyes, and shook her head
at him under his hand, slowly, wordlessly, as in
wonder. But her grip on his arm tightened.

So they knelt, in the ruddy glow of the flames, their
eyes locked.

But not for long. A sudden shouting from behind
them turned their heads thitherward, and they
scrambled to their feet. It was Archie Fraser's voice,
and he was giving directions. They could make out
shadowy figures in the smoky glare. Alec Macphail
shouted an answer. Help had arrived, obviously.

Alan and the girl considered their tree. It seemed
to have suffered no further harm, and the group to
the east that it had menaced was untouched. Their
heather-fire also, was now dying out everywhere
except in the narrow neck behind them, where it had
by-passed their little peninsula. And here there was
now a strong concentration fighting it. Grabbing
Fiona by the hand, the man ran with her through
the blackened smoking ruin, to their assistance.

In a little, Archie, almost unrecognisable so
blackened was he—as were they all, indeed—came
up triumphantly. "Och, we have it beat, Miss
Fiona," he exclaimed. "Hech, aye—but it was
warm while it lasted, whatever!"

"You think so, Archie—you're sure?" the girl
questioned, breathlessly. "I'm afraid I don't see
it, myself. That fire, over there, looks terrible. There
seems to be two fires. I'm afraid I don't quite understand . . .?"

"Och, ourselves it was lit this one, as a fire-break,

P

see you," Fraser explained. "But we hadn't just enough men in it to control it properly. But we're fine, now. The bastards—och, I beg your pardon, indeed—these damnation poachers' fire is yonder." And he pointed westwards to the tall fearsome wall of fire out of which burning trees thrust like roman candles. "But never fear—our break'll hold it, surely."

"I wonder?" Alan doubted, hoarsely. "You think it's wide enough?"

"Och, yes—it'll not cross that, at all. There's nothing left for it to burn, whatever. You'll see."

They watched, fascinated, and one by one the other men joined them, as they each finished beating out their own segment of the heather-fire. These men had all assisted at many an annual moor-burn, when, each April, the heather was fired in selected patches to enable the young shoots to come through for the grouse to feed on. They knew the technique, and had required no superintending. Fiona, it transpired, had come on, on her own, when she saw the blaze. Alec Macphail, Maclean, and two others, arriving later at the road-end in the hotel-keeper's car, had likewise perceived and come hot-foot.

With the last trees before their belt of charred ground silhouetted blackly against the blaze, they watched the fire bear down on them. Almost in silence they stared, narrow-eyed, into the smoke. It was a breath-taking, alarming, experience, just to stand and wait, before that devouring awe-inspiring devastation. But there was nothing else to be done. They had attempted all that was humanly possible. Their fire-break had been the only remedy available. They could only hope, now.

And some time in their watching and hoping, voices behind them turned all heads around. Three more men were approaching, and even above the roar of the fire authority of two of their voices was not to be mistaken.

"This is a bad business—shocking," one of them declared, with the clipped crispness of his kind. "What the devil's the meaning of it all?"

Alan heard the girl at his side draw a quick breath. "Sir Henry!" she gasped, appalled.

"Lord—is that Miss Macpherson? Dammit—I didn't recognise you! What are *you* doing here!" That was a foolish question, but probably not foolishly meant.

Fiona Macpherson was tired, strained, and she was desperately disappointed. "At the moment, I am watching our forest burn—and more than the forest!" she said, tartly.

"H'mmm. Quite. We saw the glow of it, from the hotel—came along to see if we could help," Mortman informed, "What's the cause of it all? Hikers?"

There was just a moment's silence. Then Fiona spoke evenly, deliberately. "No, Sir Henry—worse than that, I'm afraid. You may as well know, since your interests are affected. This is the work of a gang of deer-poachers. They were seen in the act, waylaid—and this is their answer!"

"You mean—they've deliberately set the woods on fire!"

"Yes."

"Well, I'm damned! The utter scoundrels. And poachers, you say? This is quite an impossible situation. Good Lord—we can't stand for this sort of thing."

"No," the girl agreed, flatly. "I imagined you'd feel rather like that about it. It affects your position quite a lot, I recognise."

"By God, it does!" Mortman cried, "It's a scandal—a dastardly scandal! This sort of thing makes a farce of all legitimate dealings—it strikes at the very root of organised society. What are you doing about it?"

"At the moment, we have just finished burning a fire-break, to prevent the blaze coming any further," the young woman said, with brittle patience. "We are waiting to see . . ."

"Yes, yes—but what about the poachers?" Sir Henry interrupted, "What's being done about them?"

Alan spoke up. "Mortman," he said, with throaty challenge, "with a forest-fire on our hands, poachers can go to hell! If we let this thing have its head, thousands of acres of timber could be destroyed— houses and lives menaced. Heaven knows where it would stop—you know how this forest runs right into Rothiemurchus. It could go for miles and miles. Poaching, compared to this, is a mere flea-bite . . ."

"The fire must be controlled, yes—but so must the poachers, young man," Sir Henry gave back, frowning. "They are the cause—this is only the effect. How d'you know they won't do it again? Where are they now? And are the police aware of this?"

"The police are here—at least, the local constable is," Fiona informed, wearily.

"And if you want to find the poachers, sir, I suggest you go and look for them!" Alan said rudely, and there was a murmur of agreement from the standers by. They were a polite and mannerly folk, these Highlanders, but fire-fighting is tiring and fretting work, and some at least were not at their most patient. Also, all knew what this was costing Fiona Macpherson, and how little able she was to afford it.

John Cameron it was who spoke then, and even his voice held a note of quivering excitement behind

it. " You won't have to look far for them, either,
I'm thinking," he cried, " Look there ! "

They all swung round to follow the line of his
pointing hand. In the darkness of the forest ahead,
north-eastwards, four red points of light were
gleaming, expanding—and quickly grew to five, and
six.

" The hell-born devil-be-damned blackguards ! "
Archie Fraser roared. " They've done it again.
They're after starting a new fire ! " And, choking, he
launched into a stream of non-translatable Gaelic.

CHAPTER XX

HELPLESSLY, utterly shocked, the group in the rushy hollow stood and stared at this supreme enormity— the forest re-fired, well beyond their fire-break. This was the ultimate cruelty. The first could have been done to provide a diversion, to enable the poachers to escape whilst the blaze was being dealt with; this was sheer vindictiveness and hate. Calculating judicious hate—the fire was being lit on a much wider front, stretching much further north-west than before.

Only Sir Henry Mortman and his anonymous friend started towards the new conflagration. The others stood still, recognising all too clearly the utter hopelessness of the situation.

"It's no good, at all," Cameron called out, towards his two gentlemen. "We'll not can stop that. It's too wide—and the most of us here are done, just. It's no good."

Alan sensed rather than heard the sob at his side, and his arm went out impulsively to encircle the girl's shoulders. "My dear!" he said. And that was all that he could find to say.

He felt her body shiver and then go tense under his grip. But she said nothing, stared straight ahead. He removed his arm quickly.

The new fire, about quarter-of-a-mile from them, was waxing and spreading with great rapidity, for the forest was thicker there, apparently. Sir Henry came back.

" We must do something ! " he protested. "Can't just stand here and watch."

"What do you suggest?" the girl asked, desperately, even-voiced.

" I don't know. But surely something can be attempted. Another fire-break . . . ? "

" No use." Archie declared. " Too thick, it is, right to the river . . ."

" The river, yes. What about the river? Can't something be done, there? "

" Not up here, the line the fire's on. If it was a bittie further down, where it's wider, and the trees are more open . . . But up here, the Bruach's only two-three yards across, between steep rock, just. The trees near touch each other at either side. Och, it'll be across yon in a jiffy, just."

" That's right," Cameron confirmed. " Sparks could be taking it across, even, to say nothing of fallen trees and branches. Och, it is just a burn, the Bruach, no more. Further down, as Archie says . . ."

" Then, can we not at least go after these damned poachers? " Sir Henry demanded. " We know they're still in the wood in front somewhere . . ."

" They're armed, you know," Fiona mentioned. " With tommy-guns."

" Are they, damn them ! " Mortman snorted. " Still, I'm prepared to have a crack at them—eh, Tony? We're not going to be made fools of by a bunch of crooks. Who's willing to come with us, and beat 'em out? "

Surprised, Alan considered the man. He had scarcely expected this. Others were staring, likewise. "Perhaps you don't take these people very seriously? " he suggested. " I think you should, you know. If they'll do this . . ." and his arm swept round to include all that burning forest, before and behind, . . . " they'll do anything. I'd say they wouldn't hesitate to use their weapons. A keeper was killed over on Dalinblair Forest, only a month or so ago, you know."

"Perhaps, perhaps. But I think the attempt should be made. I'm not going to lie down under this, young man, however *you* feel about it. I don't allow people to take a swipe at me, and get away with it!"

"At you . . . ?" It was Alan Kinnear that enunciated the words, for all of them.

"At me, yes," the other returned, sharply. "I'm the shooting-tenant, am I not? This poaching is a direct attack on my interests. It has got to be stamped out, or I may as well pack in. And I don't pack in, gentlemen, let me tell you—Henry Mortman isn't starting to pack in at this stage in his career. Now—who's coming with me?"

"Well, I'm damned!" Alan asserted, in all sincerity.

It was a second or two before the wondering Highlandmen found their tongues. Then Archie, foremost as usual, spoke out. "Och, I'll come along right enough. I've got a Luger automatic in my pocket, see you—it'll maybe be useful . . ."

"Good man."

A chorus of doubtful affirmation seemed to indicate that most of the others were prepared at least to follow Archie's lead, and Sandy Cattanach was beginning to re-establish the law's primary duty in the matter, when once again the keen-eyed gamekeeper intervened.

"Do you see what *I'm* seeing, at all?" John Cameron asked, of all and sundry. He turned his face up, sniffing the air, licked his thumb and thrust it up above his head, testing the breeze. "Well, now —what d'you think of that?" he demanded, obscurely.

"D'you mean the wind's changed, John?"
Fiona only just managed to get out, strangle-voiced.
"I do not—and that's the queer thing, whatever!"
the other announced. "But see yonder!"

At first, none of them could see what the keeper
was driving at. The red wall of flame, driving away
from them, was as frighteningly bright as ever, certainly by no means flagging. The fire was raging
quite as well as its perpetrators could have wished.
And then, Archie Fraser saw it. "My Gracious!"
he cried. "It's turning, whatever. It's sweeping
round. John—you're right, man. Look you down-
by, there."
Though it took inexperienced eyes a little while to
see it, soon it was clear to all. The fire had changed
direction—and changed it radically. Where it had been
proceeding due north-eastwards, behind the south-
westerly breeze, it had suddenly swung away round
at right angles and more, west by north. And not
only that, but its rate of travel had increased noticeably, drastically. Even the roar of it, a third of a
mile away, was appreciably louder. And yet, as they
assured themselves, the wind had not changed.
Mystified, they stared.
Archie looked at the keeper, strangely. "John,"
he said, and cleared his throat. "John—it's, it's
the . . ."
"Aye, man," Cameron nodded, slowly. "Just
that. It's the Anail, whatever."
"My God, it is! It's the Anail na Ferlas!"
Archie's voice was distinctly higher-pitched than
usual. He began to laugh, and then stopped himself,
quickly. "Just that," he cried, quietly.
Alan's tone was sharp-set, above the muttering of
the other local men. "What was that you said?" he
demanded.

Fraser coughed. "The Anail, it is—the Anail na Ferlas, the right name is. The fire's got into it."

"Ferlas . . .?"

"Aye, then—Ferlas. The Breath of Ferlas, it means, just. A wind it is, sort of."

"That is so," John Cameron agreed, soberly.

Mortman was beginning to speak, but Alan Kinnear cut in on him, urgently.

"A wind?" he said. "You mean, a special kind of wind?"

"Yes—in a sort of a way. It comes down from MacDhui, see you . . ."

"It is a current of air, coming through the Larig," Fiona declared. "A sort of down-draught, when the wind's from the south-west. Caused by the land formation, I suppose—something to do with the shape and great height of the Cairngorm massif, probably . . ."

"You mean, this is a current of air that comes down out of the Larig Ghru, occasionally, when the wind's in a certain direction . . . and it's called the Breath of Ferlas?"

"That is so," Archie confirmed. "Only it's not just occasionally, maybe. I'm thinking it blows all the time, when the wind's in the south-west—and the wind's usually in the south-west, see you. But the Anail's queer. Sometimes it blows hard, and sometimes you'd scarce can be feeling it—and that's nothing to do with how hard the wind's blowing from the west, either. I couldn't tell you what causes it. And it depends on how strong it is, see you, just where it goes when it comes wheechling out of the Larig. Mostly, it comes birling round the foot of Carn Elrig, there, and across the mouth of Glen Einich, and out this end of Loch an Eilan, getting weaker all the way. But when it's strong, it comes on round this way, round the foot of the hills—and don't I know it, that have had my stacks lifted by it right out of the stackyard at Dalnamuick! And when it's coming round here, it's blowing practically due west, see you. Like now . . ."

"Right in the face of the real wind . . . ?"

"Just that."

"Seen the same thing in the Tyrol," Sir Henry's friend Tony volunteered. "Quite simple, really, I suppose."

"Don't have to go so far as that," Mortman told them. "In Westmorland, there's a thing called the Helm Wind—comes off Crossfell, at the head of the Pennines. Devil of a thing for the local farmers. On one place it's a calm day, on the next he's having to tie his ricks down."

"Just so, sir," John Cameron agreed. "Interesting it is, right enough. But look you at that fire. While we're talking here, it's moving back fast."

It was true. The fire, running into the strong easterly draught of air, had swung round in a steep bend, a hairpin bend, and was working back westwards, not exactly on itself, of course, but alongside, as it were, at a fairly acute angle. And at speed. While before, it had only had a mild breeze behind it, now it had something approximating to a wind. They could observe its devouring progress with their own eyes. But they could see something else, too. This development had altered the entire situation. Though the fire was fiercer, faster, it was heading for a different sort of terrain.

"Archie," Fiona cried, new hope, new life, in her voice. "We can stop it now, can't we? Another break?"

"Just what I was thinking, my own self. It's running along the same line as the Bruach. Yon open ground, where the sawmill used to be . . ."

"Better than that," Cameron intervened.

" Further up. We could be saving half-a-mile of timber. There's open ground farther up—in from yon big pool. Just scrub and sticks, it is—cut there in the last war. You know . . . ? "

" Aye, so . . . "

" That's right, John."

" Good, then. But we'll have to be hurrying. Come you ! "

So began another hectic scramble through the hummocks and glades and bottoms of that heather-floored slantwise forest, to another battlefield with the ravaging enemy. They went north by east, to meet the fire—and only one or two of them all, Alan included, looked back first to see how that first fire fared. What they saw did not restrain them; their fire-break was doing its work. The baulked flames towered angrily at the edge of the charred ground, but came no further.

Following Cameron at varying speeds, the enlarged party strung itself out, straggling across the neck of untouched forest, heading a little to the left, or west, of the new line of fire. Alan was not the last, but if it had not been for Mortman and his friend, he would have been. He was not so very far from the end of his tether, that man—and had more than an inkling of it. He had reached the stage where he was, to a certain extent, disincarnate; his mind, though clear, was rigidly controlled, his will was completely in charge, and his body a mere automaton, a sensationless machine—but a machine that was running-down fast. He just managed to keep Fiona Macpherson's back in view—and he was glad that it was her back, for he tripped frequently and fell more than once, through a curious inability to lift his feet, and he would not have liked her to see him so doing. He did not like her to see him in this state, at all.

She was bound to think of him as a weakling, as it was . . . And she had not spoken a word to him, directly, since the incident of her hair, when he had said what he had said—except her explanation about this Ferlas wind, and that had been general, to them all . . . So long as he could keep her back in view, he would make it . . .

He could not know that she was aware of every trip and fall that he made, and kept her back to him only with difficulty and out of a woman's infallible sensibility. Deliberately, she chose the easiest going, and not for herself. The four of them dropped well behind the hurrying local men.

It was a strange nightmarish journey that, across the dark, shadowy, smoke-curtained, open woodland. On three sides of them, the fire held sway, from south-west to north, and all the trees and the heather and the rushes were stained red by the murky glare of it. But it was an unsteady flickering glow, and the heather was long and hid ancient stumps and dead branches and outcropping stone and innumerable ant-hills—a rough road for weary legs.

When at length they arrived at the new base of operations, with a hot gust of smoke-laden air to greet them—Ferlas Mor's hot breath, indeed—it was to find the new fire-break already well started and alight. There were eight men at work on it, now, of course, none of them tyros. It was a wide level brackeny place, where trees had grown once, though now only a dead spike or two thrust upwards out of the bleached scatter of branches, the scrub-birch, and the dying bracken-fronds. And across it, their new fires were racing and joining up at speed, impelled by that urgent wind from distant Ben MacDhui, on which came the crackling roar of the greater fire behind.

It was as well that it burned quickly, too, for they

were no great distance ahead of the main blaze—four
hundred yards, no more. Cameron's selected
terrain had been as far up as they dared go.

Already the men were racing back, to where, about
a hundred yards to the rear, they were going to make
a stand. Here, there was no burn or damp ground
to act as a base, but there was an old saw-mill road,
and by dragging all the dead wood and sticks well
back, and stamping down the bracken at the far
side, they hoped that they could stem this preven-
tive fire that they had lit.

And not only the men were racing, as Fiona and
Alan came up. Other things were running back
through that narrow gap in the circle of flames—swift
shadowy silent things of the forest, fleeing from the
ever-contracting trap, small things that scuttered and
scampered, and tall graceful deer that bounded, and
heavy-winged birds, owls, capercailzie, blackcock,
that beat their way to safety. A roebuck almost
brushed Kinnear in its swift passage, its wide white-
rimmed eyes so preoccupied with the terror behind
that it scarcely saw him.

As he joined the others, dragging at the clutching
branches, Alan thought about those wild creatures
in their panic—and suddenly something clicked in
his mind. " Good Heavens ! " he burst out. " The
poachers, themselves . . . ! "

" Just what I was thinking," the man working
at his side, said. It was John Cameron's voice.
" Aye."

" Lord—what can we do ? " The younger man
demanded. " We'll have to do something. We can't
just leave them to, to . . ."

" We're after doing the only thing that we can,
Mr. Kinnear, at this minute—stopping this fire ! "
the keeper said, forcefully. " Nothing else there is
for it, at all."

" But, if they're trapped . . . ? "

" They'll can get out the same way as the beasties
. . . if they hurry. Ourselves, we've got to stop this
fire—if we let this out of control, they've had it then,
right enough."

" I suppose so . . ."

Perhaps his gnawing anxiety about those poachers
helped Alan Kinnear, in that renewed labour.
Certainly it had the effect of taking his mind off what
he was trying to do. Not that he was capable of
toiling mightily, as he had done before; his efforts
were comparatively feeble, involuntary, dogged only.
But others made up for him. Twelve of them, there
were, to stem that tide, with Mortman and his loud-
checked friend taking their share manfully with the
rest, and Fiona a self-appointed supplier of new leafy
birch-boughs for beaters.

It was a considerably briefer struggle this, though
fierce enough while it lasted. This wind, the Anail
na Ferlas, saw to that. Also, the bracken, swiftly as
it flared-up, had not the combustibility of the tough
heather-stems; the young birches being green and
non-resinous, shrivelled rather than burned; and the
dead pine branches, debris of lumbering days,
though they blazed furiously, were not too hard to
clear away from their chosen defence line. In a few
minutes, the fire was held, except at the top corner,
where there was some heather, and it tended to spread
outwards and upwards. Archie was mobilising all
hands to this end, to cope with it, when Fiona
Macpherson's voice rang out shrilly.

" Listen ! " she cried. " Quiet, Archie ! Listen ! "

The roar of the fire was plain enough, the hiss and
splutter and the pistol-like cracking of resinous wood.
But above it and through it came something else,
faint but unmistakeable—a thin high screaming,
prolonged and horrible.

"Great God—it's the poachers . . . their women!"
Alan shouted, and was for plunging forward at once.
John Cameron's hand restrained him forcibly.

"Take it easy, Mr. Kinnear!" he urged, commanded. "Take your time. It may not be, at all—
I've heard roe scream like yon, many's the time,
and them wounded."

"Hares, too," Macphail testified.

"Sounds dam' like a woman to me," Sir Henry
declared.

"Aye, it does . . ."

"Of course it is," Alan cried. "These poachers
had two women with them. We can't leave them to
burn . . ."

"And what can you do, at all, man?" Cameron
demanded.

"We can go to them. I'm not just standing here,
and listening, while they, they . . ."

"If you can get in, they can get out, whatever,"
the keeper pointed out.

"They may be trapped . . ."

"If they're trapped, how will you be getting at
them, then? They've six men with them, you
say . . . ?"

"I agree with this young man," Mortman
announced, authoritatively. "We've got to make an
attempt to get at them."

"I'm telling you, it may be a deer—it may not
be them, at all," John Cameron was more authoritative still. "Any man going into yon furnace, and
risking his life, is a fool . . . !"

"Stop it!" Fiona cried. "I can't hear, for your
arguing. Listen—I think it's moving, the sound—
that screaming. It's coming nearer . . ."

"It is so—you're right." That was Archie Fraser.
"And if it's coming nearer, whatever it is isn't
trapped."

" Yes, but . . ."

" Damn it—will the lot of you be getting on with stopping this bloody fire . . . ! "

" Look ! " Someone on the edge of the throng exclaimed. " Over yonder. No—it's dark again . . . Now—there ! Against the flames, see you . . ."

" Aye, I see him . . ."

It was a man running, his figure silhouetted against the red glare. He was coming almost straight towards them—the only way he could come, indeed. It was not him who was screaming. As he came on, bounding and stumbling, two or three of the watchers moved a little way uphill to intercept him.

" A boy who does be valuing his own skin, him ! " Archie commented, grimly.

Like the roebuck, the running man did not see them until he was almost upon them. Then, faltering, after a swift glance left and right, he came on, his hands outstretched, babbling a stream of words in some outlandish tongue, crazed with fright.

Archie Fraser grabbed him as he came up. " Quietly now, my mannie," he said. " You're safe enough, now." And to the other. " This isn't one of the boys we saw, at all—one of the drivers he'll be, just."

The spate of words continued. " Is that Gaelic ? " Sir Henry wondered.

" By the Powers, it's not ! " Fraser cried, indignantly. " Look, you—speak English, will you ! " and he shook the prisoner like a rat.

" It not me," the man got out. " Not me, please ! I not light fire . . . No, no—I tell you. Not me . . ." And he relapsed into gibberish.

" What about the rest of your gang, man ? " John Cameron demanded, back from his fire-fighting. " Are they trapped ? Can they get out ? "

But the fellow was beyond giving them an answer.

Q

He began to sob. Disgustedly, Archie pushed him
across to Cattanach.

"Your pigeon, man Sandy—a right beauty,
too . . ."

That screaming had been stopped for a little, but
now there was another outbreak of it—a high uluant
skirling, that set them all wondering, except for
Fiona Macpherson. All eyes were clamped on the
narrowing dark stretch of wood that the flames had
not yet reached.

It was perhaps as well that they had John Cameron
with them, level-headed man. "Look, now!" he
shouted exasperatedly. "This fire is not out on us,
yet. Will you be wasting all we've done? Get you on
with the work, will you and damn these borachs."

That was wise, for their fire, though damped down,
was not entirely extinguished, and was being fanned
by that hot draught of air into little blazes again.
Most of his hearers addressed themselves to the
completion of their task—but they kept each an eye
on that exit from the fire-trap of the burning forest,
as they worked.

Fiona saw them first. "Here they come," she
called. "Two . . . three—no, four of them . . ."

Archie Fraser straightened up, threw aside his
birch-bough, and drew the Luger pistol out of his
pocket. "Aye, then," he said. And then, raising
his voice a little. "Best be ready to get down, all of
you—down in the heather. They'll maybe open up
with a burst, when they see us."

It was a strange sensation, to be standing there in
silence, ready to throw themselves flat at a moment's
notice, waiting for their fellow men escaping out of
the jaws of death—and yet who might still be minded
to blast death at *them*, in hate, panic, or a dash for
liberty.

Soon, they could see them fairly clearly—two men

half-carrying, half-dragging someone between them, and behind, another couple close together, probably one supporting another. Suddenly the screaming bubbled up again, and promptly, one of the first pair of men struck back-handedly, viciously, and the noise stopped. Obviously it was one of the women, with hysterics; the other, no doubt, was one of the figures behind. That left two men to be accounted for.

That the oncoming party did not see the waiting group before they did, no doubt could be accounted for by the fact that they stood against the dark background of the unburned forest. But probably there was more to it than that; these people were not looking for more trouble—they had had plenty, to deal with, and still had their hands full. Their minds were on what was behind, rather than on what was in front. It was obvious in every line of them. Archie Fraser was taking no great risk when he stepped forward, from behind some birch-scrub, pistol in hand.

"Come you right along, the lot of you!" He ordered, "We've got you covered—every last one of you. Come on."

The two men in front halted, one of them letting go of the woman they were supporting, who all but fell. He stepped clear, crouching, in swift reaction.

"No you don't, damn you!" Archie cried, and thrust a hand forward, menacingly.

A beam of white light switched on. Sir Henry Mortman's friend had produced an electric torch. It showed a squat wide-legged figure, torn-shirted and blackened, crouching tensely, a hand at his back. Whether he was reaching for the tommy-gun that was slung over his shoulder was not to be known, for the light revealed something else—the evil gleam of the out-thrust Luger pointing directly at him—and he froze into immobility.

Altogether, that unexpected shaft of light revealed a strange scene against the background of fire and smoke, that few who saw it were likely to forget in a hurry. Apart from the first man, there were two others, each supporting a woman—though it required some perception to recognise the first, at least, as such. She was drooping against her escort, almost completely blackened by soot—as were they all—and there was little to indicate where face ended and scalp began. Her hair had been on fire, most evidently, and was scorched right to her skull, superficially like that of a negro. Her clothes, too, were burned. The others looked in only slightly better case, their clothing torn and charred, that of the girl to the rear largely hanging in shreds, while something in the nature of a bandage was tied round her forehead. Both women had lost their ridiculous shoes. The man upholding the first had a gash in his cheek, from eye to chin, apparent even under the carbon. The expressions of the three of them were tense, set, strained; that of the woman with shock, slack and relaxed. They made a pitiful sight.

But there was nothing pitiful about the crouching individual, as he waited there apart, alert, keyed-up, ready for anything—a dangerous man, obviously, and no ready accepter of fate. That Archie Fraser recognised, it was very evident.

" You, my mannie," he said, his voice grating, " Get your hands up above your head, out of the way."

The man did not move a muscle.

" Jump to it ! B'damn—d'you think I'm scared to shoot, after what you've done ? Man, it would be suiting me fine to be putting two-three rounds into your dirty hide . . ."

"Liar ! " the other snarled. " Ye bluidy big Hielan stot ! "

" So it's you is it ! " Archie jerked. " The borach from the Cowcaddens ! Stand still, blast you ! " He took a step closer. If the man's features were unrecognisable under the grime, that voice was not. They had the leader here. " I've handled your kind before, yes—I wasn't at Bardia and Tobruk for nothing ! Up with those hands, I say . . ."

And then the fellow acted, exploding forward like a projectile, right into the midst of them, cancelling out the threat of Archie's pistol instantly; shooting would be as liable to hit friend as foe. Though it was one man against a dozen, the odds against him could be scaled down wholesale; he had surprise on his side, singleness of decision, and everybody he struck at was an enemy; it was not at a tight group that he hurled himself, but at a line, a semi-circle, only one man thick, and undoubtedly he had seen that there was a woman amongst them, and he launched himself straight at Fiona, arms flailing. She went down under his rush, and Alan Kinnear, at her shoulder, seeking to save her, was butted aside violently, and, unsteady on his feet as he was, toppled and fell with her. Archie Fraser leapt after the man, unhesitant, but he had not the other's flying start and his outstretched hand grabbed only shirt-collar, which came away in his grasp. Willie Maclean, the saw-miller, seeking to intercept from the right, tripped over Alan's legs and got a swinging buffet to the stomach that doubled him up. And there was no-one else near enough to intervene effectively—for, as has been indicated, they had been spread-out in a semi-circle, and the break-through was the work of only a second or two, requiring only a tithe of the time it takes to tell. There was plenty of them to throw themselves after the fugitive, but no more to obstruct.

That is, except Sir Henry Mortman. He had been standing a little to the right of Fiona, and seeing the thug rushing towards him, fists up, had taken a prudent step or two backwards. As Alan fell, he stepped still further back, to avoid entanglement, and so it was that he was exactly opposite the poacher when Willie Maclean stumbled in his attack. The backhanded swipe at the saw-miller threw the fellow just a degree off his balance, and towards Mortman. The older man was suddenly galvanised into action, shed the weighty majority of his years and dignity, shouted "Schoo—oo—ool!" in a falsetto and mildly ridiculous fashion, and threw himself at the runa-gate's feet, arms wide, in a caricature of a Rugby tackle. And the other tripped, staggered, and fell headlong.

Before he had risen to more than his knees, half-a-dozen men were upon him.

From just behind, in the heather, Sir Henry's voice came excitedly, "Hooray! Up the School! Well tackled, b'Gad!"

"'Well, I'll be coopered!" John Cameron said, heavily. "Just listen to that!"

CHAPTER XXI

To Alan Kinnear, as to certain others no doubt, it
seemed a long walk back to the road and the cars.
Archie Fraser and Sandy Cattanach with the
prisoners, were away in front, the dangerous Low-
landman bound with the sling of his own tommy-gun.
John Cameron and a group of volunteers were
remaining behind to keep a watch on the fire; the
second fire-break seemed to have done its work and
halted the blaze, but it would not do to leave it
unobserved—the wind might change; the Forestry
fire-squad from Glenmore was to be sent for.
Mortman and his friend walked with Fiona, and
incidentally Alan, and though they wore no seven-
league boots, the latter had his work cut out to keep
up with them. He did not want to walk at all, in
fact. He wanted only to lie down there and then in
the inviting heather, and let the world go by. Perhaps
Fiona Macpherson knew just that, and that was why
she kept just a pace or two ahead, with the two
Englishmen, the while she regulated the rate of
progress and picked the way judiciously. It is to be
doubted if she heard more than a word or two of
what Mortman was saying.

And, curiously enough, he was saying plenty.
There was no holding Sir Henry down. He was in
tremendous fettle. Undoubtedly, he looked on him-
self as the hero of the night—as perhaps he was.
Quite gone was his chill reserve and stiff correctness.
He chuckled and slapped his thin thigh, nudged his

friend in the ribs, and more than once took Fiona's arm—though that was scarcely a practical procedure over that terrain. And he dealt at some length and particularity with the technique of catching poachers, putting the fear of death into hikers and such-like, and generally keeping the countryside in a whole-some condition. Spirit was what was wanted, it appeared, determination—guts, if Miss Macpherson would pardon the vulgarity. It was no good running away from things, shutting one's eyes and hoping for the best. They all knew about the Highlanders' *laissez faire* complex, but tonight they had had just a little sample of what could be done, with decent leadership and just a modicum of the spirit that made Old England what she was.

For a taciturn man, Sir Henry waxed almost eloquent. And somehow or other, his eloquence carried them as far as the road.

Both Mortman's and Alec Macphail's cars had been left as far up the road as they could get—at the felled tree. Macphail, Archie, and Sandy Cattanach, were waiting beside them, with the prisoners and another couple of guards, when Fiona and her party came up.

" Too many in it for Alec's car, altogether," the constable pointed out, very much in charge now. " Can we be putting two-three of them in your car, sir ? "

" Of course, Officer, of course. That is, some of the, er, cleaner ones," Sir Henry acceded. " It will give me quite a lot of satisfaction to convey these scoundrels safely into durance-vile, where they belong."

The bound leader of the captives said something brief, forceful, but mercifully largely unintelligible; he had cut and swollen lips to talk out of, now, to add to his other difficulties.

" Quiet, you ! " the law said, authoritatively. " I'd be pointing out, sir, that it's K'ussie we'll have to be taking these borachs to—I've no room for them all at Coraigbeg. Och, but it's not that far, at all . . ."

" That's all right, my friend—Kingussie it is. I'd run these people farther than that, b'Gad—I'd run 'em right into the dock at Inverness, or wherever it is, for that matter, with pleasure—and into goal afterwards ! After all, they're really my poachers, aren't they ! " And Sir Henry beamed on them all.

Into the wondering silence, Archie Fraser observed, " Just that, indeed," doubtfully, for want of anything better to say.

" How long will they get for this, d'you think, Officer ? " Mortman went on, genially. " For arson, assault, illegal possession of firearms, poaching, theft, and wilful damage to property ! The maximum sentence, eh ? How about three years ? Three years would just suit me nicely—eh, Miss Macpherson ? Just the period of my lease. Could anything be more suitable ? "

Fiona's quick intake of breath was not lost on Alan Kinnear, somewhat bemused as he was, alean against the gleaming side of the Rolls-Royce—nor on any of the local men there. Their glances flickered between the girl and Mortman, consideringly.

" You . . . you are still thinking of taking up that lease then, Sir Henry ? " she got out, with some evident difficulty.

" Of course I am, m'dear—definitely. Y'know, in three years or so, I think I could make something of this place—I do indeed. A little drive, and decision, a little old-fashioned determination, is all that's required—and some straight thinking. Given that, Glencoraig could be quite a decent proposition. We'll deal with the hiker-problem as we've dealt with these poachers. We'll mend these deplorable roads, put some drainage in hand, get another keeper or two on the place, and generally smarten things up. Eh, Tony? I'm not a man who does things by halves, b'Jove. Believe me, in three years, you'll hardly know the place ! "

" I do believe you," Fiona assured, but faintly. She swallowed. " But I'm very grateful, just the same . . ."

"What d'you mean—just the same ? " Mortman looked a little surprised. But his ego, released by sheer elemental physical action, for possibly the first time in forty years, was too surely in the ascendant tonight for any doubts, for any preoccupation with nuances and shades of meaning in the reactions of these curiously erratic-minded Highlanders. He turned to Cattanach. " Well, bundle them in, Officer. Better put that floor-mat on the seat first, though—I don't want the upholstery ruined. They're dirty as sweeps—though some of the rest of us are not much better, eh ? Ha—ha. Now—which ones am I getting ? The women, and this dago-fellow ? Very well. Only, I must have them adequately guarded, y'know . . ."

" Och yes, sir—Angus here, and Donald Mac-Vicar'll squeeze in the back there, too, easy. In you get, now. Archie and me will be managing the other three in Alec's car, fine."

" We will so," Archie confirmed. " I've got my Luger, here—damn't. I haven't had a shot with it yet, at all ! "

" Man, wheesht you, Archie—the less we're hearing about yon, the better. I'll be coming to take it off you any day now, whatever." He pushed Donald MacVicar's lengthy person into the Rolls, and got the rear door shut, with some difficulty. " Och, it's as well, I'm thinking, that yon other two creatures escaped on us, back there—or some of us would be having the long walk, this night."

"That is so," Macphail agreed. "But six out of eight is no' bad, at all—and their transport, too . . ."

"Aye—but with all the drive and the determination that was in it, like the gentleman said, we should have been having them all!" That was Archie Fraser, satirically. "Och, yes—eight out of eight, it should have been. Nothing else. Look at the leadership, we had . . ."

"H'mmm," said Sandy Cattanach and Fiona Macpherson, together. Also, the front door of the Rolls slammed shut, and the self-starter whirred. "Sorry I've no room to give you a lift, Miss Macpherson," it's owner mentioned. "But your car's just down the road, you say? Good. Off we go, then. I'll see you at Kingussie, Officer. Tally-ho!" And purring majestically, the big car slid forward in the brilliant path of its great headlights.

"Aye, so," Archie observed, soberly. "The ways of the Lord are just wonderful, whatever. Aren't we the lucky ones!"

"Archie Fraser," the girl cried, "you have an ill tongue in your head. Take him away, Alec, before I get annoyed with him."

"I will so, Miss Fiona—right away. You've got these bright lads stowed away in the back, there Sandy? In you get beside them, Archie—you and your Luger."

"Aye, then. I'm just hoping they'll be trying a bit escape, on the way." He looked out of the open window, back to where Alan stood in silence. "There's not been that much out of Mr. Kinnear, this whilie," he said. "You all right, Alan man?"

"I'm all right," Alan said.

"Tired, just—eh? A right through-other poacher-catcher you ! What you're needing is drive, decision, and determination, whatever . . ."

" Archie . . ."

" Right, you—very well, so." Fraser agreed, hurriedly. " You will be looking after the invalid, then, Miss Fiona ? A right handful, as invalids go, too—and don't I know it ! "

" I will," the girl promised. " And, Archie—I want to say how grateful I am, really, for all you and Mr. Kinnear have done today. You have been wonderful, just spendid. If it hadn't been for you . . ."

" There would have been no fire, at all ! Maybe we'd have done better not to have interfered," Fraser suggested. " Och, no—you've nothing to thank me for, Miss Fiona—not a thing. If there's anyone to be thanking, it's Ferlas Mor ! "

There was silence for a moment or two. That was not a joke. None of them there was inclined to treat that subject too lightly. Better not to talk about it, at all.

" Aye, then," Alec Macphail said, at length. " Uh-huh. Just that. We'll be off then, Sandy—or yon toff'll be waking up the whole of K'ussie, seeking the police-station . . ."

" That's right, man Alec. Off with you. Goodnight, Miss Fiona—and you, Mr. Kinnear."

" Goodnight, Goodnight. And thank you, all."

" *Slan leat* ! " Archie cried, " *Tha àm math a tighinn*. Up the Macphersons ! Man, Alan—they've got a right queer motto, the Macphersons—Touch the Cat but a Glove ! Take you heed to it, will you . . ." The rest was lost in the roar of the accelerating engine —no purring Rolls, this. But a few words came back to them as the car lurched off down that uneven track " . . . or I'm telling you, Seana Macdonald will be having to find herself a new lodger ! "

Into the quiet that succeeded, the girl spoke, carefully, " My car is about half-a-mile down the road. Will you wait here, Mr. Kinnear, while I go and fetch it up ? "

Alan took his time to answer, but he appeared to be marshalling his unruly thoughts rather than finding any difficulty about coming to a decision. " You will not," he answered her, with no shade of uncertainty. " And a while back, you were calling me by my Christian name ! "

" Only once," she said, but without his certainty. " And only in retaliation. Only because you had done the same thing, yourself."

" And have I stopped doing it, then ? "

" I don't know." She shook her head. " I don't know, at all." This was not the forthright and decided mistress of Glencoraig.

" Then, for your information, I have not, Fiona Macpherson—and will not, either, until you tell me to."

" I don't think I will do that, Alan," she assured him, gravely.

" I am glad of that," he acknowledged, as gravely. They were very serious, both of them. " That is one step forward we are, anyway—even if there is a long road ahead of us, yet."

" Long, is it ? Not so very long, perhaps." Just the beginnings of a smile quivered at the corners of her mouth—though, of course, the man could not see it. " Only half-a-mile, Alan." And quickly. " Can you make it, that far, with me—tired as you are ? "

" Yes, I think so. I think I could make it farther than that, with you beside me. If you were to go beside me, I think I could go on . . . to the end of the road, Fiona."

She said nothing to that, only turned and began to

walk down that rutted track beneath the trees, but
unhurriedly, waiting for the man to fall into step
beside her. And after a little, watching his progress
out of the corner of her eye, as they went, she spoke.

"Take my arm, if you like, Alan. There is nobody
to see us, now."

"Nobody to see us now," he repeated, thoughtfully, and nodded, as though to himself. "Yes. But
you are kind," he acknowledged. "I will take
whatever you give me, of your kindness."

So arm in arm they followed their road, and
thought their own thoughts.

Presently Alan Kinnear observed, out of those
thoughts, deliberately. "Fiona—I think I am
possibly a little light-headed tonight. And because a
man may sometimes be forgiven for what he says
when he is light-headed, I am plucking up courage to
say what I would . . ." Carefully he corrected himself, ". . . what I *might* not dare say otherwise.
You follow me?"

"I think I do," she answered, small-voiced.

"What I want to say, you see, is that I was not at
all light-headed when I spoke to you that time under
the tree, the blazing tree. You know?"

She did not speak.

"You remember?" he insisted.

"Yes."

"I was not light-headed, then."

"You were excited. I was excited a little, too. It
was rather an exciting time, wasn't it?"

"Yes." He turned, to look at her searchingly, in
that dim light. "Yes—I see what you mean." And
he shook his head, but heedfully, for the head he had
was not to be shaken lightly that night. "But I
meant what I said, then . . . and I mean it now!"

At his side, her footsteps faltered just a little.
"Yes . . . but will you mean it tomorrow, or the next

day? You see . . ." And then she could no longer restrain herself, and her words came out in a rush. " Oh, Alan—I want you to be sure of yourself. Not to be carried away, on—on an impulse. Tonight you are overwrought. It has been a terrible day for you —and you are still a sick man. It must have been a fearful ordeal, a fearful strain. You can't be yourself, tonight. You are nearly all-in, I know—I have been watching you. Wait, Alan. Say no more tonight . . ."

" And if I have not the courage tomorrow, or the next day? What then? "

She gulped. " I must take that chance," she said, as evenly as she could.

" You . . . you mean . . .? Good Lord, d'you mean . . . ! " He tugged at her arm, that he held, urgently. " And you still don't want me to speak, tonight? "

" No . . . yes! Oh dear, I'm a little light-headed myself, I think ! And I'm afraid, Alan, afraid . . ."

" Afraid of what? "

" Afraid that . . . oh, my dear, I'm afraid that, being light-headed too, I'll blurt out that I love you, desperately, that I want you, need you, that I've loved you ever since, when you were ill, and you clutched my arm like you are clutching it now, you . . ."

" Fiona Macpherson ! " he cried, and his voice rang out strongly now. " Will you be quiet! Will you have some decency, girl ! Me, it is, that started this—will you give a man a chance? It is not for you to talk like that . . ." He stopped, abruptly. " Listen," he demanded, almost indignantly, " is there such an almightly hurry to get to that car of yours? "

She shook her dark head. " No—not any more, Alan."

"Thank heaven for that," he sighed. "Look, there is some heather here, too—and I have been wanting to sit down in some heather for hours and hours and hours. Will you come and sit down there, with me, my dear—for I have something to tell you? Something that will not wait until tomorrow, or the next day—something that will not wait another minute! Will you?"

"Alan, dear," she said, "I wish I could say no— but I can't. Not any more."

"Not any more," he agreed, decisively. "Ever!"